A TWO-SI...

It was difficult enough for Gemma to refuse to wed John Delevan when he was not only one of the most attractive and attentive gentlemen she had ever met, but also the beloved brother of Gemma's best friend, Lucy.

It was even harder to keep the man Gemma adored, Captain Godwin, out of the clutches of exquisite Coralee Fairmont, the reigning belle of the ton, who had never met a man whose head she could not turn and heart she could not capture.

Gemma had a dangerously seductive suitor to resist . . . a ravishing rival to vanquish . . . and a growing doubt about whether her heart's desire was to win or to lose. . . .

DOROTHY MACK is a native New Englander, born in Rhode Island and educated at Brown and Harvard universities. While living in Massachusetts with her husband and four young sons, she began to combine a longtime interest in English history with her desire to write, and emerged as an author of Regency romances. The family now resides in northern Virginia, where Dorothy continues to pursue both interests.

A Prior Attachment

Dorothy Mack

A SIGNET BOOK

NEW AMERICAN LIBRARY

For Susan,
who inspired the creation of Gemma

NAL BOOKS ARE AVAILABLE AT QUANTITY DISCOUNTS
WHEN USED TO PROMOTE PRODUCTS OR SERVICES.
FOR INFORMATION PLEASE WRITE TO PREMIUM
MARKETING DIVISION, NEW AMERICAN LIBRARY,
1633 BROADWAY, NEW YORK, NEW YORK 10019.

SIGNET TRADEMARK REG. U.S.PAT.OFF. AND FOREIGN COUNTRIES
REGISTERED TRADEMARK—MARCA REGISTRADA
HECHO EN DRESDEN, TN, U.S.A.

SIGNET, SIGNET CLASSIC, MENTOR, ONYX, PLUME,
MERIDIAN and NAL BOOKS are published by
NAL PENGUIN, INC., 1633 Broadway, New York, New York 10019

First Printing, May, 1989

1 2 3 4 5 6 7 8 9

PRINTED IN THE UNITED STATES OF AMERICA

1

Soft though it was, the tap on the door seemed to have a galvanizing effect on the woman reclining on a chaise longue fashioned of intricately carved mahogany and upholstered in sea-blue velvet. An observer might be pardoned for assuming she was waiting in no little anxiety for just such an event, since her worried gaze had been fastened on the door, but her reaction to the sound would cast some doubt on this theory. She started violently and her fingers sought and gripped the book lying unopened in her lap with knuckle-whitening tension. The voice that gave permission to enter was barely strong enough to penetrate the paneled wood, though she summoned up a singularly sweet smile to greet the girl who peeked inquiringly around the door.

"You sent for me, Mama?"

"Yes, dearest. Do come in. I was afraid I had missed you. Mrs. Benedict thought you had formed the intention of gathering flowers on the grounds."

"And so I have, now that the rain has stopped," replied her daughter gaily, displaying a large basket over one arm as she came all the way into the room. "The flowers in the main reception rooms are perfect, of course, but I remembered how Lucy was used to admire the sloes in the blackthorn hedges, and I thought I'd gather some for her bedchamber."

"A nice welcoming touch," the older woman agreed.

A small silence ensued while the girl waited expectantly, her eyes following her mother's gaze to the thin fingers that fiddled with the pages of her book. "Did you wish to charge me with an errand, Mama?"

"No, no, thank you, dearest." Large shadowed dark eyes fleetingly surveyed the waiting girl; then dropped again to her lap. After another short interval the woman indicated a boudoir chair covered in the same sea-blue velvet with a flutter of her fingers. "Sit down for a moment, Gemma. I'd like to talk to you."

When the girl had obeyed this command, her mother seemed to find it difficult to initiate the conversation for which she had expressed a desire, but at last she laid aside her book and took a deep breath. "You have been looking forward to Lucy's visit with a good deal of pleasure, have you not, my child?"

Gemma bounced a little in her chair. "Of course, Mama. It seems an age since we've met. I scarcely saw anything of Lucy in town once the Season really got started, and then, you know, she contracted the influenza in the spring, and Mr. Delevan thought it advisable to send her into the country to recuperate. I was working it out in my mind just this morning. Lucy and I haven't set eyes on each other since April, though we have corresponded, naturally."

The duchess smiled in sympathy with her daughter's bubbling expectancy. "I have to tell you that we are also to have the pleasure of entertaining Mr. John Delevan while Lucy is here."

Gemma's eyes widened in surprise. "Lucy's brother? It was my impression that Mr. John Delevan was busily involved with his career in the law."

"So I comprehend, but your father has invited him to accompany Lucy."

"*Papa* has? I did not know that he was acquainted with Mr. Delevan. For some reason or other I have not yet met him myself."

"I believe your father is slightly acquainted with the young man." After another short hiatus the duchess continued, selecting her words with great care. "He especially desired me to request that you extend yourself to make Mr. Delevan's visit enjoyable."

"Of course I shall. I have long wished to make the acquaintance of Lucy's brother. She speaks of him so often and so fondly that I almost feel as though he were my brother also."

The older woman sat up straighter, swallowed dryly, and plunged. "As a matter of fact, your father is very . . . hopeful . . . that you and Mr. Delevan will find, on longer acquaintance, that you like each other well enough to make a match of it."

Gemma stared at her parent in dawning horror and leapt out of her chair as though it had become too hot to be borne. "Did I hear you correctly, ma'am? Did I hear you say Papa would like me to *marry* Mr. Delevan?"

"I believe he is very set on it," said the duchess, burning her bridges behind her.

"But I am going to marry George! You know we have been as good as betrothed these two years past." Gemma's voice rose in pitch and volume with each succeeding word, and her mother winced and fell back among the pillows on the chaise with whitening cheeks.

"Please, dearest," she begged nervously. "You might be overheard by one of the servants."

"It's immaterial to me if the whole world hears," declared the young girl rebelliously, though she lowered her voice in automatic compliance. It shook with passion, however, as she reiterated her protest. "You know it has been an understood thing that George and I should become formally engaged when he returns to England. Now that Napoleon has abdicated, I have every hope that he will send in his papers quite soon. I do not believe he would care to be a soldier in peacetime."

"I know that there was an attachment between you the last time George was home, but he did not apply to your father for permission to pay his addresses. After all, you were no more than a child at the time."

"I wasn't! I was turned seventeen and I have always known my own mind. I have loved George since I was a little girl."

Her mother smiled faintly at this indignant pronouncement, but she shook her head too and said with a gentle regret, "Your father could never countenance such an unequal match, my child. George is a younger son and his prospects are no more than respectable. You—"

"I care nothing for that!"

"I don't suppose you do at your age, but others must keep your best interests in mind."

"You mean Papa, of course. If *I* do not care for a position of the first consequence, why should it concern my father? You have taught me to hold house; I shall make a good wife for a man of modest means. And George is not entirely without prospects, you know, nor dependent on his army pay. He will have Stanton Lodge for his own." Something in the expression on her mother's face caused the girl to abandon her arguments. "Will nothing make my father give his consent?" she demanded straightly.

"I . . . I fear not."

Gemma bit her lip fiercely and stalked over to the window in the square apartment. After a moment while she fought for control she said in a very different tone, "If it means waiting until I am of age, I am resolved that I shall marry no one but George, Mama. My father cannot compel me to wed Mr. Delevan."

This resolute speech was delivered over her shoulder while one hand played with the blind cord. The duchess eyed her daughter's straight back and for a moment was able to relax the rigid control she had imposed over her features to allow the sympathy and pain she felt for this beloved child's distress to show in her eyes. By the time Gemma had turned to face her with a touching assumption of dignity, her emotions were veiled once more. She watched her daughter bend to pick up the basket that stood near her chair, and begged, her tones betraying anxiety, "Gemma, you will treat Mr. Delevan with all the courtesy owing to a guest in our home?"

"Naturally, Mama," she replied dully. "Mr. Delevan has the double recommendation of being my friend's brother and my father's guest."

The duchess thought it prudent to ignore the slight stress placed on the word "father's", but there was still one more item of news that it was her duty to impart before her daughter quit the room. She sighed and took her fences with a rush. "Mr. and Miss Delevan will not be our only guests for the next few weeks," she began, avoiding her daughter's suddenly narrowed glance. "Your Aunt Sophronia and your Cousin Coralee will be arriving tomorrow for an extended stay."

"Oh, no, not my cousin," wailed Gemma, instantly reduced to childishness by the weight of this fresh disaster. "Why did you not warn me, Mama?" she demanded, turning on her trembling parent with gritted teeth. "That was all that was wanting to spoil Lucy's visit."

"I did not learn of it until today, dearest," pleaded her mother in extenuation. "Your father told me an hour ago that Sophronia was bringing Coralee here to remove her from the vicinity of an unsuitable young man who had been dancing attendance on them ever since they arrived in Brighton."

This interesting piece of information failed to mitigate the disaster as far as Gemma was concerned, though she did speculate aloud on the amusement they might expect to derive from the situation should Coralee's abundant charms and documented propensity for flirtation succeed in diverting the attention of Mr. Delevan from the original object of his visit. By the time she had put this happy thought into words and considered it for a moment, the frown had cleared from her brow and she was looking decidedly mischievous.

The duchess protested. "Gemma, you are not to encourage Coralee to flirt with Mr. Delevan! Your father will be furious if such a thing should happen."

"Encourage her, Mama? I shouldn't dream of it," came the dulcet reply. "All that is required is for me to show the least interest in Mr. Delevan for Coralee to make a dead set at him."

"Gemma, such vulgarity! Please do not employ such expressions in the presence of your aunt. You know what she is." Her grace had almost started up from her chaise and was wringing her hands in great agitation.

"In fact," pursued her undutiful daughter, disregarding this last plea, "it will not even be necessary to stimulate an interest in Mr. Delevan. I daresay he is so rich that he need be no more than one degree more prepossessing than an orangutan to catch Coralee's interest. She'd flirt with anything in trousers just to keep her hand in, but rich as his father is, Mr. Delevan must be considered a matrimonial prize."

"Gemma, stop! You will bring on one of my palpitations," moaned her sorely tried parent, and indeed she was looking so pulled that her offspring's conscience smote her. Casting aside the basket, Gemma subjected her trembling mother to a quick embrace and bent her best efforts to soothing that poor lady's disordered nerves with faithful promises to mind her tongue when in her formidable aunt's company.

"Yes, but Gemma, you will try to get along with Coralee this time, will you not? I know you girls rubbed each other the wrong way as children, but you are both young ladies now and the least we can expect is that you will remember that Coralee is our guest and behave accordingly." Tears gathered in Lady Carlyle's dark eyes and threatened to spill over. "Your father will be so angry if your conduct merits censure. He will say I have allowed you an unbecoming degree of freedom—he was against sending you to Miss Climpton's Seminary from the beginning, but it was so lonely here for you with Peter away at school, and I thought . . . I thought—"

"Shush, Mama, don't talk. Here is your vinaigrette. Breathe deeply," commanded Gemma, becoming increasingly concerned with the consequences of this lamentable interview on her fragile parent. The duchess frequently suffered from an irritation of the nerves, and the present occasion was shaping as a severe trial to her fortitude. "I promise I shall treat my cousin with all the consideration due to a guest and I shall try not to regard her sly digs. And I promise further that my aunt shall have no cause to complain of me to my father this time.''

The frantic grip on her hands loosened as the duchess relaxed into the depths of the pillows, clutching feebly at the small aromatic bottle her daughter held beneath her nose. ''Thank you, dearest,'' she whispered. ''I know all this has been a great disappointment to you when you were anticipating Lucy's visit so eagerly, and I am well aware that Coralee can be difficult.''

''Coralee,'' said her daughter in succinct summation, ''is a jealous cat.''

''I know she is,'' was the unexpectedly candid reply, ''but you will never succeed in convincing any gentleman of this fact, so I beg you will not demean yourself by seeming to notice if she implies things to your discredit in that sweet insinuating manner of hers. Half of her barbs are too subtle for the masculine mind in any case.''

Gemma gave a delighted chuckle at such a show of spirit from her gentle mother and managed to coax a smile from her lips before settling her among the cushions with vinaigrette handy and blinds drawn to keep out the sun that was trying to burn away the remaining clouds.

Her own smile vanished the second she closed the door behind her. In the brief span of fifteen minutes her peace had been cut up and all her pleasure in anticipating Lucy's visit had been destroyed. Under any other circumstances she would have been eager to meet, and predisposed to like, John Delevan, but it was going to be the worst kind of embarrassment to have to consort on a daily basis with a man who was coming for the express purpose of making her an offer she could never accept. If only her father had given her some hint of his intentions in this quarter, she could have written to Lucy to make her sentiments known. She had given her schoolfriend some inkling of her feelings for George two years ago and could have trusted her to alert her brother to the situation. At least it would have pre-

vented this beastly visit from taking place. And to
complicate matters still further, they were to have the
double misfortune of Aunt Sophronia and Coralee to
cloud her delight in Lucy's presence.

Gemma's feet had reached the east terrace without
benefit of her brain's guidance. She paused on the flags,
unsure whether she still wished to embark on a quest for
flowers with her thoughts in such turmoil, or whether it
might not be advisable to seek her bedchamber for a
quiet hour in which to compose her disordered mind
before the influx of guests was upon them.

She had half-turned back when a mad scratching at
one of the French doors decided her in favor of a walk.
Her mother's Pekingese, Homer, was frantically
signaling his desire to accompany her on an outing,
yapping and wagging his absurd brush of a tail. Her
mood lightened at the sight of his doggy enthusiasm and
she opened the door and accepted his ecstatic gratitude
as he danced around her, licking any part of her
anatomy she was so unwise as to present to him.

2

With a reverberating crack rendered even more virulent by the fact of its being high summer, the fast-moving clouds parted and generously fulfilled their promise of rain.

"Whew! Almost left it too late," admitted the man entering the carriage with more agility than grace as he threw himself into a corner after hastily shutting the door against the almost horizontal fall of rain. He removed the hat perched atop his crisp brow locks and shook drips of water from it before placing it tenderly on the seat beside him. A small frown appeared as he caught sight of one brown shoulder while depositing the hat. The frown deepened to a grimace once he had divested himself of his tan gloves and confirmed his fears that his new coat, delivered just last week from no less a tailor than the great Weston, had indeed received a wetting.

The other passenger in the luxurious carriage had been observing this pained pantomime through a pair of uncommonly fine gray eyes into which a smile had crept. "You seem a trifle overanxious about a slight wetting, John," she commented in an attractively low-pitched voice with a hint of amusement coloring its tones.

"Well, we are nearly there, I believe. I would not wish to present an off appearance when meeting your friend and her family for the first time." The gentleman did not look up as he continued to apply his handkerchief to the damp patches on his shoulders, and this ineffectual blotting action, or perhaps some slight awkwardness in his manner, deepened the lady's amusement.

"Then I must be grateful, I collect, that the inclement weather and your burning desire to present a point-device appearance at Monteith Hall have combined to give me the pleasure of your company for the last few miles of our journey."

This uncomplaining remark, uttered with sweet seriousness, brought the man's head around to face his companion for the first time since entering the chaise. An answering gleam enlivened his bright-blue eyes though all he said, and that mildly, was, "Now, Lucy."

Ignoring this weak rebuttal, the lady continued, warming to her grievance, "And to think that I dispensed with the services of a maid on the trip in the mistaken belief that I was to have my brother's company. Was ever a person more basely deceived than I? Even Addie's chatter would have been preferable to two days of rocking and lurching solitude."

The insensitive creature sitting at his ease across from her was apparently too calloused to be even minimally affected by this piteous tale. "Now, Lucy," he reiterated in the same mild tone, "you know you insisted on sending Addie to the shore for a rest because she can't seem to shake that lingering cough. There was never a question of taking her with you. And there was never any question of my riding inside either." The smile in his eyes spread to his lips. "You know I get queasy after a half-hour in a closed carriage."

The lady's lips quirked in response but she permitted a sigh to escape them. "You never were a good subject for teasing, John. You never give one the satisfaction of seeing you rise to the bait, and you're always the first to laugh at yourself. Totally unaccommodating."

At this ludicrous complaint her companion burst into laughter and was joined by his sister an instant later. The smile lingered as the man asked sympathetically, "Tired, love?"

"Not really," admitted Lucy. "Slightly bored perhaps, though the scenery has become rather lovely in the last few hours—or it would be, if this torrential shower were not obscuring the view completely. I like the low, rolling hills and the vistas of Wiltshire." With one white gloved hand she rubbed a circular area in the window to clear away the fog created by their breathing, and peered out hopefully. "I can barely see the edge of the road at the moment. Poor Joseph must be drenched by now."

"I fear so, but the air is warm and we are less than five miles from our destination if Joseph's last estimate was correct."

"Thank goodness! I fear I am not the stuff of which good travelers are made. I am much too impatient to arrive at my destination."

A look of concentration knitted his brows. "You have not, I think, visited Monteith Hall before, have you, Lucy?"

"No. Gemma invited me once when we were still at school, but Mother became ill and I had to return to London. I never went back to Miss Climpton's."

Lucy's face had grown still and closed. He knew she was thinking of their mother's death two years before and the shattering effect it had had on their father, and he spoke quickly to distract her. "What is Lady Gemma like?"

Enthusiasm replaced the unnatural gravity of his sister's expression. "Oh, Gemma is a sweetheart! Lively, impulsive, always eager to be out and doing—in short"—on a tiny spurt of laughter—"all the things I'm not. And she is the loveliest girl imaginable."

It was impossible for John to look at Lucy with the disinterested eye of a connoisseur, but he didn't think it was merely his partiality that found *her* one of the loveliest girls imaginable. He tried to survey his sister's features objectively as she recounted one of Lady Gemma's pranks while they were at school together in Bath. He conceded that, being neither divinely fair in the English tradition nor fashionably dark, she was less likely to make an immediate impression than some other young ladies, but he considered her combination of rich chestnut-colored hair and fair skin quite eye-catching. Nor was there any doubt in his mind that her large gray

eyes, set under clearly defined dark brows and thickly
fringed with preposterously long black lashes, could
hold their own against those of any blue- or black-eyed
beauty in the kingdom. Her face was a classic oval and
her features regular though unspectacular. A shade
taller than average, she carried her generously curved
slimness with the unconscious dignity and grace of a
young queen. Peering at his sister through half-closed
lids, he concluded that, when animated as she was at
present, Miss Lucinda Delevan was a match for the
prettiest girls who were trotted off to Almack's year
after year to acquire husbands.

Loath though he was to admit it, this attractive
animation of Lucy's was rather the exception than the
rule, however. His sister generally presented a quiet,
composed appearance, and those beautiful eyes of hers
had a disconcerting habit of scrutinizing people in a way
that threatened to penetrate their most dearly held
disguises. She deplored sham of any sort, and in her
quiet, well-bred fashion, often without any words at all,
was entirely capable of stripping a prospective suitor of
all his protective coloring and reducing him to the bare
bones of his character.

And here she was, already one-and-twenty, with no
prospects of marriage before her at present and,
seemingly, no concern for her future. Although the
daughter of a wealthy banker had not possessed the
social credentials to make it possible to obtain vouchers
for Almack's, Lucy had acted as their father's hostess
since their mother's death and had led a fairly active
social life following their period of mourning. Despite
having his own rooms at Gray's Inn, John kept in close
contact with his family and was well aware that a
number of men, several of them quite well-connected,
had dangled after Lucy in the last year. He was aware
too—from his father, not his sister—that she had
refused no less than three offers during this period.

Once when he had commented on the continued
absence of a particularly persistent visitor to the big

house in Hanover Square, Lucy had told him serenely that the gentleman in question would no longer be calling on them. In addition to being undeniably handsome, the young man, a scion of an ancient family once powerful in the land but now much reduced in material circumstances, had seemed to possess all the attributes of breeding, education, and address to make him acceptable to any lady, and he had appeared devoted to Lucy. When John had mentioned this, his sister had replied with perfect composure and no trace of regret that the gentleman had also been devoted to Mr. Delevan's impressive fortune, and unfortunately for his hopes, this had been the greater devotion.

Watching the vivid face of the girl sitting across from him, her body swaying easily with every motion of the coach, John recalled the dismay that had spread through him on that occasion at his sheltered young sister's recognition and calm acceptance of such a situation. It wasn't cynicism precisely, and she evinced no bitterness that she should be sought after primarily for her material assets, but he was a bit chilled and uneasy at the casual way she had turned her back on a golden opportunity to lead the one kind of life for which a girl in her circumstances had been reared. He had come to the suitor's defense with an awkward but honest appraisal of him as a man of honor and principle who would treat his wife with every consideration and who was evidently prepared to form a sincere attachment to Lucy. She had heard him out without interruption or contradiction but with a queer little smile on her lips that had vaguely disturbed him. When he had stumbled to a halt, she had said quite gently that she accepted the validity of everything he had argued and that perhaps, had she loved the man, she would not have dismissed his suit without giving it more serious consideration.

Brother and sister were bound by close ties of affection, but he had experienced all the embarrassment of a diffident young man where the deepest emotions

were concerned. Lucy had taken pity on him with a
swift change of subject. They had not again discussed
her matrimonial prospects, and she continued to play
the role of a young woman completely content with her
lot, satisfied to remain her father's hostess and
companion. The one glimpse she had permitted him
beneath the surface serenity, however, had destroyed
her brother's illusions of this score. Lucy had a great
capacity for devotion to those she loved, and this
potential would be stifled forever if, as he feared, the
ranks of those eager to court her should gradually thin
when it became generally known that the banker's
daughter looked with favor on none of her suitors. Unfortunately, short of playing matchmaker, the mere
thought of which role filled him with horror, he had not
been able to conceive of a single constructive action that
might advance the cause of his sister's eventual
happiness.

Of course, thoughts of a sister's—even a much-loved
sister's—future were not constantly uppermost in the
mind of a young barrister struggling to carve a niche for
himself in his chosen profession. No doubt his mind was
straying to Lucy's prospects today because of the recent
and most unexpected conversation with their father that
had resulted in his accompanying her on this journey—
which reminded him that he had not been completely
truthful with her when she had evidenced delight at his
generosity in offering her his escort to Wiltshire.

With a smiling glance at Lucy, who had finished her
story of her friend, he made a partial rectification of the
omission.

"I did not tell you before, my dear, but I shan't be
leaving Monteith Hall immediately. I have been invited
by the duke to remain for a visit."

"John, how delightful! But why did you not mention
it long since? There has been ample opportunity in the
past two days, surely."

After an almost imperceptible hesitation, her brother
replied casually, "I had not finally decided that I could

square it with my conscience to remain away from my work for more than a few days when we embarked on the trip. Distance has helped to persuade me that a break would be a good thing."

Lucy accepted this explanation without question and repeated her pleasure in having her brother's company for an extended period. "We shall have such good times," she declared enthusiastically. "Gemma was always the center of activity at school."

"Shall I like her?"

"You could not *not* like Gemma," responded Lucy with conviction.

"She sounds a bit of a featherhead."

This provocative remark drew, not the pointed defense he had expected, but a delicious gurgle of mirth from his sister. "I know it must seem so from what I've said," she admitted readily. "Gemma can appear bird-witted at times, and I have the mortifying conviction that you will construe anything else I tell you about her in the same vein, but I promise you it is not so. The fault is mine for not being able to describe her accurately, to get to the essence of her. Ridiculous things just seem to happen when Gemma is around, though it isn't at all her doing . . . most of the time," she added in a con-scientious attempt to be a scrupulous reporter.

John raised one brown eyebrow and said in polite accents, "I must accept your lucid explanation of the lady's character and beg you to describe her appearance to me."

But Lucy had noted the amusement he concealed im-perfectly. She tossed her red-brown curls, setting the blue flowers adorning her straw bonnet stirring, and pressed her soft lips into a firm line.

The other eyebrow elevated at her negative response. "Are you also unequal to the task of describing the physical attributes of the 'loveliest girl imaginable?' " he inquired, and added with mock concern, "Poor Papa! I wonder if he knows quite what a waste of money your expensive education was?"

Her lips twitched. "Wretch! But I believe I shall let you form your own impression of Gemma without any coloration from me." She adopted a lofty manner. "Then we shall see whether or not I have set the case too high. He laughs best who laughs last."

"That puts me in my place right enough. Lady Gemma has a staunch champion in her old schoolmate," he said idly.

Lucy's reaction to this remark was more serious than he could have anticipated. "Yes, odd as it must seem when one considers her obvious assets and her background, I have always felt rather protective of Gemma. Of course I am almost two years her senior," she mused to herself, "and she is smallish and appears rather delicate, though she's actually tough as whitleather. Perhaps that accounts for it."

John ticked off on his fingers the attributes mentioned by his sister. "Small, tough, lively, impulsive, in need of protection. If you thought to increase my desire to make the acquaintance of your unusual friend, you have succeeded beyond your wildest imagination. You see me all eagerness for the honor."

Lucy glanced at him sharply and doubted.

Little though she knew it, John's drawled accents were contrived to conceal the truth of what he had just said. In talking with Lucy he had finally decided not to reveal, at least for the present, his exceedingly good reason for wishing to meet Lady Gemma Monteith.

The blunt fact of the matter was that his grace the Duke of Carlyle was extremely desirous of repairing his dissipated fortunes by arranging an advantageous marriage for his only daughter. Who better as candidate for her hand than the son of a man so anxious to see his children established among the hereditary aristocracy that he was prepared to disgorge an extortionate sum of money to accomplish this feat? Naturally these great designs would be impossible of accomplishment without the consent and cooperation of the children concerned. Lucy, John was aware, had tacitly recorded her disinclination to further her parent's scheme by calmly turning away a succession of would-be suitors.

That left himself.

John glanced out the window at his sister's bidding and agreed that the storm seemed to be tapering off. His frowning gaze remained fixed on the green vistas hazily revealed through the diminishing rainfall, but his thoughts were unrelated to the scenery. Mr. Delevan had been deeply disappointed in his only son's refusal to spend his days in the fashion popular among the sprigs of the nobility, by devoting the larger share of his time and energy to the crucial question of the correct wardrobe in which to pursue various sporting and social activities that were pleasurable enough in small doses but, to him at least, insupportable as a way of life. The elder Delevan deplored his son's decision to take up the law as a full-time pursuit, but he was a fond parent and allowed himself to be persuaded that, far from being dry and dusty, the law was an ever-changing, constantly fascinating subject to his son and offered a challenging arena in which to make a name for himself. As John had pointed out, he had inherited his sire's driving energy and capacity for hard work and would be bored to extinction by the aimless life of a dilettante. Mr. Delevan had reluctantly abandoned his dream of supplying his son with the enormous largess required to cut a dash in society, comforted eventually by a growing sense of pride as John's modest successes began to earn him the respect of his colleagues. This almost unacknowledged but unmistakable pride was John's justification for having circumvented his father's dearly held scheme.

But if the senior Delevan had had to abandon his dream of a life of gilded leisure for his heir, one result had been to make him cherish even more tenaciously that other dream of seeing his grandchildren firmly established among the aristocracy. His own wife had been of gentle birth but had harbored few social ambitions. Theirs had been a loving and harmonious

marriage, the gentle Mrs. Delevan deferring in all public
matters to her more forceful spouse. Over the years the
children gradually learned that their mother had her
own methods of controlling her husband's more extravagant starts, and John had no doubts that had she still
been alive, her quiet influence would have been exerted
for their benefit when it came time to choose a life
partner.

However, she had not survived a brief, painful illness,
and her death had left her husband bereft. In those first
months his state had been pitiable indeed. Fortunately
his relations with his children were excellent, and with
their support and affection he had gradually emerged
from the depression that had left him bewildered and
indecisive for the first time in his existence. He was only
lately beginning to resemble his former self. John could
not suppress a slight uneasiness at the way Mr. Delevan
had come to depend so entirely on Lucy, almost putting
her in her mother's place, but on the other hand, he
harbored a strong suspicion that this dependence made
it easier for his sister to refuse the offers of men she
could not care for.

Which situation left John as the logical vehicle for the
consummation of his father's hopes.

Women had never come very much in his way. There
had been one or two brief intense spells of calf love
while he was an undergraduate, but since embarking on
his law career, John had neither time nor the inclination
for courtship or even dalliance. His father, immersed in
his own grief, had left him alone of late, not even
inquiring eagerly about the eligible females he might be
meeting, as had been his habit in the past whenever his
son had spent any time in company with friends of his
Cambridge years. Therefore, it had come as a complete
shock when, after answering a summons to his father's
office at the bank, he had been presented to the Duke of
Carlyle, and on the departure of that noble personage
following ten minutes of general civilities, he had been
informed   that   his   parent   was   in   the   process   of

negotiating a marriage contract between his son and the duke's daughter.

His first stunned disbelief mastered, he had been on the point of registering a categorical denial of any matrimonial interest in an unknown female, no matter what her lineage, when he had had the misfortune to look more closely at his own parent. The sight of his father alive with pleasurable expectancy and more like his old self than for the past two years had triggered an unexpected surge of pity and filial affection that had considerably toned down his subsequent response. He had retained enough sense of self-preservation to keep from agreeing to the marriage, but in the course of a lively interview that saw his father return to his old juggernautlike form, he had admitted to having no prior attachment to any other lady that would preclude an alliance, and later agreed not to give his final refusal of the match without first meeting the lady concerned. At least, this last was the sense of what he intended to convey, but upon later reflection, he could not overcome the sinking feeling that his parent had interpreted this rather loosely to mean that, unless he took Lady Gemma Monteith in instant and irremedial dislike, a marriage would assuredly take place. Presumably the young lady's wishes in the matter were not to be consulted.

A sudden thought somewhat reversed the sense of creeping doom that had kept pace with the wheels bringing them to Monteith Hall. Perhaps the duke had no stronger hold on his daughter than Mr. Delevan on his son. A lively, unpredictable young woman answering to the description Lucy had given him might be well able to extricate herself from a proposed match that did not meet with her approval.

John Delevan's worst enemy could not accuse him of being set up in his own conceit. He was aware of and grateful for a good brain, and equally aware and not overly concerned with the fact that his person did not resemble a Byronic hero or a figure of high romance. In fact, he decided with mounting cheerfulness, he was very probably the last man in the world to appeal to the sort of girl Lucy had described to him.

A glance across at his sister took in the presence of a half-rueful smile as she indicated the breaking cloud cover outside with a slightly smudged white gloved hand.

"I apprehend that this means I shall arrive at our destination in lonely splendor, after all," she said with a resigned sigh.

"Well, yes, I think I shall ride this last bit if you would not object too strenuously," replied her brother meekly. "I have been feeling rather queasy for the last mile or so. And if the sun should appear, it will dry my coat," he added with happy inspiration.

Lucy sternly quelled a smile. "It is my firm conviction that you don't know what it means to be queasy. You are the slyest thing in nature, John."

"No, no, I protest. You do me a grave injustice," he complained straight-faced as he replaced his modish hat at the correct angle and gathered up his gloves from the green corduroy seat preparatory to taking his departure. "Would you be so obliging as to pull the check rein, my dear sister?"

His dear sister complied with this request but gave it as her opinion that he would be well-served if his beautiful new coat arrived at Monteith Hall liberally splattered with the mud created by the recent storm.

"Now, Lucy," said John for the third time before bestowing a brilliant valedictory smile on her as he left the carriage.

3

Lady Gemma Monteith and her canine companion set off across the smooth lawns of her ancestral home in the direction of the lane that led to the post road. This was reached by traversing a shallow belt of trees that concealed the grounds from the view of anyone arriving from this direction until the trees gave way to an encircling wall of brick that was eventually breeched by a Jacobean gate house giving onto the avenue that led to the main entrance of the hall. Beyond the belt of trees a thick high hedge bordered the lane, and this was Lady Gemma's destination at the moment.

One destination was as good as another as far as Homer was concerned, and except for repeated short forays to chase down the source of various woodland noises, he took his job as his mistress's companion seriously. From hard-won experience of his frenetic style, Gemma kept one eye on his progress. Her vigilance kept her from tripping over him on one of his ill-judged rushing returns, but her swift sideways maneuver to avoid stepping on the pup resulted in a dirty wet mark made by a branch brushing across the hipline of her dress. After relieving her feelings in a burst of scolding, to which Homer was as usual impervious, she proceeded on her way, having mentally accepted the necessity of changing her gown before their guests arrived. The sodden condition of the path endorsed the precautionary wisdom of wearing a pair of old half-boots instead of her sandals. They were already disgracefully mud-covered, but at least her feet were dry.

The blackthorn hedge, when she reached it, was still glistening with raindrops, and Gemma was markedly damp by the time she had clipped a generous quantity of the white blossoms and placed them in her basket. There were one or two scratches disfiguring her hands and wrists, and having forgotten to put a handkerchief in her pocket, it had been necessary to dry her hands on the skirt of her gown, a procedure that had not enhanced its appearance. The sloes were lovely, though, so Gemma did not regard a little inconvenience when she pictured what would be Lucy's surprise and delight to find masses of them in her bedchamber.

Lady Gemma's sartorial condition would have remained a minor inconvenience had not Homer gotten himself entangled in the hedge. It was necessary to lay her basket aside and squat down to free the pup. In the process, Gemma found herself hooked on a branch of the hedge. It had become inserted in the low rounded back of her bodice when she tried to rise after rescuing Homer. It jerked her back onto her heels, and such was the awkwardness of her position that she could neither twist her head sufficiently to the rear to see, nor reach a hand to the proper spot to pull the branch away. Any attempt to get to her feet was going to result in a huge tear in one of her favorite gowns, not to mention the possibility of a corresponding tear in her flesh. She might have been able to use the shears to some good effect, but they were in her basket just tantalizingly out of reach. Homer's yelps were rising to a crescendo as he ran to and fro, trying to entice her into a game, and she had just about decided there was no recourse save a ruined dress when she became aware of the sound of hoofbeats approaching in the lane beyond the hedge during a pause between barks.

"Is that you, Peter?" she called in ringing tones. "I need your assistance desperately. Tie Rufus up and come through the gap a little farther along."

The hoofbeats stopped abruptly, then continued on for a bit. Gemma tried to follow the movements behind her but Homer's barking made that all but impossible.

"Quiet, you idiotish animal! It is entirely your fault

that I find myself in this ridiculous predicament in the first place." A second later she exclaimed, "Thank goodness you came along just at this moment," as the welcome sounds of a body brushing through the small gap in the hedge reached her ears at last. "Pray unhook my dress from this malevolent branch before I grow roots," she begged, craning her neck and rewarded by an oblique glimpse of polished Hessians and fawn-colored inexpressibles making their way toward her. She was still trying to reach Homer to cuff him into silence when she felt the fingers of one gloved and one ungloved hand at her back. It seemed but an instant before the hands had moved to her waist and lifted her to her feet. Gemma turned a laughing glance over her shoulder and encountered the intent blue-eyed gaze of a stranger.

"You're not Peter," she accused, spinning to face him fully.

The stranger drew in a long breath and smiled. "Alas, no, but the urgency of your request and the awkward nature of your situation led me to believe that you might prefer to accept any prompt assistance rather than await Peter's arrival, no matter how swift."

"Well, you are very right about that," she conceded frankly. "I cannot remember when I've been so uncomfortable."

The man heaved an exaggerated sigh of relief. "Then perhaps I need not fear that my presumption has put me quite beyond the pale before ever we have been introduced."

"On the contrary, I believe that even among the highest sticklers it is considered perfectly permissible to abandon formality in the middle of a rescue," she replied, adopting his tone of mock gravity. Huge near-black eyes laughed into blue before the girl swooped down and retrieved her basket.

"You must allow me to thank you most gratefully, sir, for a very timely assistance," she declared, and on impulse broke off a clump of the flowers in her basket and presented it with a flourish to her rescuer, who accepted the token with a graceful bow.

"Would you be so kind?" He indicated his lapel, and Gemma obligingly and unselfconsciously inserted the flowers in his buttonhole. She stepped back to admire the effect, then turned her steps toward the gap in the hedge.

"Have you left your horse tied in the lane, sir?" For the first time curiosity appeared in the dark eyes. "Were you heading for the hall?" she inquired as he suited his pace to her shorter steps.

"Yes," the man replied, sweeping off his modish beaver hat and turning to face her squarely. "May I introduce myself? My name is John Delevan and I . . . Is something wrong?"

Long black lashes descended to conceal the flicker of dismay that had appeared in her eyes at his words. "No, of course there is nothing wrong. It is just that if you are Mr. Delevan, Lucy must not be far behind; in fact, I hear a carriage in the lane now, and just *look* at the picture I shall present in greeting her!" This last was added in a despairing wail.

Mr. Delevan took full advantage of the permission accorded him to study the discomposed girl at his side. Even now she had not mentioned her name, but he had guessed her identity from the instant laughing brown eyes had met his in a glance brimming with rueful mischief when she had thought him the unknown Peter. He had understood in a flash why Lucy had found it so difficult to describe her friend. It wasn't easy to describe sunshine either; one simply gravitated toward it. Now, as he took in muddy boots, crumpled sprig muslin gown with patches of damp and streaks of dirt, a charming straw bonnet set slightly askew on dusky curls, and one delicate wrist bearing an angry scratch, a smile very like his sister's—did he but know it—appeared in the bright-blue eyes.

"I would suggest that there is nothing to be done but carry off the situation with a high hand," he offered calmly, "*after* you straighten your bonnet."

The basket of flowers was unceremoniously thrust into his hands as Gemma's flew to her hat to rectify matters. "Quickly, let us catch the chaise in the lane," she urged, slipping through the gap in the hedge on the words.

Perforce, Mr. Delevan followed her and the darting little dog, his progress considerably slower, thanks to the minuscule size of the gap and the bulky basket he carried. His driver had already started to obey her signals to stop when he arrived beside his horse. Lady Gemma had not waited for him but had sped after the braking chaise, waving and calling to Lucy, whose smiling face had appeared at the window. By the time Mr. Delevan retrieved Blackbeard and caught up with the chaise, his groom had opened the door and Lucy had tumbled out into the arms of her friend. They were both laughing and talking at once, with the yapping dog circling them, watched benevolently by Henry and less patiently by the coachman, who was eager to see the end of the journey. Mr. Delevan gave the latter an understanding wink and approached the absorbed girls with a purposeful air.

"May I suggest, Lady Gemma, that you join Lucy in the carriage for the last few yards. You'll be able to get a running start on catching up on all your news." A friendly smile accompanied the words as he extended a hand to assist her into the carriage. Lady Gemma looked a trifle surprised at such high-handedness but allowed herself to be maneuvered thus. He handed Lucy in, then the dog, and closed the door before recalling the basket of flowers he had in his turn thrust into his groom's unwilling hands. At this point he decided Henry's ruffled feelings must be temporarily sacrificed in the interests of getting to their destination, and he swung himself up onto Blackbeard's back after giving Joseph the signal to start.

Inside the carriage Gemma was repeating her delight at having the company of her dearest friend. "You look quite recovered from that dreadful influenza, I am thankful to see, but we shall spend hours and hours outdoors this summer. That will bring the roses back to your cheeks," she predicted, casting a knowledgeable eye over her guest's features.

"It sounds a delightful program," Lucy agreed, "but you know I am naturally pale, especially compared with you." She surveyed her hostess's healthy olive complexion with an affectionate smile.

"Oh, I am as dark as a gypsy, of course; there's nothing to be done about that."

Lucy was well aware that Gemma rated her physical attributes very low, despite considerable evidence that others were drawn to her glowing dark looks. She had come to the conclusion that it must simply be a case of the grass being greener, a romantic longing to be different from one's everyday self. She had meant to observe her brother's first reaction to her friend, but they had put that beyond her power. "How did you and John come upon each other?" she asked, her first pleasure in seeing Gemma giving way to curiosity.

"He rescued me. I was caught on a piece of hedge and called to him, thinking it was my brother Peter I heard in the lane," Gemma explained, and looked slightly affronted at Lucy's gurgle of laughter.

"Just what I would have expected. You haven't changed a bit."

"It was purely an accident," her friend replied, on her dignity.

"Of course, but it could only happen to you." Lucy assessed the other's crumpled appearance with interest and smiled more broadly.

"Fustian!" declared Gemma roundly. "It could have happened to anyone. . . . Well, perhaps not to Coralee," she admitted, grimacing.

"Is Coralee your cousin, the one you said you couldn't get on with as children?"

"Yes, and we still don't get on together. She is excessively good to look at and disgustingly accomplished and has a talent for making me seem *farouche*. I always show to disadvantage in her company."

"Nonsense, Gemma. You go along in company quite

comfortably," argued Lucy in a practical spirit.

Her companion's face was a study in regretful resignation. "You shall have a firsthand opportunity to judge for yourself, I'm afraid. My mother told me today that Coralee and my aunt are coming for a long visit. Such a hideous stroke of luck, when I was so looking forward to having you all to myself."

Lucy quirked an eyebrow at the gloomy tone but contented herself with a noncommittal murmur.

The coach had entered on the avenue of chestnut trees now and she was straining for her first glimpse of Monteith Hall. Gemma forgot her gloom in mischievous anticipation of her friend's reaction.

She was not disappointed. As they swept around the last curve, the main front of the hall was revealed in all its complexity.

"Goodness!" Lucy was startled into a faint ejaculation. "It looks like something out of a fantasy, but delightful," she added in case Gemma should be offended.

Mr. Delevan, riding beside the groom, was in the happy position of having his first impression of the Duke of Carlyle's principal seat uncensored, but in any case, it was Henry whose reaction was recorded.

"Well, if that don't beat the Dutch," he exclaimed in patent disbelief. 'You'd have thought somebody would have pulled the place together. It looks as if every man jack of them what was living in the place had a hand in designing it."

John could not but agree with his groom that Monteith Hall struck one at first glance as being unplanned, almost haphazard in design—certainly it made no pretense of striving for any kind of symmetry with its irregular bays and rooflines—but on continuing to regard it as he came closer, he conceded a definite charm about the whole that overcame its architectural deficiencies. Clearly Tudor in conception and period, its rosy brickwork and mullioned windows, oriels, and partial timbering in some of the bays produced a harmonious effect that was augmented in his eyes by the ivy

growth that was extensive without in any way adding a
dreary touch. He let his glance climb to the profusion of
tall molded chimneys that, in conjunction with the
crenellated tops of some of the bays, made the roofline
even more picturesque.

Just at that moment the carriage pulled up before the
entrance porch, which, John noted with interest, was
surmounted by the arms of Henry VIII. The huge oaken
door was already open, forcing his attention from the
peculiarities of the architecure to the butler and his sub-
ordinates who were deploying themselves in readiness to
assist the arrival of the guests.

John had to restrain a chuckle as the butler betrayed
his calling by permitting a momentary expression of
astonishment to cross his long, ascetic face when the
first person out of the carriage proved to be his young
mistress, who declined his assistance, tossing an airy,
"Hullo, Stansmere. Will you help Miss Delevan?" as
she jumped lightly down despite the squirming pup in
her arms.

The duke's reaction to the sight of his daughter an
instant later brought no similar inclination to amusement, however. Most of John's attention had been
focused on the scene beside the carriage, but he had
detected from the corner of his eye the imposing figure
of his host approaching from the doorway.

"Gemma, what is the meaning of this? How came
you to be in such a disgraceful condition?" he
demanded in a well-modulated voice that nevertheless
seemed to thunder into a sudden silence.

His daughter started and bit her lip before replying
coolly that she would explain it to him presently. She
deposited the yapping dog on the ground and shooed
him into the house before the irate duke could cuff him.

"May I present my dear friend, Miss Lucinda Delevan, Papa?" she said as Lucy descended from the
chaise.

The duke responded charmingly, bowing over Lucy's
hand with a show of flattering interest that her brother
suspected was an automatic reaction in one accustomed

to a lifetime of success with the fair sex. In his turn, he was made graciously welcome by his host, who then attempted to present his daughter, though it was evident by the set of his mouth that he was displeased by her disheveled state.

"I have already had the extreme felicity of meeting Lady Gemma, sir," John said smoothly, interrupting the duke's apology for her appearance.

"We had the good fortune to spy Gemma in the lane," Lucy continued, taking over for her brother. "It was marvelous to have her personal escort at the end of a long journey." She sighed suggestively, but the duke refused to be put off the scent.

"Walking in the lane scarcely seems an adequate explanation for the state of your dress," he commented to his silent daughter in a tone from which all previous warmth had departed.

"I was picking flowers for Lucy's bedchamber and, with Homer's help, got myself dirty," she said briefly, no note of apology present in her explanation. "Now I propose to escort Lucy to her room so she may put off her bonnet before tea."

"Thank you, Gemma dear. Oh, are these the flowers?" as John offered the basket to his hostess with a smiling bow. "How lovely! You remembered how much I admire sloes. Thank you so much."

Gemma eased her guest away from the men, grateful that John Delevan had made a remark about the facade of the hall that demanded her father's attention long enough for the girls to make a silent entrance into the house. For a moment her shoulders sagged a little. She had been so looking forward to spending a quiet summer with Lucy, but everything had conspired to go wrong from the moment her mother told her of the expanded guest list. Well, she still had Lucy, and she was determined not to allow the others to ruin this visit.

Beside her, Lucy noted the sudden air of resolution about her friend's bearing and wondered as to the cause as she allowed herself to be led up the heavily carved wooden staircase.

4

It was a full half-hour before the residents of the hall, both permanent and temporary, assembled in one of the main saloons for the scheduled refreshments. By that time, Lucy had been installed in a spacious bedchamber located in the same corridor as her friend's in the oldest wing of the house, and she had amply gratified her hostess by her spontaneous pleasure in being assigned a room furnished with the ponderous carved furniture prevalent in the seventeenth century. She exclaimed over the original bedhangings of crewelwork, faded with the passage of time but still strong, and gazed out the casement windows to admire the view of smooth lawns sloping down to an ornamental lake.

Lady Gemma then left her guest to freshen up in privacy while she hurried to her own room to remove her boots and change into another gown after removing as many of the signs of her recent activities from her person as possible. There was nothing she could do about the red scratches on her wrist except try to dull them with powder, but she washed her face and hands and revived her flattened coiffure with a quick brushing. The dark curls were enhanced by a yellow ribbon that matched her prettiest new muslin, a dress she had worn only once before, which had elicited a rare compliment from her father.

The fact that Lucy and her brother had both tried to mitigate an embarrassing confrontation with her parent just now had touched her heart. They had shown themselves sensitive to nuances in the atmosphere, and she was resolved that the beginning of Lucy's visit should not be further clouded. Hopefully, her father would be pleased with her restored appearance and they would brush through the tea-drinking ceremony with no additional display of his displeasure.

Long before dinner was over that evening, Gemma was regretting her placatory behavior, however. The duchess had joined them for tea, and after greeting Mr. Delevan kindly, had begun questioning Lucy about her recent illness with a gentle concern. She had always liked this sensible girl and considered her a good influence on her volatile daughter. At any other time Gemma would have been delighted to share her parent with Lucy, but this monopoly today had played directly into her father's hands.

The duke was at his wittiest, entertaining Mr. Delevan with the latest sporting stories from the London clubs and keeping his daughter firmly in his orbit when she would have joined the ladies' talk. Not that his grace was ever guilty of being obvious; he was a man of the town, a superb conversationalist, and a talented raconteur who could on occasion even give a convincing appearance of listening attentively to others. Mr. Delevan proved to be an appreciative audience: interested, quick to catch the point, and once he even succeeded in capping one of his host's stories. Her father's choice was no slow top, Gemma was compelled to admit. She had a shrewd notion that Mr. Delevan did not spend all his days mewed up in a dim dusty office, buried to his shoulders in legal tomes.

As the evening wore on and the duke became increasingly affable and expansive, his daughters spirits became correspondingly weighted. Now she bitterly regretted the impulse that had caused her to bestow a boutonniere on the last man in the world she wished to encourage. A lingering hope that the gesture might have gone unnoticed was extinguished during tea when she caught her father's speculative glance fixed on the white blossoms wilting against the dark-brown coat of his guest. That he was sufficiently needle-witted to make the association was attested to by his suddenly benign countenance and the swift smile for his daughter, though no remark was made. His daughter's spirits slipped another notch.

Mr. Delevan's manner toward a girl he had just met could not be faulted, but Gemma derived no comfort from this. She'd have preferred a patent show of indifference to his exemplary civility but was not so unreasonable as to expect such from a man whose very presence indicated the opposite of indifference. Whether there was anything at all of a personal nature to be read in Mr. Delevan's courtesy was a question his host's daughter could not have determined even had she wished to do so—which she passionately did *not*—because acute embarrassment and distress over her own hapless position prevented her from being able to meet the gentleman's glance for more than the fraction of a second. It required all of the social sense painfully acquired during her London Season to enable Gemma to play her part in the cosy family evening without revealing her mental agitation; and by the time the ladies retired—at a thankfully early hour, since Lucy was a bit fatigued from traveling—she had, in desperation, formed the firm intention of laying all her cards on the table before Mr. Delevan at the earliest possible moment. It was inconceivable to her that they could engage in daily intercourse while Mr. Delevan remained ignorant of the attachment between herself and George. It would be the grossest inconsideration to let him continue in the mistaken belief that she was free to consider his suit.

This resolve once taken, Lady Gemma was able to bid her friend good night with a cheerful air and an easier conscience. It was not until she was about to climb into her own bed that it struck her that she had no idea whether Lucy was aware of the contemplated match between her brother and her schoolmate. This unwelcome possibility gave birth to a new worry that her refusal of Mr. Delevan might wound Lucy and drive a wedge into their friendship. This new problem would have given her troubled spirit a difficult time indeed had not the sleep of total mental exhaustion claimed her healthy young body very shortly thereafter.

The following morning Lady Gemma arose at an early hour, animated by the urgent need to carry out the decision taken the previous evening with respect to Mr. Delevan before her father's machinations could become obvious to everyone. This time she dressed quickly, with no thought to pleasing the duke, and was nearly finished by the time her maid entered the room. Thinking her mother might not have had the opportunity as yet to request that Mrs. Benedict detail one of the young housemaids to wait on Lucy during her stay, she sent Polly along to her friend's room and spent the next few moments rehearsing what she would say to Mr. Delevan. A very little consideration served to convince her that there really was not a tactful approach to such a delicate subject. In the fullness of time it might be possible by oblique references to George to impress upon Mr. Delevan that her affections were already bespoken, but her father's behavior indicated he was not prepared to allow this new acquaintance to ripen at its own unaided pace. This being the case, there was no alternative to a direct confrontation. Bracing herself for the ordeal, she went down the hall to knock at Lucy's door.

"Oh, I do like that!" Lady Gemma passed an approving eye over her guest's crisp lilac cotton gown with its dainty white pleated neckline below a narrow frilled ruff. She closed the door and came into the room to wait while Polly finished brushing out Lucy's shining chestnut tresses.

"Am I late for breakfast?"

Intercepting her friend's quick glance at the French clock on the marquetry table desk, Lady Gemma shook her own dusky curls. "No, we need not go down for another twenty minutes or so. Quite often Papa and Peter will have been riding before breakfast, and Mama never leaves her rooms much before noontime. Her constitution is not strong, you know."

"I liked your mother so much when she would visit you at school. I hope having us here will not be a strain on her."

"Oh, no. Mrs. Benedict and I see to it that Mama is not troubled unnecessarily with the small household crises. Dealing with Papa's demands is quite as much as she can manage in general."

"While I am here, you must let me help too in any way I may." Lucy made no comment on Gemma's reference to her father, though she was already beginning to suspect that her friend did not enjoy the kind of warm relationship with the duke that existed between Mr. Delevan and his children. "Shall we meet your brother this morning?" she asked, hoping to hit on a happier topic. In the next instant she wished she had confined her remarks to the weather as Gemma took her underlip between her teeth, anxiety furrowing her smooth brow.

"I trust so, or the atmosphere at table will be sulfuric. Peter is at a stage of life where he much prefers the company of his male contemporaries to that of his family. He delights in evading my father's watchful eye and absenting himself from home, sometimes for days on end, though he well knows there will be a reckoning due when he does come home. I once asked him why he continues to defy Papa's edicts, and he told me the freedom was worth the punishment."

"He does not sound so very different from most young men of his age to me," said Lucy tolerantly.

"Do you think so?" Gemma brightened. "Mama and I go about in a constant quake that he will do something so reckless there will be no smoothing it over with Papa. It takes a terrible toll on my mother's nerves when my father and Peter are on the outs."

Lucy nodded in wordless sympathy, marveling at her own lack of preparedness for this visit. She had not given a thought previously to the possible existence of undercurrents in her friend's family life. It was a decidedly thoughtful young woman who entered the breakfast parlor a few moments later, alerted to small nuances in the atmosphere.

The first meeting with the Marquess of Gresham, who seemed refreshingly uncomplicated, passed off very well. Lucy knew him to be just a year senior to his sister, but was surprised to find him quite unlike her in looks, favoring, as he did, his paternal parent while Gemma had inherited the warm dark coloring of her mother's Italian ancestors. He was not as large as the duke, standing just above middle height, with the slim build of youth, but father and son shared the same slightly aquiline cast of countenance and golden-brown hair. Both possessed light-blue eyes set under straight brows. There was little sign as yet that the young marquess would develop the penetrating, somewhat sardonic gaze that rendered his father's aspect so formidable at times. He was dressed carelessly, with a Belcher handkerchief around his neck that drew forth a scathing comment from the duke that did nothing to dampen his high spirits. He returned Lucy's frank appraisal with the same masculine appreciation his father had displayed but without the older man's ease of expression, and he greeted her brother with ready friendliness.

"It will be a pleasure for Gemma to have the company of an old friend," said the marquess, looking up from the plate of eggs and beef he was demolishing to smile widely at Lucy. "There is never much doing around here in the summer. I hope you won't find it unbearably dull after London."

"I'm sure I shan't. Just being in this lovely countryside will be a treat for me."

"How could life possibly be dull, Peter, with Aunt Sophronia and Coralee coming for a nice long visit?" Gemma did not see the quickening interest in Mr. Delevan's eyes at her tone of bogus innocence; she was anticipating her brother's reaction to her little bomb.

Peter did not disappoint her. After nearly choking on a mouthful of food, he bent a look of pop-eyed horror at his sister's sweetly composed features. "Good Lord,

not—" He broke off under a quelling glare from his
father and amended hastily, "I mean, I was not aware
that my aunt and cousin meant to honor us with a visit
this summer."

"Perhaps if you stayed at home more often, you
would know more of the family's affairs. My sister and
niece arrive today, and naturally I shall expect you to do
your part to entertain your cousin while she is with us."
His grace forestalled any attempt on his son's part to
articulate the mutiny writ clear on his face by declaring
his intention to conduct Mr. Delevan around the estate
after breakfast. "I trust we may hope for your company
also, Gresham."

The mention of Mr. Delevan's name recalled Gemma
to the need to speak privately with that gentleman.
"May Lucy and I come too, Papa?" she put in swiftly,
unconsciously easing what might be considered the
unease of their guests at being present at a family
squabble by diverting attention from the rebellious
Peter.

"My dear Gemma, Miss Delevan has been cooped up
in a carriage for two days. I am persuaded she would far
liefer employ her time this morning in a relaxed tour of
the old parts of the house." Turning to Lucy with a
charming smile, the duke added, "You appear to me
someone who will appreciate the fine linenfold paneling
in the queen's room and the original hangings, Miss
Delevan."

"Oh, yes, indeed I shall."

Seeing the sparkle of anticipation in her friend's eyes,
Gemma conceded herself outgeneraled and accepted her
defeat with good grace, firmly suppressing the sense of
frustration that gripped her whenever her glance
chanced to fall on John Delevan calmly eating his
breakfast with every appearance of enjoyment. His
friendly smile seemed to demand a like response, but
after responding to it at one point, she experienced an
absurd pang of guilt, as though to smile at Mr. Delevan
was to betray her love for George. With a concerted

effort she shook off this mood and prepared to enjoy a morning with Lucy.

The morning passed happily and all too quickly. Lucy's obvious pleasure in exploring the rambling structure that had evolved over the years communicated itself to her friend, who was able to see her home through fresh eyes. As expected, the state rooms, which had been prepared for a projected visit by Queen Elizabeth that never took place, were of paramount interest. The series of square rooms, one following another with their doors lined up for the ease of the royal progression, were preserved intact as far as the original paneling and tapestries were concerned, though the furnishings had been updated at the whim of subsequent owners and their ladies. One mantelpiece still bore the arms of Queen Elizabeth over it, and there was a gloriously carved wooden overmantel in the withdrawing room that had probably been executed at a later date by Grinling Gibbons, who was known to have worked in the area. All the rooms boasted plasterwork ceilings of geometric design and exuberantly carved doors in the Tudor arch shape.

Lucy fell in love with a sumptuously carved and upholstered daybed with an exquisite shell-shaped head, but in general she found the paintings of more interest than the bulky furniture. "This is a charming study of the young queen," she enthused, stepping closer to admire a painting in the royal bedchamber.

"Which is more than one can say for that gruesome copy of the Holbein portrait of her father in the anteroom."

Lucy giggled at Gemma's delicate shudder of distaste and agreed. "Having that forbidding face so near one's bedchamber would certainly drive away my sleep."

The girls amused themselves by trying, and failing, to discover some likeness to the present duke or his son in the two old portraits of ancestors dating from the time of the early Stuarts that were enshrined in the state rooms, and Lady Gemma promised her guest a visit to the picture gallery on another occasion to pursue this quest further among what she slightingly referred to as a plethora of family portraits accumulated down through the years. By the time they had wandered into a newer wing and peeked into the main guest rooms used by the present duke, it was nearly time for lunch.

The pleasant task of showing Lucy around the hall and answering her numerous questions had successfully diverted Lady Gemma's attention for hours, but the sight of Mr. Delevan's brown head in the dining parlor brought her problems rushing to the forefront once more. It was imperative that she seek a private interview with him—and the sooner, the better, for the sake of her peace of mind. But how to accomplish the feat without arousing the curiosity of every other member of the household was a puzzle that occupied her almost to the exclusion of eating.

In the ordinary way, shyness was not an affliction that troubled Lady Gemma, nor was Mr. Delevan's person particularly intimidating or off-putting. Once granted the opportunity and the requisite privacy, she felt confident that she could make the necessary explanation in a way that would spare his feelings and permit them to deal together without strain thereafter. Numerous opportunities would doubtless arise without her contrivance in the course of time, but time was of the essence. Coralee and Aunt Sophronia would be upon them before the day was over, and her cousin's sharp eyes and instinct for news gathering were forces not to be underestimated. She was bound to spot any little maneuvers of her uncle's aimed at throwing her cousin and Mr. Delevan together, and there would be no restraining that mischief-making tongue of hers.

By the time the meal ended, the duke's daughter was in a highly developed state of tension, unsure whether to act or not to act, and, incidentally, more in sympathy with Hamlet's indecision than she had ever expected to be back in her school days when she had read the play. Then, while she sat paralyzed by doubts, the situation resolved itself with the ease of a drawer sliding into its grooves.

Lucy, who had crooned lovingly over the superb pianoforte in the music room that morning, expressed a diffident desire to practice upon the instrument if no one would be disturbed. She was promptly commanded by the duchess to regard it as her own at any time during her visit, since all the family enjoyed music without a single member being in any way disciplined enough to practice regularly. Her grace then requested an interview with her husband concerning some household matters. Peter announced his intention of riding into Bath that afternoon. The duke's questioning glance fell on his guest, but before he could inquire the latter's wishes, Mr. Delevan remarked idly that he had glimpsed a lovely garden that morning that he would enjoy exploring. Perhaps Lady Gemma would be so kind as to direct his footsteps?

Avoiding the satisfied gleam in her father's eyes, Lady Gemma demurely expressed herself willing to guide their visitor on a tour of the gardens, hoping she had been able to disguise her eagerness as filial obedience.

"Don't neglect to take a hat, dearest. The sun is strong today," warned the duchess as the luncheon party scattered to its various pursuits.

"Yes, Mama," said her dutiful daughter.

Twenty minutes later, Lady Gemma was conducting her father's houseguest along the neat, graveled paths of the rose garden. Mindful of the ostensible reason for this tête-à-tête, she made a conscientious effort to deliver a brief history of each variety that caught Mr. Delevan's fancy. Again he proved an attentive and encouraging audience, so much so that she forgot for a time her real purpose and discoursed with mounting enthusiasm on her favorite flowers, unaware of the charming picture she presented in her deep-pink dress with its white sash and little neck ruff of goffered lawn. Obligingly, Mr. Delevan directed his attention to all the

specimens she extolled, but it returned each time of its
own accord to the vivid countenance of his hostess. A
tiny smile hovered on his lips as she lifted her face to the
sun's rays with sensual enjoyment. He gestured toward
the straw bonnet dangling over her arm by its pink
ribbons.

"Was I mistaken or did I hear you promise your
mother to wear a hat on this perilous expedition?"

For a second she looked disconcerted until a lambent
glance detected the quizzical gleam in his eyes.
Incredibly thick lashes descended to conceal her
expression. "I promised Mama to *take* a hat," she
corrected primly, "so you *are* mistaken sir."

"A thousand apologies, Lady Gemma," he replied
solemnly, acknowledging the hit with an exaggerated
bow. "As a barrister, I should never be guilty of
imprecise interpretation, but I beg you will not heap
ashes on my bowed head."

"How nonsensical you are!" She chuckled and
resumed her strolling pace along the curving walk. "Ah,
here is Mama's favorite, the Belle de Crécy. Isn't this a
perfectly beautiful specimen?"

"Perfectly beautiful," he agreed.

Something in his look, which wasn't directed at the
rose, caused the rich color in her cheeks to deepen.
"You did not even look at it," she scolded, then
continued to babble in sudden embarrassment. "I
suspect you are a fraud, sir. It strikes me that your
interest in our lovely garden is merely assumed."

"No, no, I protest! It is you who are mistaken this
time." Mr. Delevan exhibited a wounded expression.
"My interest in *all* the lovely things in your garden is
quite sincere."

There was nothing but friendly raillery to be heard in
his voice, but Lady Gemma found herself hurrying into
speech. "Mr. Delevan, may I speak to you quite
plainly?"

"Yes, of course." He was all polite encouragement,
but the bright-blue eyes engaging hers were now neutral
in expression.

She resisted a cowardly urge to look away and faced him, a small valiant figure reflecting an unconscious dignity. "Mr. Delevan, my mother told me yesterday that my father wishes me to . . . to marry you." She paused expectantly, but he remained silent in the wake of such unexpected frankness. "Is it true?"

He ignored her question for the moment, posing one of his own. "Has your father spoken on this subject to you?"

"No, he has not!"

Mr. Delevan looked faintly perturbed but did not speak, and Lady Gemma's impatience burst forth. "You have not answered my question, sir."

"Yes, it is my understanding that your father would like you to marry me," he replied, meeting her anxious gaze with honest eyes.

She expelled a pent-up breath. "Mr. Delevan, I am so very sorry, but there can be no question of our marrying. I am promised to another."

The smallest of frowns appeared between his brows. "Does your father know this?" he asked quietly.

"He chooses not to, but he is well aware of the attachment between George and me," she exclaimed in some bitterness. "This is an intolerable situation!"

"It is rather awkward to be sure. However, you must not distress yourself, Lady Gemma. I would not dream of pressing an unwelcome suit upon you."

"You are too kind, sir," she broke in, almost stuttering in her eagerness to thank him. "Of course, I knew that a brother of Lucy's must be understanding. This is an unpleasant surprise for you too, and I most earnestly beg your pardon."

"You must not," he said firmly. "It is rather for me to apologize for being the instrument, however unwitting, that has caused you distress. Naturally, I shall make my excuses and return to London straightaway."

At this suggestion the girl facing him on the garden path lost some of her rich color and her fingers twisted around one another in mute agitation. "I have no right to ask you to remain under the circumstances, sir," she said in a low voice, staring fixedly at a lovely yellow rose bush, "but Papa will be so angry with me." She closed her lips tight against any further cowardly utterance and squared her shoulders as if to accept a burden.

The man watching her laughed out unexpectedly, drawing startled brown eyes to his. "That we cannot allow," he declared in a remarkably lighthearted tone for one who had just lost a well-connected bride. "If it is your wish, I will stay—on one condition."

"And that is?" A slight wariness manifested itself in her manner.

"That you cease to treat me with that touch of reserve I remarked from the moment I mentioned my name," he said, and smiled at her. "I should like us to be friends."

"Done!" She responded instantly to the invitation in that infectious smile. Her spirits rebounded and she stuck out her hand in the time-honored gesture of agreement.

Mr. Delevan accepted the small hand with alacrity and gently squeezed her fingers. "It's a bargain," he promised.

Unfortunately, the person against whom this tacit alliance had been formed, came upon them at just the moment when they stood close together clasping hands.

"Gemma, my dear child, your mother wishes a word with you," boomed the duke in jovial accents. "I will take over your duties as guide for the time being."

Mr. Delevan didn't turn a hair at this unexpected interruption, but the duke's daughter jumped back, dropping his hand as though it were red-hot. She blushed furiously in mingled annoyance and discomfiture and took herself off before she could further betray her agitation. The fact that her departure under the circumstances might be construed as flight could only be deplored, not avoided.

5

Two hours later, Mr. Delevan's unhurried progress across the first-floor gallery was arrested by a chorus of notes coming from the music room, though chorus was rather too flattering a word for the eager but not entirely harmonious sounds masquerading as music, he decided, altering his course to approach the open door. The air of preoccupation, or perhaps indecision, that had rendered him nearly oblivious to his surroundings just a moment before vanished, to be replaced by a look of keen enjoyment as he stepped into the room and absorbed the scene at the pianoforte.

Visually, the two girls engrossed in the music they were attempting to produce presented a picture that would charm anyone whose appreciation of feminine beauty and appeal had not absolutely atrophied. Lucy, cool and serene in a gown of lavender with a white collar, was seated at the instrument, intent on getting a phrase correct. Lady Gemma, with her hand on her friend's shoulder as she peered at the music, was a vibrant creature in deep pink.

"No, no, that's too high, Lucy. Cannot you play it in a lower key?"

"If I do, the low part then becomes too difficult for female voices. Try it again, Gemma." Her fingers ran over the keys as she sang the phrase in question. "There! You can do it if you get a running start," she said coaxingly, then winced in exaggerated pain at her partner's croaking rendition. Stiffling a giggle, she suggested that the aspiring singer might be more successful if she came at the phrase full-voiced. "Try it once more."

"What I really need is a ladder to reach that high

note," her friend muttered darkly, "but this will have to do." She seized a spindly legged gilt chair and dragged it over to the pianoforte. Lucy watched in laughing disbelief as the raven-haired girl proceeded to climb on top of the seat.

"Now, let's try it again," Lady Gemma proposed, "from the beginning."

Lucy shook her head, still laughing, but obediently struck the opening bars.

Musically speaking, the duet that ensued was not likely to gain a place for the performers on the professional stage, John Delevan opined in his role as uninvited music critic, but they were certainly enjoying themselves mightily. Lucy's voice, well-trained and true, had not the power to reach the back of the room and was rather drowned by Lady Gemma's strong performance in the lower registers. The latter tended to go off pitch and crack entirely on the higher notes, but mindful of Lucy's advice, she was making a determined assault on the difficult part. As she gathered strength for the key test, she forgot her somewhat precarious position atop the delicate chair seat, removing the balancing hand from its curved back in order to throw her whole body into the effort.

"She's going to fall," Mr. Delevan told himself with fatalistic calm, and he moved forward purposefully, just in time to catch his hostess as she teetered off the chair.

For a second the three figures were motionless, as though taking part in a tableau. John was unaware that Lucy had ceased playing, though he had heard her gasp as her friend fell. He stood looking down at the unruffled bundle of femininity in his arms, an odd little smile on his lips. He was watched in turn by his sister with a sharpened interest that escaped his notice, since his vision was wholly filled by two velvety brown eyes that stared solemnly up at him, then blinked.

"I missed my note," said Lady Gemma sadly.

A crack of laughter broke from Mr. Delevan and he

set his delicious burden on her feet with a reluctance he could only pray had gone unnoticed. For another instant he kept a steadying arm around her shoulders until she could regain her balance.

"Dearest Gemma," cooed a somewhat breathless voice from the doorway, "Uncle Ernest said I was to come straight up to the music room, but I'll go away again if I am *de trop.*"

Three heads turned as one to the figure poised in the entrance. She withstood their scrutiny with the smiling self-possession of one confident of her appeal. Indeed, the extravagantly high-crowned silk bonnet setting off her golden curls to admiration could not have been carried off by any female the least bit insecure in her own estimation, so daring were its lines.

Lady Gemma rallied first. "Hallo, Coralee. Sorry not to be downstairs to greet you, but I didn't hear your arrival." The words were welcoming, but Mr. Delevan was quick to note that neither Lady Gemma's expression nor her voice carried any notable degree of warmth.

A tinkling laugh brought his attention back to the vision in the doorway. "Small wonder you didn't hear our arrival. The noises I heard as I came up the stairs would have drowned a hunt," declared Coralee, gliding into the room under three pairs of eyes. For a second or two her attention was concentrated on the glove she was drawing carefully from her hand, and the three pairs of eyes followed the action, avoiding one another's glance. When the newcomer looked up again, her audience's attention was riveted to her. Flashing a smile from one bemused face to another, she arrived at her cousin last of all.

"Now, Gemma dear, you must introduce me to your fiancé," she commanded playfully, slanting a glance at Mr. Delevan's uncommunicative face. "What a naughty girl to keep such delightful tidings to yourself! Mama will be thrilled for you."

"What maggot have you got in your head now,

Coralee?'' demanded her red-faced victim, finding her voice at last. "I am not betrothed to Mr. Delevan.''

"*Not* betrothed?'' The golden-haired girl looked from her cousin to Mr. Delevan in patent bewilderment. "But when I arrived just now, you were in his arms. I mean . . . Oh, I do beg your pardon, and yours, sir, for being such a goose as to misunderstand.'' She cast her eyes down, the picture of pretty confusion.

Mr. Delevan, taking in his sister's expressionless countenance and Lady ·Gemma's seething speechlessness, intervened. "The unromantic truth is that you happened along just after I had the good fortune to be able to prevent Lady Gemma from suffering a fall, but you must not tease yourself, ma'am. It was a natural mistake under the circumstances. Alas, I cannot claim the honor of being Lady Gemma's fiancé.''

The new arrival directed a pitying look at her cousin. "You poor thing,'' she gushed. "How fortunate this gentleman was on the spot to catch you.'' She cast her large blue eyes around the room as if seeking the source of danger. "What did you fall from, Gemma dear?''

"A chair,'' her cousin replied shortly.

The blonde's exquisite eyebrows elevated a trifle. "A chair?'' she echoed in puzzlement.

"I was reaching for something.'' Lady Gemma pinned her cousin with a stare that dared her to continue the subject, and after a crackling instant, the latter shrugged and turned her attention to Mr. Delevan, making good use of long silky lashes as she pointed a decidedly flirtatious glance at that gentleman. "You must think me a positive ninny to jump to conclusions like that, Mr.—?'' she turned an inquiring look on Lady Gemma.

"This is my friend, Miss Delevan, and her brother, Mr. Delevan. My cousin, Miss Fairmont,'' said this young lady, performing the introductions ·in a perfunctory manner, having, if Mr. Delevan were asked his impression, her work cut out for her to swallow her spleen.

"I am persuaded this has to be Lucy!" Miss Fairmont turned her battery of charm on the other girl present. "Gemma was forever rattling on about her friend Lucy. You must know that we have all been longing to make the acquaintance of such a paragon."

Lucy extended her fingers to meet those of Gemma's cousin, wondering in some amusement how, from such a flattering description, she could possibly be left with the idea that all and sundry had been bored to extinction by tales of herself. "I shall try to live up to my advance notice," she returned coolly, with a smile as wide as Miss Fairmont's.

The latter then directed her attention to Mr. Delevan once more, fixing his eyes with her beautiful blue ones as she declared her pleasure in the acquaintance in such melting terms that any gentleman so regarded might be forgiven for imagining he had made a conquest. Mr. Delevan, unimpressionable by nature, felt no inclination to preen himself but was so obliging as to return the compliment by gazing at Miss Fairmont with frank admiration and responding with his most elegant bow as he retained her hand just enough longer than the time permitted by good manners to justify the look of triumph she flicked at her cousin.

Lady Gemma had her temper well in hand by now, but Mr. Delevan was beginning to recognize her moods and he was in no doubt that the little smile adorning her lips at present contained a measure of contempt for the susceptibility of the male of the species to feminine wiles. He smiled inwardly as he made a mental wager with himself that the little brunette would scorn to employ those feminine wiles that were an integral part of her cousin's arsenal. He had not come to any conclusion yet as to whether or not she was conscious of the weapons she herself possessed in abundance. Those eyes, for instance . . . When he had unhooked her from the hedge yesterday, the first sight of those heavily lashed, deep-brown eyes full of mischief and warmth had affected him like a blow over the heart. And her

very lack of artifice was a potent attraction in itself, at
least to a man like himself, who had never had the time,
or perhaps the inclination, to peel away the layers of
conventions, tricks, and posturings like so many leaves
of an artichoke to get to the heart of any woman whose
surface attracted him. He had always suspected that,
unlike the artichoke, the results might prove indigestible
in many cases.

After an acquaintance of less than five minutes, he
was willing to postulate that Miss Coralee Fairmont
might have been designed to prove his theory. She was a
raving beauty at first glance. There was no denying that
an impartial eye chancing upon the three young women
exchanging somewhat stilted pleasantries would tend to
linger longest on Miss Fairmont by virtue of exquisite
sculpturing and delicate coloring. In stature she was
between Lady Gemma's fairy proportions and Lucy's
tall, generously curved womanliness, being of moderate
height with a nicely rounded figure and delicate wrists
and ankles. There was only one word for the modeling
of her features: perfection. Nose, eyes, lips, cheekbones—all were beautifully crafted individually and had
been assembled by a master artist in a countenance
whose planes would be lovely fifty years hence, though
he would not dare vouch for her expression. She had
treated them to a succession of appealing poses—gaiety,
bewilderment, blushing confusion, invitation—but at
one point the sly malice had almost peeked through, and
it would not be a feat beyond comprehension to picture
those lovely features compressed into petulance, or
those melting blue eyes chilling to ice chips. When Lady
Gemma was upset or unhappy, her heart-shaped face
lost the sparkling vitality that was its most essential
characteristic, rendering her almost plain, but it was
impossible to conceive of her entirely devoid of warmth.

Mr. Delevan had remained somewhat outside the
girls' chatter during the past few minutes, but now he
was drawn in by Miss Fairmont, who apologized
charmingly for monopolizing the conversation. "As a

matter of fact, Uncle Ernest expressly desired me to tell you that tea will be served in the blue saloon directly.''

At this point Lady Gemma recollected her manners and declared that she, for one, must immediately descend to the saloon to welcome her aunt, but the others were free to drift in later if they desired to make any repairs to their appearance. ''And you will no doubt wish to put off your bonnet, Coralee, delectable though it is. Your usual room is ready for you. Would you like me to show you the way?''

Miss Fairmont declined an escort, and the group disbanded for the moment.

The rest of the day passed quite pleasantly, although Mr. Delevan had no reason to alter his first impression that the cousins were something less than devoted to each other despite the nostalgic rendition of several incidents from their shared childhood that was indulged in by Miss Fairmont's formidable parent during tea and dinner.

Mr. Delevan found Lady Sophronia Fairmont to be a handsome woman of majestic though well-corseted proportions, whose regal graciousness must have been the result of her upbringing as the only daughter of a duke. Certainly her marriage to a plain mister, no matter how wealthy, would not have endowed her with a commanding manner only lightly disguised by a thin overlay of feminine reticence on those occasions when she ran headlong across one of her brother's decisions. Fairer in coloring than he, she had inherited the family tendency toward the aquiline, being the possessor of a haughty Roman nose that, mercifully, had not descended to her daughter. For that blessing at least, the long-deceased Mr. Fairmont must be allocated the credit. After a few hours in Lady Sophronia's dominant presence, Mr. Delevan was convinced that marrying the duke's daughter had been the last independent decision the late Mr. Fairmont had been permitted to make.

Lady Sophronia was the apotheosis of graciousness to the Delevans. She treated her sister-in-law with an

affectionate condescension not quite untinged by the
contempt in which persons who contend that all life's
vicissitudes can be mastered by an unrelenting
resolution hold those unfortunates who cannot always
muster the requisite degree of resolution. She inquired
after the state of the duchess's health, promised at a
more convenient moment to reveal the ingredients of a
new tonic guaranteed to bolster shaky nerves, and dismissed her hostess from her consideration except to
compliment her on her cook's way with a salmon
mousse. Her attention alternated from interrogating her
brother on the status of tenant families known to her
from her youth to monitoring the conversation among
the young people.

Tonight the party was diminished by one, for the
Marquess of Gresham had not returned from his day's
activities in time to grace the family board at dinner,
much to his father's ill-concealed annoyance and his
mother's scarcely better-disguised anxiety that some evil
may have befallen him. In the face of this parental
ferment, Lady Sophronia permitted herself no more
than two or three semioblique observations on the
undisciplined and inconsiderate nature of modern youth
and proposed a hand or two of whist.

During the past several hours Mr. Delevan had made
the interesting discovery that the lively coquettish Miss
Fairmont of the music-room encounter was another girl
entirely when under her mama's all-seeing eye. Even
Lady Gemma's usual high spirits were reduced to
demure propriety in her aunt's company. However,
when the duke agreed to a game of whist and Lady
Sophronia said, "Come, Coralee," in her imperious
manner, her daughter attempted to squirm out from
under the maternal thumb.

"Cannot my cousin play in my stead, Mama? I have
the headache a little from traveling."

Mr. Delevan noted the flash of dismay that passed
across Lady Gemma's expressive face, but before he
could offer himself in her place, the duke spoke up,

"Gemma can't tell a spade from a club, she has no card sense whatever." His disarming smile lighted on his niece. "Tell you what, puss. You and I will be partners, and if we win, I'll buy you the prettiest dress in Bath next week."

Coralee's face cleared immediately and she tucked a small hand under the arm her uncle presented. "It's a bargain, Uncle," she said gaily, and ignoring her mother's admonition not to employ vulgar phrases gleaned no doubt from her cousin Peter's vocabulary, she tripped over to the game table by the duke's side, her headache apparently forgotten in the wake of a challenge to her skill.

The duchess had located the cards and was making her way toward the same spot while Lady Gemma and Mr. Delevan rallied to aid Lady Sophronia in gathering up all the various accoutrements that she seemed to take with her everywhere. Lady Gemma handed her aunt her reticule, a work bag, and the case containing her spectacles, which she would need for playing cards. As Mr. Delevan solicitously draped a large paisley shawl about her ladyship's shoulders, he closed one eyelid in the suspicion of a wink, bringing a responsive gleam to Lady Gemma's eyes. She lowered them quickly as her aunt turned to thank her attendants before making her way over to the card table, where the other players awaited her deliberate approach with the patience acquired by familiarity.

The three nonplayers immediately fell into an easy conversation. Lucy and Lady Gemma had their needlework at hand, but neither girl set another stitch in the lively hour that followed. They kept their voices low so as not to disturb the cardplayers. Lady Gemma had confided that neither her father nor his sister allowed any light conversation at the table when they were engaged in one of their marathon contests, each regarding nonessential verbiage as injurious to concentration.

"Poor Mama will have need of a soothing tisane

before sleeping tonight, what with Peter's shabbing off
when he well knew Aunt Sophronia was due to arrive,
and then having to be her partner at whist. Usually Papa
and Aunt play together and all poor Mama has to do is
lose graciously, which I assure you she does very well,"
she explained seriously, and looked a question when
Mr. Delevan emitted a soft laugh.

"It was nothing, a private thought. Miss Fairmont
seems to stand up to the ordeal very well," he said, to
change the direction of her thoughts as Coralee's voice
rang out in triumph.

"That card takes the trick, Uncle."

"Oh, yes, Coralee is a fine player; my aunt trained
her."

Since neither Lucy nor Mr. Delevan felt they had anything further to contribute in this connection, the talk
shifted to other subjects.

From time to time the duke spared a glance for the
young people grouped near the fireplace. Judging from
his expression, the sight of the three engaged in comfortable conversation seemed to afford him considerable satisfaction. Miss Fairmont, following his gaze on a
couple of occasions, looked a trifle thoughtful but
returned her attention to her cards. With a new dress as
incentive, she was calling upon all her skill in playing up
to her uncle's game. In this effort she was aided by the
duchess, always an erratic player given alike to flashes
of brilliance and strange lapses, both equally inexplicable to her husband, who generally avoided
partnering her. Tonight her play was uniformly poor,
and the duke and his niece were well ahead when the son
of the house strolled in at ten-thirty, still in the casual
garb he had worn at lunch.

The intervening nine hours had not improved the
young marquess's appearance. If the Belcher handkerchief tied around his neck in place of a cravat had
seemed inappropriate at lunchtime, it was doubly so in
the evening with the addition of numerous creases. Mr.
Delevan's quick eyes noted that his blue coat was

missing a button and the morning's carefully windswept arrangement of his gold-streaked locks, known as the Brutus, was now merely windblown. Evidently young Gresham had had enough to drink to dissolve his sense of discretion, for he advanced boldly into the room, declaring cheerfully that he had remembered on his way home that his aunt and cousin were arriving today and thought he must just pop in and welcome them before retiring. He treated the assembled company to a bright, vacuous smile before making his way toward the card table, where his aunt had drawn herself up stiffly. It was a blessing—albeit a small one—that he was perfectly steady on his feet.

At Mr. Delevan's side, Lady Gemma sat unmoving, but he could feel the tension in her bearing, and a glance at the duke's rigidly controlled features was sufficient to assess his lordship's censure. The duchess was covering her son's progress with disjointed questions about the reason for his delay, the possibility of some accident befalling him having been uppermost in her mind for hours.

Peter looked astounded for an instant, then swept away her worries with a careless wave of one hand. "What could happen to me in Bath?" he asked in honest surprise. "I ran into some fellows I knew and we got to talking and the time just flew by." Turning to Lady Sophronia, who had removed her spectacles and was studying him with no discernible pleasure, he bowed over her hand with a flourish. "How do you do, ma'am? I trust you had a pleasant journey?"

"As pleasant as traveling ever is, thank you, Gresham, given the state of these beastly roads. I daresay it is not necessary to present you to your cousin?"

"Lord, no, ma'am," agreed her nephew, turning with relief to the smiling girl at his left. "Though I must say you've certainly changed for the better since I last saw you, Coralee."

Fortunately, this tactless speech did not appear to

offend his cousin, who giggled and replied demurely, "Would that I could return the compliment, Peter, but really, that costume!" Raised eyebrows and a pointed look at the neckcloth completed her remark.

Peter grinned, unabashed. "I have no ambition to be regarded as one of your dandy set, thinking of nothing more interesting than the cut of one's coat or the perfection of one's cravat."

"How fortunate," murmured Miss Fairmont sweetly.

The marquess was not so befuddled as to be taken in by the look of studied innocence on his cousin's lovely face. "Some things haven't changed," he drawled. "You still have a viper's tongue, Coralee."

Everyone save Lady Sophronia, who had bristled up for an attack on her nephew, regarded the arrival just then of Stansmere and the tea tray with thankfulness. Conversation became general when the duke inquired into his guests' wishes for the next morning. Lady Gemma was urging a morning ride, should the weather prove promising, when her brother, who had evidently been trying to reverse the effects of a prolonged fast, judging by his repeated forays on the trays of sandwiches and cakes, spoke up between mouthfuls.

"Almost forgot. Guess who I ran into in Bath tonight—old George! Had no notion he was coming home. Did you know, Gemma?"

Had Peter not immediately turned his attention to the vital task of selecting another sandwich, he could not have missed the radiance that sprang to his sister's face before she got her expression under control. Certainly Mr. Delevan noticed it, and if the look of annoyance that replaced the duke's benevolence for an instant was anything to go by, so did her father. The duchess sucked in a breath and concentrated her regard on the contents of her teacup after one swift peek at her daughter's face.

Realizing that Peter, sandwich in hand, was awaiting her reply, Lady Gemma denied any prior knowledge of George's intentions in a sedate voice that revealed nothing of her feelings.

"He said he'd ride over to pay his respects tomorrow. He told me he's selling out," her brother confided to the company at large, explaining for the benefit of the Delevans that George Godwin was a friend and neighbor who had been with Wellington's army for the past four years. "Having old George around will liven up our dull existence. He's a great gun, is George, up to every row and rig." Peter fell silent, munching on his cake and presumably contemplating the benefits that would secure from the presence of their old friend in their midst once again.

"Well, I have a bone to pick with George Godwin," declared Miss Fairmont to the surprise of everyone present.

"Nonsense, you were a mere child the last time you met Captain Godwin," her mother stated positively. "If he offended you, doubtless you invited it by following him around like a tantony pig."

Lady Gemma had turned to her cousin in surprise. "Whatever do you mean, Coralee? What bone have you to pick with George?"

The blond beauty tossed her curls and put up her chin with a distinctly challenging air. "He called me a scrubby brat the last time we met. I shall make him take that back." The calm confidence with which Miss Fairmont uttered this statement jolted a crack of laughter from her uncle and sent Miss Delevan's eyes to her friend's in quick apprehension.

"I'll back you to do just that, puss!" The duke's former mood of joviality, shattered since his son's entrance, surged back in full rein as he leaned forward and pinched his niece's chin playfully.

Mr. Delevan's eyes sought Lady Gemma's, as had his sister's, to offer comfort, but if she felt at all threatened by this turn of events, it was not to be discovered in her manner.

"George would not have meant to hurt your feelings, Coralee," she assured her cousin earnestly.

Miss Fairmont lowered long lashes, then swept them

up. "I shall still make him take it back," she said with a glinting smile.

Mr. Delevan, saying good night to his sister in the gallery later, surprised her by asking in a cautious undertone if she knew Miss Fairmont's age.

Lucy's eyes searched his for a moment before she answered, "Why, yes, Gemma was saying only this morning that Coralee's eighteenth birthday is next month."

"Only seventeen! Good Lord, I'd have supposed her to be older than her cousin from her self-possession and her . . . her . . ."

"Her forward manner?" suggested Lucy dulcetly. "She's a born flirt, if that's the word you are seeking."

"Now, Lucy, your claws are showing, my dear," reproved John with a quick grin that was gone almost as soon as it appeared. "I hope this George of hers is the constant sort," he growled, spinning abruptly on his heel and leaving her staring after him openmouthed.

6

Mr. Delevan's first opportunity to assess the constancy of Captain Godwin did not come until late afternoon on the following day. When the enlarged family met together for breakfast, the duke raised the subject of the morning ride proposed by his daughter the evening before, but Lady Gemma seemed to be having second thoughts on the matter. She apologized for having forgotten the existence of some household tasks she had promised to accomplish for her mother, and then went on to point out the rather threatening aspect of the sky to the west, which might indicate the wisdom of postponing the ride till another day. As the duke's face started to take on an aspect as threatening as the sky, Lucy hastily declared her preference for spending a quiet morning indoors if the others would excuse her. Coralee followed suit, declaring herself unable as yet to contemplate the motion of a horse without arousing symptoms of travel sickness. It was decided that the male members of the party would not allow anything as negligible as possible poor weather to interfere with an outing, with the result that the house party split up along gender lines for the morning.

Mr. Delevan played out his role of a guest willing to fall in with all the host's plans for his entertainment with the calm good temper that always distinguished his behavior, but today it was in the nature of mechanical courtesy. His imagination kept returning to the hall, where two out of the three resident young women were eagerly anticipating the arrival of a gentleman, unknown as yet to Mr. Delevan but about whom he was beginning to entertain the liveliest curiosity. It was most probable that the captain would pay a morning call, which would mean that Mr. Delevan would miss the first meeting in two years between Lady Gemma and the man she loved. He would also miss the captain's reaction to Miss Fairmont, who had evidently been a mere adolescent on his last visit home, not that Mr. Delevan could picture Miss Fairmont as having been in any way an awkward adolescent. The girl was a honey pot and must always have been lovely to look at. Ah well, though he might not be present at the initial encounter, doubtless the captain would be a frequent visitor to the hall. There would be ample opportunity to observe the relationships existing among all the parties. The logical question as to what possible interest these relationships might have for a virtual stranger he preferred for some obscure reason not to address at the moment.

When everyone reassembled in the small dining parlor used for breakfast and lunch, it needed only one sharp glance from normally lazy blue eyes to inform Mr. Delevan that the promised call had not been made. Lucy was her usual collected self, smiling a general greeting to the masculine contingent as she slipped into her chair. Miss Fairmont's brilliant smile slid over her relatives to linger on Mr. Delevan. Lady Gemma smiled too, but it was an absentminded effort that barely disturbed the smooth surface of her cheeks.

On an acquaintance of less than two days, Mr. Delevan had learned to judge her mood by the depth of the twin dimples that dented those cheeks. He had discovered a smile was not necessary to bring them into play—even a rueful grimace would do the trick. It was only when she remained utterly still that they disappeared completely, except for the ever-present one in her chin. Those dimples were a source of fascination to the young barrister. He had never seen their like and found himself anticipating their appearance as their owner reacted to the scene around her.

Now he thought, poor baby! He hasn't come and she is determined to conceal her disappointment. To aid the process and, incidentally, distract the duke's attention, he initiated an animated discussion of the places they had gone on their morning ride. Lunch passed off very smoothly with Lady Gemma contributing her share to the conversation. Only when her brother teased her about her inability to read the weather, as proved by the still-sunny skies, did she look a trifle conscious.

"I still hold that we shall see some rain before sunset, and sooner rather than later," put in Mr. Delevan, accepting as his reward a grateful look from warm brown eyes.

In the event, Mr. Delevan and Lady Gemma were proved good weather prophets, for the sky clouded over rapidly during lunch and burst open shortly thereafter. A glimpse of Lady Gemma's small person, taut with impatience as she stood staring out at the rain, was mute evidence of how little satisfaction she derived from having her judgment vindicated. Obviously, the rain would keep Captain Godwin away at least during the early part of the afternoon. His old friend would have to content herself with the thought that the reunion would be all the sweeter for the anticipation.

As it happened, Mr. Delevan was a witness to the initial meeting between the alleged lovers, and sweet was not among the terms he would have employed to describe the event. He had gone off to play billiards with Gresham after lunch without seeking any conversation with the duke's daughter. It was considerably later in the afternoon when he saw her again and under circumstances that caused him to forget the proprieties momentarily.

"Gemma!" he cried, rushing forward. "What has happened?"

Anyone might be pardoned the lack of preface, but Lady Gemma didn't even notice. She had just entered the passageway through the door that led to the kitchen area, and she was dripping wet or, to be more precise, half of her person was emitting a stream of water while half remained dry. She wiped a hand across wet curls, brushing them behind her ear as she addressed herself to the concern in Mr. Delevan's manner.

"It is nothing, sir, merely a stupid accident. I went to the kitchens with a message from Mama. One of the maids had been washing down the flagstones in the scullery. I imagine she was preparing to empty out the wash water just as I passed. I saw her slip on the wet flags, and naturally I jumped forward to try to save her from falling."

"Naturally?" he murmured with a little smile and an inquiring lift to his voice.

"Of course." Lady Gemma looked her surprise. "The poor girl could have injured herself in a fall on that stone floor."

"I take it that you saved her from this fate and"—pointing to the bedraggled skirt of her yellow gown—"this is the result?"

"Yes," she replied ruefully. "The bucket dropped and splashed us both. And now I'd best excuse myself and go upstairs to change before anyone else sees me in this condition." The dimples made their appearance as she smiled up at him. "You seem fated, or cursed, to see me always at my worst."

He returned her smile but replied with theatrical intonation, "Though it distresses me to contradict a lady, you must allow me to tell you that you do not have a 'worst.' You are unfailingly appealing, though often damp."

Lady Gemma dropped him a mock curtsy. "Thank you, kind sir, and now I must dash before those voices I hear approaching discover me in this state."

She headed for the back stairway at a near run and had just reached it when her father's hearty tones halted her in her tracks.

"Ah, there you are, my dear. I thought I heard your voice. Here is an old friend who is desirous of seeing you again."

Lady Gemma's back was to Mr. Delevan, but he knew the struggle it cost her to obey her parent's summons when her instincts prompted a quick escape. Reluctantly, her hand left the newel post and she turned to face the two men who had entered the hall. She made no motion toward eliminating the distance between them, but sudden happiness wiped out embarrassment and irradiated her face as she breathed, "George!"

The younger man must have possessed splendid eyesight, for the smile on his lips faded as he took a few precipitate steps forward. "For heaven's sake, Gemma, what have you been doing to yourself? You're all wet!"

"If you've forgotten my daughter's propensity for falling into awkward situations, then you don't know her as well as you think you do, my boy," said the duke indulgently.

Mr. Delevan, standing unobserved a few feet away, reminded himself once more that this was his host, and remained silent with an effort.

The remark elicited a responsive chuckle from Captain Godwin. "I confess I had forgotten, sir. Whatever mischief you've been up to, Gemma, I am delighted to see you again, and I'll be even more delighted when you've repaired the damage. How did this come about, if one may ask?"

Color had flooded Lady Gemma's cheeks at her father's words, but now it receded as she slowly withdrew the hand Captain Godwin had briefly squeezed. Her dark eyes searched his, and the soft mouth trembled into a smile. "Welcome home, George. Mr. Delevan will tell you how I came to be in such a state. If you will excuse me for a bit, I shall retire to repair the damage before rejoining you."

Mr. Delevan watched as his hostess ascended the stairs with commendable poise before he turned to acknowledge the introduction being made by the duke.

He saw a man of four- or five-and-twenty, a bit younger than himself, and as much the personification of the ideal of masculine beauty as Miss Fairmont was its feminine counterpart. Captain Godwin topped John's own moderate stature by two or three inches and his erect military bearing accentuated the athletic proportions of his physique. His coloring was not dissimilar to that of Lady Gemma, his hair being as dark and wavy as hers and his brown eyes a few shades lighter. Add to these qualities handsomely chiseled features, a gleaming white-toothed smile, and an air of easy assurance, and it would be perfectly comprehensible if Mr. Delevan felt himself reduced to an insignificant figure by comparison. He did indeed study the captain thoroughly with his mild blue gaze, but if he nurtured any uncharitable emotions such as jealousy or dislike, nothing of this was discernible in the pleasant manner in which he responded to Captain Godwin's friendly greeting.

In fact, despite one instinctive spurt of chagrin at his first glimpse of the splendid soldier, Mr. Delevan had made a discovery that allowed him to remain in perfect charity with Captain Godwin. Put into its simplest terms, it was this: Captain Godwin did not love Lady Gemma as she deserved to be loved; he was therefore unworthy of her, and he *wasn't going to get her!*

In the grip of the euphoria immediately resulting from such a momentous decision, Mr. Delevan was easily able to look upon his rival with goodwill not unmixed with the contempt a man feels for the stupidity of another when he proposes to gain by it.

He was not allowed any time to reflect on the significance of the moment, however, for the duke, unaware that his candidate for son-in-law had ever considered turning down the honor, was sweeping both young men ahead of him, figuratively speaking.

"Shall we adjourn to the blue saloon, where we can raise a glass to your safe return in comfort, George? Your friend will be thinking himself abandoned indefinitely by a lot of inhospitable savages."

"Oh, Ollie won't mind, sir. He likes his own company; in fact, I had the deuce of a time persuading him to come along today. He's turned into a regular hermit since he caught it at Toulouse." The captain moved forward at the duke's bidding but slowly, in order to enlighten their ignorance about his friend.

"Ollie and I served together in Spain for three years under the duke. We came through Salamanca and Vitoria without a scratch, and then in April, when we chased old Soult out of Toulouse, Ollie caught one ball in the left arm and another grazed his cheek. Made rather a mess of it, actually, though it doesn't look so bad now the redness is fading somewhat. The doctors say he should have regained the full use of his arm by now, but he can't move it at all. I finally talked him into coming home with me to try what the waters of Bath could do for the arm, but he's not in a humor for society at present. Never was much for the ladies anyway—too abrupt for their liking, I collect—but since his betrothed threw him over after the injury, though he was determined to break it off himself, he's been like a bear with a sore head. He's the best of good fellows ordinarily," he added hastily, as if fearing his bald recital might have prejudiced his listeners against his comrade-in-arms.

They had reached the door to the blue saloon by now and stepped in to find a stern-featured man idly glancing through an issue of the *Gentleman's Magazine*. While the duke summoned the butler and gave him an order, Captain Godwin made Mr. Delevan and Major Barton known to each other.

When he stood up, Major Lord Oliver Barton was even taller than Captain Godwin and, despite the stiffly held left arm, gave an immediate impression of latent strength. His shoulders, under a well-cut blue coat, were massive, and though there wasn't an ounce of superfluous flesh on the bulky frame, he had heavily muscled thighs and large hands and feet. His face was lean with prominent cheekbones and a square jaw that did nothing to alleviate his distinctly forbidding aspect. A jagged scar running diagonally from the corner of his eye to his earlobe aggravated the effect. The men bowed with perfect civility, but Mr. Delevan's friendly manner met with no appreciable thawing on the part of Major Barton.

Nonetheless, by the time Lady Gemma returned, the gentlemen were embroiled in a serious discussion of the probable course of political events in Europe now that the allied sovereigns had departed after their ceremonial visit celebrating the end of the war. Mr. Delevan had

leveled a look at Captain Godwin to see how his last
point had been received when he saw something that
caused him to swivel his head ninety degrees to the right.

The captain's air of polite attention had given way to
a rapt stare directed over Mr. Delevan's right shoulder.
He straightened as though jerked by a string, and the
fingers of one hand made a minute adjustment to his
cravat. It did not require an extraordinary intellect to
guess that the opening of the door behind Mr. Delevan
had signaled the arrival of a member of the fair sex, but
while getting to his feet a second later, he reinspected
the captain's face seeking a more precise explanation.
Three extremely attractive young ladies had entered the
room together, yet Mr. Delevan received the impression
that it was the sight of Miss Fairmont that had been
responsible for Captain Godwin's reaction. A veiled
glance at Lady Gemma told him nothing; she was
making her smiling way across the room to take the
captain's extended hands.

"Much better," he approved, casting a knowledgeable eye over the frothy confection of green and white
ruffles she had donned. "Now you look as I often
pictured you, the perfect remedy to the barren Spanish
plains." He dropped her hands to smile at the girl who
had glided silently to his side during this exchange.
"And this, of course, is young Coralee. If I may be
permitted the license of an old family friend, *you* are
not at all as I remember you. How dared you grow up
the minute my back was turned!"

Miss Fairmont's big blue eyes warmed with laughter
and her pretty teeth gleamed through parted lips as she
expanded under his playfulness and the obvious
admiration in his gaze.

"May I assume, then, that you no longer consider me
a 'scrubby brat?' " she inquired demurely.

The captain looked taken aback for a second but
rallied quickly. "If ever I said anything so ungallant,
which I take leave to doubt, the provocation must have
been extreme," he declared forthrightly.

Miss Fairmont flirted her eyelashes at him. "You did

indeed say it, and the provocation *was* extreme. I wouldn't allow you and Gemma to shake me off so you might disappear into the rose garden together.''

Captain Godwin laughed good-humoredly, but Mr. Delevan thought he detected the faintest flicker of embarrassment on his handsome face. Certainly he avoided looking at Lady Gemma, whose cheeks had reddened at her cousin's words.

Recalling her role as hostess, she hastily addressed herself to the present situation, beckoning Lucy forward to be made known to Captain Godwin.

John watched with approval as his sister responded to the captain's practiced gallantry in a cool pleasant manner. Major Barton was then summoned to his friend's side to be presented to the ladies.

There could scarcely have been a greater contrast between any two men in similar circumstances. Captain Godwin exerted himself to charm each young lady in succession, his interest apparently captured by their attractiveness and individuality. Major Barton acknowledged each introduction with a stiff civility belied by the cold indifference of his expression. As far as John could tell, this repelling lack of interest applied equally and impartially to all three ladies.

With respect to the girls themselves, he saw that Lady Gemma's natural warmth was checked and altered into slight hesitancy as she met his arctic look bravely but briefly, turning aside with relief when he removed his attention from her to bow to Lucy in turn. Lucy remained unmoved alike by his scarred visage and unencouraging manner, greeting him with calm good manners that concealed her thoughts. Her neutrality was overset a moment later, however, when Coralee, who had remained on the far side of Captain Godwin, turned to accept the major's bow and caught her first glimpse of the scarred left side of his face. Her audible intake of breath and instinctive recoil, though quickly controlled, could not have escaped Major Barton's notice, but not by so much as the quiver of a muscle did he betray any reaction. Mr. Delevan was persuaded he

must have intercepted the fulminating look Lucy sent in
Coralee's direction, but his only response was a slight
deepening of the sardonic curl to his lips.

"Shall we all make ourselves comfortable?" As
daughter of the house, Lady Gemma ushered the guests
to seats. "My mother and aunt will be down directly,"
she assured her father.

Lord Gresham arrived before she finished speaking,
followed within a minute or two by the senior ladies,
each of whom greeted the newcomers in the style
dictated by her personality. Lady Sophronia was all
regal condescension while the duchess welcomed her
guests with gentle warmth.

The expanded party was very merry, if the noise level
was a fair measuring stick. Captain Godwin, as the
returning hero, was very much the center of attention,
good-naturedly attempting to answer a veritable barrage
of questions from Gresham, Lady Gemma, and Coralee, all talking at once. Lucy was drawn into his orbit
also, and to a lesser degree and for a shorter time, her
brother. Even Lady Sophronia interrupted occasionally
with a demand for information of various relatives or
acquaintances who had served in the Peninsula and
might therefore be thought to have come in contact with
Captain Godwin. The duchess alone made no effort to
engage his attention.

During the next half-hour, Mr. Delevan noted that,
whenever she thought herself unobserved, her gaze
would revert to Captain Godwin with an air of
speculation that he had not discerned in her manner
until now. He would have given a lot to be privy to her
conclusions, but he had already begun to suspect that
the quiet duchess was long practiced in keeping her
thoughts and feelings to herself. That her husband did
not as a rule invite her opinion and participation in
matters under discussion had also become apparent
early in the acquaintance, though he could not have said
with any confidence which was cause and which result.

He and the duke remained slightly apart from the

main focus of conversation—John because he did not like to see Major Barton slighted, however unintentionally, and the duke in order to satisfy his curiosity about the last weeks of the campaign from the lips of someone who had been on the scene. In the beginning, Captain Godwin had called on his friend for corroboration of several points in his tales of army life in Spain, but Major Barton's monosyllabic responses were not conducive to requests for further elaboration, and he was gradually abandoned by the young people. Mr. Delevan found him quite conversable when pressed, and though he did not volunteer his opinion on the political queries raised by the duke, his observations on the conduct of the war were rational and thought-provoking.

When the callers at last rose to take their leave, they were strongly pressed to remain for dinner. The majority of those present later held to it that Captain Godwin would have allowed himself to be persuaded had not the major made it so plain that he considered the visit had lasted long enough. However, when the invitation was repeated for the next day, the latter said all that was polite in accepting, as did the captain with rather more enthusiasm, and the men were permitted to depart with suitable expressions of goodwill.

At dinner that evening and later in the saloon the returned soldiers furnished the main topic of conversation, at least among the females of the family. Captain Godwin was pronounced to be all that was amiable, his manners examined and approved for their unselfconscious ease, his address admired, his loyalty and concern for his unfortunate comrade praised, his character extolled. The unfortunate comrade himself came in for a minimal share of the conversational airing, it perhaps being deemed better to remain silent where one could not wholeheartedly approve. In any event, it was unanimously agreed that the return of the soldiers would lend a much-appreciated zest to the social affairs of the neighborhood in the weeks to come.

7

The young ladies of Monteith Hall were correct in their assumption that the social life of the locale would increase with the addition of two returned soldiers in their midst. The war that had cost individuals and the nation so much was over at long last and celebrations were the order of the day. The city of London had barely recovered from the recent round of festivities during the visit of the allied sovereigns, which had included, in addition to parades and official presentations, a masquerade ball given by the members of White's in honor of the conquering hero, the Duke of Wellington, to which four thousand people had been invited. There was even a plan afoot to clean up the London parks in preparation for a great celebration to be held in August commemorating one hundred years of Hanoverian rule.

Though nothing on this scale was to be contemplated in the country, the general air of thankfulness and triumph gave expression to a rash of informal balls, picnics, and private festivities among local hostesses who vied with one another in providing the most-talked-of entertainments to welcome the returned heroes.

Although Lady Gemma had invited Lucy for a visit with the primary intention of providing a healthful summer environment to complete her recovery from influenza, the advantages accruing to the addition of two eligible males to the neighborhood were not to be ignored. Captain Godwin's father, Sir Humphrey, was renowned for his gregarious nature, and he and Lady Godwin could be expected to celebrate their son's safe return and welcome his friend with bountiful hospitality at the manor, Lady Gemma predicted on the morning following the formal call of the captain and Major Barton. The unsettled weather continuing another day, the three girls were cozily ensconced in the music room. Lucy was helping Gemma trim a hat, and Coralee was practicing scales at the pianoforte.

"Mama has sent a note to the squire bidding him and Lady Godwin to dinner tonight. She felt they would not wish to part with George so soon after his arrival."

"Is there not a brother also?" Lucy asked idly, revolving the straw bonnet on her hand in order to gauge the effect of the spray of artificial flowers she had just finished sewing onto its curving brim.

"Yes, Malcolm. Naturally he will be invited too."

"What is he like, the older brother? Is he as handsome as the captain?"

"There is a strong family resemblance, but Malcolm is not so big as George. He's of a quieter nature too, less outgoing. He is eight-and-twenty, I believe, enough older that he was never a part of our games and activities when we were growing up."

"Is he married?"

"Not yet, but if rumor is correct, he is on the brink of contracting an engagement to one of the Biddlesford girls from Little Menda. I do not know what is holding him back. Letitia Biddlesford has been making cow's eyes at him for almost a year."

"Perhaps he cannot bring himself to engage to live with that cackling laugh of hers for the rest of his life," suggested Miss Fairmont with cheerful brutality as she played a dashing arpeggio.

Lady Gemma chuckled but offered a mild protest. "Letty Biddlesford may not possess any extraordinary degree of beauty, and she does have a rather irritating laugh, especially when she is a trifle nervous, but you must admit that she is an amiable girl, Coralee, and will make Malcolm a fine wife."

"Why must I admit any such thing?" inquired Coralee equably, halting her finger exercises for a moment to stare at her cousin. "*You* may call it amiability, but *I* call it rather a simple want of wit or decision masquerading as amiability. She has no thoughts or opinions of her own, so finds it prudent to agree with anything proposed by someone else. In short, she has more hair than wit.''

"No, that is too unkind, and not really true. I will grant you that Letty is not precisely needle-witted, but she doesn't want for common sense and her principles are fixed. There is nothing about her that would unfit her to be the wife of someone in Malcolm's position."

Miss Fairmont shrugged her shoulders. "Unless he has a prejudice against a bore with a cackling laugh for a wife," she retorted unarguably before returning her attention to her beautifully kept hands as they danced over the keys.

Lady Gemma pulled a comical grimace for Lucy's benefit but refrained from prolonging a fruitless discussion about people entirely unknown as yet to her friend.

She was in a mood to be tolerant of all mankind's foibles at present, Lucy thought, regarding her school chum with affectionate understanding. Though Gemma had volunteered nothing of her sentiments concerning George since his appearance on the scene, some slight previous knowledge of the attachment, plus a close friend's intuitive awareness, told her that Gemma was on fire with well-contained excitement and anticipation. She would have taken her oath that her friend was in love with the dashing captain and could only wish that the gentleman's emotions were to be read so easily. Certainly there was affection and pleasure in the renewal of friendship, but Lucy had sought eagerly and in vain for some sign of a deeper attachment on his part. She reminded herself that a man's tender ego might well prevent him from wearing his heart on his sleeve, so to speak, before he had some cause to believe his devotion was returned. It made sense, good sense. Then why, against such convincing rationalization, did the nagging thought persist that she could discern no sign of love on his part because none existed?

And then there was his reaction to Coralee Fairmont. For a long moment Lucy's deliberate gaze rested on the girl at the pianoforte. Captain Godwin had been struck in a heap by her loveliness. This was scarcely surprising, of course. Any man who failed to respond to the age-old appeal of a beauty as perfect as Miss Fairmont's must be lacking discrimination indeed. Her brother John had looked as admiringly and as long at Coralee as had Captain Godwin. A frown appeared on Lucy's smooth brow as her concentration was turned inward. John had looked often and admiringly at the lovely blonde, but was there a difference in the quality of his appreciation perhaps? His sister had learned it was rarely possible to tell what John was thinking if he wished to conceal those thoughts. If she were forced to describe his attitude toward the gorgeous Coralee, she'd have to call it a blend of admiration and amusement and concede that he did not seem concerned with concealment of either. Now that she came to comparisons, it occurred to her that there was more of amusement in Captain Godwin's attitude toward Gemma than toward her cousin. In fact, his demeanor toward Gemma last night was strikingly similar to that of John toward Coralee. The implications of this line of thought, though highly intriguing, would have to await a more propitious hour, however, for Gemma was demanding Lucy's opinion of the newly decorated bonnet, which she had just placed on her head.

"Let me see it in profile. Oh, yes, I do like the effect of the flowers on the brim dipping toward one ear."

"Coralee?" Gemma twirled slowly in front of the pianoforte to give her cousin a view of the hat from all angles.

"Very fetching," drawled Miss Fairmont, sparing the dark-haired girl a quick look before executing a series of rippling notes. "I am persuaded George Godwin will find it to his taste, if it is for his benefit."

Gemma turned away without deigning to reply to the unspoken question, but Lucy saw her pull in the corners of her mouth.

With the possible exception of Major Lord Oliver Barton, who, while comporting himself with punctilious civility and providing no grounds for legitimate complaint about his demeanor, still managed to set himself at a distance from the others, the members of that first dinner party enjoyed themselves hugely. The Delevans were pleased to find in Sir Humphrey and Lady Godwin a good-natured and unassuming pair who welcomed the brother and sister to the neighborhood with genuine kindliness. Sir Humphrey was a bluff, hearty individual with no pretensions to excessive gentility; he came from sound English stock that had been on the land for uncounted generations. His wife's birth was better than his, but neither was animated by the least desire to shine in any society removed from their own locality. They were unimpressed with the distinction conveyed by dining at a ducal table and had been on perfectly comfortable though scarcely intimate terms with the Monteith family for unnumbered years.

If Lady Godwin had an envious bone in her body, which was doubtful, its sole expression would have been in the desire that the duchess's pastry cook might somehow impart some of her skill to her own Mabel, whose many good points did not, unfortunately, include a light hand with the puddings to which Sir Humphrey was highly partial. She was even able to view her hostess with no lessening of goodwill toward one who, though less than five years her junior, threw her own ample proportions and gray hair into stark relief in contrast to her grace's slim elegance. If the truth were known, Lady Godwin often experienced a vague sympathy for the duchess, who struck her as being a woman whose gentle manners strove constantly to conceal some rooted unhappiness. When she compared her own contentment with Sir Humphrey to the life the other must lead as the duke's wife, she felt she had not far to look for the cause of this suspected melancholy.

The last guest, Mr. Malcolm Godwin, though lacking something of his younger brother's brilliance in company, possessed an attractive smile and conducted himself with a pleasing diffidence that did him no disservice with the older generation. Indeed, Lady Sophronia later described him as a very pretty-behaved young man, an encomium with which the three girls willingly expressed the unqualified agreement she expected.

No entertainment had been planned for what the duchess termed a simple family meal, but knowing the elder Godwins' fondness for cards, she hinted her sister-in-law into proposing a game of whist while the younger element amused itself by making music. Coralee was prevailed upon by her aunt to give them all the pleasure of a few songs, which she did readily enough after the requisite display of hesitation and modesty considered proper to the occasion. The applause and admiration that greeted her performance was real, for she possessed a good strong soprano that she used well, and nothing could have improved upon the exquisite picture she presented accompanying herself at the pianoforte. In her pale-yellow muslin with gold ribbons adorning the tiny puffed sleeves, she was the epitome of youth and beauty. Small wonder that most of the gentlemen present wore expressions bordering on the fatuous when at last she excused herself with a laugh and a graceful apology for taking up more of their time than was seemly. The protests following upon this remark were quite sincere; Major Barton's finely chiseled lips actually stretched into the semblance of a smile as he offered the comment that he had rarely been privileged to witness such superb breath and vocal control in an amateur, while Captain Godwin was heard to declare in fervent tones that he for one could listen to Coralee all night with indescribable pleasure.

"I know when I am being offered Spanish coin," objected Miss Fairmont. "You would be bored to tears if that were to happen."

The captain interrupted to protest dramatically that she did him a grave injustice, that she cast aspersions on his veracity, indeed on his very honor.

Miss Fairmont held up a staying hand. "Enough!"

she said on a gratified laugh. "I apologize for the imputation, but you must see the advantage from my point of view in stopping while my audience wishes more. Besides," she added, glancing around at her cousin with a glinting smile, "it is time to share the stage with someone else. Gemma?"

Lady Gemma's flawless complexion lost some of its rich color as she demured hastily, "You know I have no voice, Coralee. It would spoil the memory of your fine performance."

"Nonsense, you are too modest, my dear cousin," purred Miss Fairmont. "Why do not you and Miss Delevan sing that charming little ballad I heard you rehearsing the other day when I arrived?"

Lady Gemma's eyes, bright with distress, sought her friend's in wordless appeal and found her equal to the occasion.

"Unfortunately, we have not yet completely learned that song, but if John will assist us, there was an amusing little French song we were used to sing at school." Lucy's countenance was serene and untroubled as she smiled at the company in general before directing it at her brother.

Mr. Delevan readily assented. "It will be my pleasure, as long as you two girls promise not to drown me out." Under cover of the murmur of laughter that greeted this plea, he extended a hand to help Lady Gemma to her feet as Lucy seated herself at the instrument. The tiny brunette had recovered her poise by now, strengthened by an encouraging look from the duchess, but he could sense her unwillingness, and he gave her hand one comforting squeeze before releasing it.

Thanks to Mr. Delevan's powerful baritone, which, despite his professed anxiety, was entirely capable of dominating the female voices, the trio performed very creditably and even conceded another number to popular demand. After that, it was a simple matter for Gemma to suggest that the gentlemen try some three-part harmony. With the exception of the major, who declared flatly that he didn't sing, they were agreeable to the suggestion and eventually produced some better results than their lack of practice might have promised.

All in all, it was a pleasant evening, but as she parted from Lucy at the door to her friend's bedchamber, Gemma struggled with a vague sense of disquiet that she wished to believe was no more than simple disappointment at not having managed a single private moment with George as yet. Naturally she was disappointed—any girl in her situation would be—that the demands of general civility had precluded their achieving even a short tête-à-tête. It was no one's fault of course; tonight marked just their second meeting since George's return, and so far they had met only in company. Even as she counseled the patience that was so difficult of achievement for one of her impulsive nature, the nagging thought persisted that lovers could communicate in a room full of humanity. An exchange of glances could enclose them in their own private world. She shivered a little as she climbed into bed at last but attributed the chill to her dawdling pace at making herself ready for sleep. Tomorrow would be a brand-new day that would surely provide an opportunity to renew the closeness she and George had attained before he had gone off to war.

The small dinner party marked the beginning of a regular intercourse between the younger members of the two neighboring families. Most days would find the gentlemen from Godwin Manor engaged for some activity with varying members of Monteith Hall's current residents. Sometimes the men would go out together, but often, if the weather was especially promising, the ladies would join them in their rides about the locality.

To Gemma's silent but deeply felt chagrin, Captain Godwin made no attempt in the days that followed to single her out for any distinguishing attentions. She waged constant battle with the jealousy that gnawed at her spirit when he flirted with the obliging Coralee. He flirted charmingly with herself and sometimes with Lucy also, but the best will in the world to believe otherwise could not convince her that her share of his compliments was greater than that accorded to the other girls. A stiff-necked pride she had not known she possessed enabled her to conceal her wounds, but she bitterly regretted having displayed her heart to Mr. Delevan. Not that that gentleman of the exquisite manners and innate kindness ever betrayed his knowledge by the flick of an eyelash; on the contrary, his tactful presence and discreet social skill ensured that all appeared serene on the surface. Though grateful for both the breeding and the kindness, she was too frequently reminded of the awkward situation in which she had placed herself and was hard put to behave without consciousness in the presence of George or Mr. Delevan. However, even this uncomfortable state of affairs took on an aspect of normalcy as the days passed in outwardly pleasurable activity.

The captain and Major Barton, occasionally accompanied by Mr. Godwin, fell into the habit of calling at Monteith Hall about teatime. On less clement days they might drop in earlier and while away the afternoon playing billiards before joining the ladies for tea.

On one such rainy afternoon Captain Godwin and Major Barton wandered into the billiard room, where a game of sorts was going on amid general hilarity. All the young ladies were present with Lord Gresham, but there was no sign of Mr. Delevan. Major Barton, whose useless arm prevented him from engaging in this activity, though he was still a bruising rider, inquired for Mr. Delevan and was told by Lucy that her brother could be found in the duke's library.

"He had several business letters that needed answering," she explained, cue stick in hand. When the major stated his reluctance to disturb Mr. Delevan under the circumstances, she was firm in disabusing his mind of any such notion. "I am persuaded he will be glad of company by now, sir, for the letters have occupied him for the best part of two hours. In fact, it is my opinion that John invented the letters as an excuse to avoid teaching me to play billiards," she confided with a smile in her smoky-gray eyes, "though he put on his most heartrending wounded expression when I dared to suggest that he might be guilty of such ignoble conduct."

For just a second the major's hard eyes reflected an answering gleam of amusement. "I see you know your brother very well, Miss Delevan. There are no illusions left."

"I have always preferred the truth to illusions no matter how comforting the latter might be," she responded in a more serious vein than his light rejoinder would have called for.

Those cold eyes studied her with more interest than he had yet manifested in any of the female residents of the hall before he replied, "I too prefer the unvarnished truth, but I find few females are of like mind. My compliments, ma'am."

Though noting the bitter curl to his lips, Lucy could not resist entering an objection to this sweeping condemnation. "The folly of cherishing illusions, sir, can scarcely be regarded as strictly, or even primarily, a feminine failing." Her tone was deceptively soft and did not match the challenge in eyes and tilted chin.

Major Barton acknowledged this by a deepening of his ironic expression but deferred his acceptance of the challenge. "It seems we have a difference of opinion that might prove . . . instructive . . . to explore at a more convenient time," he allowed, adding outrageously as he eyed the cue stick in her tightened grip, "at a time when you do not have a weapon in your hand. But I am interrupting the game. With your permission I'll retire and seek Mr. Delevan."

He bowed and was gone before Lucy could close her surprised mouth. She stared after him for a moment, digesting this provocative utterance. When the others demanded her attention to the contest in progress, she was still undecided as to whether or not she had received a snub.

Miss Delevan speedily found herself in the unenviable position of having a surfeit of teachers. There was no problem in grasping the principles of the game, but the acquisition of the skills required to direct a little ball at the desired angle was another matter entirely—a matter for a lifetime of practice, based on the talent she had thus far displayed, she decided privately. In any case, it was with a sense of relief that she eventually relinquished the cue stick to Miss Fairmont, who had challenged her cousin Gemma to a game of one hundred up.

In the next fifteen minutes the expression of unholy glee that had enlivened Lord Gresham's features at this challenge was amply explained. After stringing, Coralee had first play and promptly put her ball behind the balkline to make matters difficult for her opponent. It was an admirable strategy but totally ineffective as Gemma methodically set about racking up a nearly unbroken string of winning and losing hazards and cannons that left everyone but her brother gasping in astonishment. Captain Godwin, who had offered to mark for the contestants, couldn't contain his admiration at one particularly difficult shot off the side cushion.

"My God, Gemma, where did you learn to play billiards like that?"

Gemma looked a trifle sheepish. "I was used to sneak in here when I was a little girl and practice by the hour when I should have been practicing my music," she confessed. "Only when Papa was in an especially indulgent mood would he allow me to play with him and Peter, so I was determined to become adept enough to be a worthy opponent."

"Well, I would say you have succeeded." Captain Godwin laughed. "I don't mind admitting that I shouldn't care to take my chances with you if any very large sum of money was at stake. That last shot was a beauty!"

Lucy stole a look at Coralee, whose initial surprise at Gemma's prowess had rapidly turned to chagrin. She had been watching Captain Godwin through narrowed eyes, but now she addressed her cousin with a gaiety that sounded genuine.

"I am willing, nay, *anxious* to concede this game to you, Gemma dear. You have me totally outgunned. It must be comforting to know that you have at least one accomplishment, even if it is rather an unfeminine one."

"Oh, I would not agree that skill at billiards is Gemma's sole accomplishment," said Lord Gresham, coming to his sister's defense with a considering air and a bland smile calculated to infuriate his cousin. "She can't sing or play as well as you, but she's a very graceful dancer, and the horse she can't ride don't exist. Which is more than can be said for you, cousin."

"Peter," said Lady Gemma warningly.

"Oh, dear me, I never meant to imply that dearest Gemma had *no* feminine accomplishments. I have often remarked on her talented performance on the dance floor, have I not, Gemma?" Without waiting for a response from Gemma, who was looking acutely uncomfortable by now, Coralee faced her male cousin with a glint in her eye that gave the lie to her silky tones. "I would not dream of evaluating my own performance on the dance floor, but riding is another matter. I consider myself quite as accomplished in the saddle as Gemma."

"Hah!" was her cousin's inelegant but expressive retort.

Gemma intervened before the antagonists could descend to nursery level. "Coralee is quite right to be miffed, Peter. You know she is a fine rider."

"All I said was that *you* can ride anything on four legs, which makes you a better rider in my book."

"Well, there is only one place to settle such a question, and it is not a billiard room," George said. "Would you agree, Miss Delevan, that a race between the ladies is the only fair way to judge?"

Lucy twinkled back at him. "I would agree that a race would decide who had the faster horse," she temporized.

"Oh, in that case," declared Gemma, entering into the spirit, "Coralee is lost because my Fleurette is the fastest creature on four legs."

"Nonsense, Gemma. Fleurette is a nice-enough little mare but she cannot match my uncle's White Star for speed," objected Coralee.

Gemma was adamant. "She can over a long-enough course."

"Now we have a question that can be put to the test," said the captain, "if the ladies are willing."

Both ladies attesting to their willingness to engage in a race, there remained only the details of time and place to arrange. Peter proposed one complete circuit of the ornamental water as a fair test course, and the first fine afternoon was decided on for the contest.

Mr. Delevan and Major Barton were sitting in the library idly discussing some of the reform measures due to come up in the next parliamentary session when Peter looked in to advise them that everyone was adjourning to the blue saloon for tea. Mr. Delevan's lazy gaze ran over the young marquess, returning to dwell on his attractive countenance alight with mischief.

"You look like someone who has lost a penny and found a pound," he commented. "What's afoot, Gresham?"

Peter's grin was smug. "Thanks almost entirely to my efforts, we are due for some rare sport," he boasted. "Gemma and Coralee have agreed to a horse race around the lake. I'm backing my sister to win. Would either of you like to wager a pony on the outcome?"

Mr. Delevan laughed at his audaciousness but said sternly, "No, you young scapegrace. You are well aware that it would not do to have your sister or cousin the subject of a wager."

"Strictly a private wager, no one will ever hear of it,"

promised Peter. "Very well, not a pony, then, but there could be no possible exception to a nominal bet of five pounds just to make it interesting. Any takers?"

"Not I," repeated Mr. Delevan. "I also think Lady Gemma will win."

"I'll take you up on it," said Major Barton, un-expectedly entering the lists. "Miss Fairmont strikes me as being the keener competitor."

"Done. And you are wrong, there Major. Gemma has just finished wiping up the floor with her at billiards and she is far and away the better rider, though I will say for my cousin that there isn't an ounce of fear in her. No need to fear she won't throw her heart over a fence."

Major Barton's raised eyebrow was his only comment on this analysis, but Mr. Delevan stared with renewed interest at the young man lounging in the doorway as he gathered together his correspondence preparatory to quitting the room.

"Is your sister a good billiards player, then . . . for a female?"

"She's a good billiards player for a Captain Sharp," Peter retorted bluntly. "If she were not my sister, I'd make my fortune taking her around the country and exhibiting her at fairs." He sighed wistfully for lost opportunities and noted the skeptical expressions of both men. "Do not take my word for it if you think I'm trying to ride on your backs; take her on yourselves, if you dare."

"How does it come about, this skill in a man's game?" Mr. Delevan asked curiously as the three headed down the corridor toward the stairs.

"Practice of course, and a marvelous precision of eye, but what I presume you are really asking," Peter answered with a shrewd glance at Mr. Delevan, "is *why* she took such pains to acquire the skill." For a moment the lively young man looked more thoughtful than was his wont. "I am persuaded Gemma has often wished she was born a boy; she was forever tagging after me, trying to do everything boys do and resisting instruction in the sort of household activities girls commonly engage in. But my father finally took notice of her hoydenish behavior and permitted Mama to send her to a seminary for young ladies. After a few years they turned her into a girl, more or less," he finished as they approached the blue saloon.

"Amen to that," Mr. Delevan announced in prayerful accents that caused his companions to burst out laughing as they entered the room where the others awaited them.

Attracted by the pleasant sound, they all looked to the laughing trio. When pressed to share the joke, however, the gentlemen proved united in a disinclination to divulge the cause of their merriment, though their evasive tactics differed according to their various characters. Major Barton indeed employed none: he merely ignored the general request for enlightenment and accepted a glass of sherry from his host. Peter assumed an air of mystery and declared that his lips were sealed, and not even a session on the rack arranged by a bearded inquisitor of Spanish ancestry would suffice to break his silence.

Coralee gave a scornful toss of her head. "It was no doubt some crude example of so-called masculine humor, unfit for feminine ears."

"At least nothing that would translate," Mr. Delevan said with a sympathetic smile. "Have you never noticed how few samples of humor can bear up under intensive scrutiny? Most just crumble away to dust."

"Now that you have thrown sufficient dust in our eyes, come have a cup of tea," recommended his sister, patting the sofa cushion beside her.

Mr. Delevan accepted a cup from the duchess, who bestowed her sweet smile upon him, and took the seat next to Lucy. In the buzz of resumed conversation about the room, he inquired into the success of the billiard lesson.

Lucy closed her eyes in pretended anguish. "I fear I

did not cover the name of Delevan with glory in my first lesson," she confessed, adding with a air of puzzled discovery that increased her brother's appreciation that it was not so easy as it first appeared to direct the balls accurately. Just then her eye chanced to fall on the major, sitting quite close, ostensibly engaged in conversation with the duke. Some inner certainty that she could not have explained convinced her that, though his gaze was fixed politely on his host, his ears were straining to catch the exchange between herself and John. Fortunately, her brother was discoursing a little on the intricacies of billiards, because she found herself unaccountably tongue-tied. She knew she had been caught staring at the major a moment ago when he had entered the room, but the truth was simply that she had been fascinated by the change the act of laughing wrought in his appearance. Years were subtracted from his age, the habitual dourness vanished for an instant, light came into those obsidian eyes, and she glimpsed the man he must have been before the adversities of war and the cruelties of human nature had taken their toll. It had been over in a second; his mouth clamped once more into a straight line and a furrow grooved his brow as his gaze skimmed her with arctic indifference before passing on to his host.

The incident, if indeed an occurrence of less than two seconds' duration could be so dignified, had consisted of precious little—a man's laugh, a girl's interested glance, and his refusal to receive the interest—but it had left her strangely shaken and she welcomed the comfort of John's nearness.

Through a veil of thick lashes she made a surreptitious study of as much of the major's countenance as was available to her inspection. The unmarked side of his face was quite impressive, she realized for the first time. Decided cheekbones, a square jaw, and straight thick brows over deep-set eyes contributed to an aggressively masculine effect that was only slightly redeemed from harshness by the sensitive modeling of his mouth, apparent only on the rare occasions when its owner was thoroughly relaxed. His face would be an absorbing study for a painter or sculptor, she decided with quickened interest.

"Another cup of tea, Lucy?"

"What? Oh, no, no more, thank you, John," she replied, glancing past her brother as he moved off carrying his cup for a refill. The major's closed face confirmed what she had already sensed: his attention was now totally removed from her. Since this was what was wanted to restore her usual composure, she could only attribute her lack of heartfelt relief to something perverse in her nature.

Conversation during the tea party ranged over subjects as diverse as the warlike attitude of the former colonists in America on international waters to an upcoming puglistic exhibition in the next county for which Peter was eager to make up a party, but not once did it touch on the nearer prospect of a sporting contest right on the premises. This failure to mention a projected event that might be of interest to almost everyone present in the saloon was the result of the tacit complicity of the young people, who intuitively comprehended the necessity of circumventing the prohibitions of the plan for a horse race that might be expected from the two mothers of the respective participants.

8

Two days were to pass before the anticipated ladies' race could be scheduled, for the weather remained intermittently showery and uncertain.

Life at Monteith Hall proceeded much as usual. After an early-morning ride and breakfast, the duke went about the business of the estate, accompanied, on those occasions when he could locate him, by his heir, who would reach his majority before the year was out. Lord Gresham's lack of interest in his inheritance was a sore point with his sire, who had finally been compelled to demand his presence in Wiltshire for the summer. Since being sent down from Oxford the previous spring, Peter had got caught up in a set of sporting mad youths whose escapades, unfortunately, were not confined to the healthy outdoor aspects of sport but also embraced gaming in all its less salubrious forms from cock-fighting to faro. The atmosphere at the hall had been sulfuric early in the season as Peter, cut off from his cronies and chafing under the compulsion to dance attendance on his family, had, by his sulky behavior, nearly worn his loving mother and sister to emotional shreds, so anxious were they to avoid, for his sake, any explosions of wrath from the duke. The addition of the Delevans as guests had eased the strain of the family situation at once, and the arrival of the military segment further heightened the promise of an enjoyable summer.

Most mornings found the ladies engaged in their various sewing projects in the duchess's sitting room. The look of strain faded from her sensitive face after a week of close proximity unmarred by any of the incessant squabbling that had rendered Gemma's and Coralee's shared childhood obnoxious to their elders.

Lucy thought her hostess looked more relaxed than at any time since her arrival. She knew that her own presence as a buffer and peace-keeping force was partly responsible, and was happy to be of some small service to her friend's mother. The duchess had always treated her with kindness on the few occasions when they had met previously, and a closer acquaintance saw the forging of a sympathetic bond between them that transcended the gap between their ages and stations and was a source of deep gratification to the girl, who still felt the loss of her own mother so keenly.

Lucy had no opportunity to be private with Gemma on the day following the proposal to hold a race, and no word of the upcoming event was breathed in the presence of the senior ladies. On the second day, when the skies showed some promise of clearing, she observed with no little amusement that Gemma and Coralee seemed almost to be trying to outdo each other in mutual cordiality. Each was in near raptures of admiration for the handwork of the other and pressed her cousin to accept any of the colored silks she might possess that the other did not. Lady Sophronia viewed this state of affairs with smiling complaisance, remarking two or three times to her sister-in-law that she had always predicted that all that was wanting for the girls to become the best of friends was the clearer judgment that came with increasing maturity. Each time, the duchess agreed in a serene voice, but Lucy noted that her considering gaze lingered on her daughter after Gemma called upon Lucy as an impartial judge to cast her vote with her own in favor of the superiority of Coralee's embroidery. Hiding her exasperation, Lucy delivered herself of what she hoped was a diplomatic opinion, hedged about in considerations and smothered in adjectives designed to render it pleasing to all and intelligible to none. It did not escape her notice that though Miss Fairmont met Lady Sophronia's approving glance with perfect composure, Gemma was careful to avoid her parent's speculative eye.

When they separated to freshen up for lunch, Lucy and Gemma branched off toward their rooms in the old wing. Once beyond Coralee's hearing, Lucy seized her friend's elbow and stopped her progress to announce, "I am serving notice here and now that I shall judge no more sewing contests during my visit, *or* singing contests, *or* sketching contests. Do I make myself clear?"

Her assumed severity was too much for Gemma's composure. The mask of bland innocence she had adopted in the sitting room cracked like a window hit by a stone, and her laughter rang out. "Oh, Lucy, I beg you will forgive me," she gasped between peals. "It was wicked of me to propel you into that farcical scene, but you were perfectly wonderful, I promise you. Not a word under four syllables, and I still don't know what you said or whose work you most admired!"

Lucy grinned. "Well, Miss Sly-boots, you and your cousin may think you have thrown up a smoke screen, but although Lady Sophronia may still be in the fog, your mother knows you are up to something."

"Mama possesses a sixth sense about the things I get up to," Gemma admitted. "I shall have to avoid her for a bit."

"The weather definitely looks like breaking. Do you think you may run the race today?"

"Possibly. I'll be glad to have done with this intrigue. I fear I am not cut out to be a conspirator."

"Your incorrigible brother has been trying to persuade me to place a wager on the outcome. Shall you win?"

"Oh, yes."

Lucy examined her friend's calm countenance with real curiosity. "You seem very sure," she ventured a bit hesitantly. "From what I have seen, Miss Fairmont is a competent rider and White Star strikes me as being the stronger horse."

Gemma's lips twitched and her eyes brimmed with mischief. "And so he is over a short course," she agreed, "but Coralee is bound to cram him right from the start, and Star doesn't like to be pushed. Besides which"—she paused to let her words sink in—"he likes company. Whenever he hears another horse close behind him, he slows down to let it catch up to him." Hand on her door latch, she smiled in sympathy with Lucy's sudden giggle. "That is why Papa has made him available to Coralee. He intended him for a hunter but wasn't able to train him out of that trick."

"How fortunate that I was too downy a bird for Gresham's plucking," said Lucy with satisfaction, and a deplorable use of cant that sent her friend into her room shaking her head over the vulgar influence she had imported.

At luncheon Gresham announced that the three gentlemen from the manor were hoping the young ladies might care to ride with them that afternoon. The girls referred the request to the elder ladies with graceful remarks to the effect that they would defer to their plans, and on being urged to go out for some beneficial air and exercise, accepted the invitation in civil terms.

"Will I have White Star saddled for you, Cousin?" inquired Peter casually, "or would you perhaps prefer Columbine?"

Gemma, with a superior knowledge of her cousin's mentality, continued to eat her sliced lamb, displaying no interest in the question, but Lucy held her breath until Coralee replied with equal casualness, "Oh, not Columbine, I think. White Star suits me best."

"And Smoky for Miss Delevan?" asked Peter, turning to Lucy with the tiniest of winks.

Lucy exhaled, nodded, and lowered her eyes to her plate as the duchess shifted her glance from her son to her guest.

The grass bordering the lake was not yet dry, though the sun had been shining warmly for some time when the riders assembled at the spot Peter had chosen as the starting and finishing line. He was in tearing spirits, and the others, oddly silent now that the moment had arrived, were content to leave all the organizing to him. The lawns sloped gently down from the western elevation of the hall toward the water, but the land surrounding it was essentially flat and grass-covered except where a narrow stand of trees abutted the lake at about the three-quarter point of the course. After several days of gray skies, scudding clouds, and wind-whipped water, the natural world seemed to have paused for breath. A pale-azure sky unmarked by clouds lent color to still water centered in a smooth ring of emerald green.

In her sapphire-blue habit and hat, Coralee blended perfectly with her setting as she sat unmoving on the coal-black horse with the white blaze, her expression as unruffled as the scenery, while she listened to Peter's instructions. It was the first time in a fortnight of observation that the beautiful blonde seemed genuinely uninterested in her effect on the attendant male population, and it struck Lucy of a sudden that this was a measure of the importance she attached to this silly race.

Lucy glanced over at the group a few feet away where Lady Gemma, fulfilling her role as hostess, was issuing an invitation to tea in her mother's name. She made an appealing picture as she laughingly tried to calm the fidgets out of Fleurette, whose chestnut flanks almost matched the color of her riding dress. The playful antics of the mare reflected her eagerness to be off and moving after going unexercised for several days.

Major Barton edged his big bay closer to Lucy to remark that Lady Gemma and her horse appeared to have a very good understanding.

"Gemma is good with all animals," agreed Lucy with a smile. "I believe she sat her first pony at the the tender age of three."

His eyes shifted to Coralee, who was bringing White Star into position under the direction of Peter and Captain Godwin. "Very capable young ladies," Major

Barton murmured, "but why"—looking down at Lucy in quizzical fashion—"are there not three fair entrants in this race?"

A gurgle of laughter broke from her lips. "If it has escaped your attention that the quietest horse in the stables is always assigned to me, then I shall take care not to lose face by confessing my deficiencies as a rider. I'll say instead that it was a badly managed business," she declared gaily.

"But not too late to amend, surely. A word in Gresham's ear—"

He *had* to be teasing, but Lucy's hand shot out of its own accord to stay his on the bay's reins. "Don't you dare!" she squeaked in faint alarm.

Attracted by his sister's soft squeal, John sidled closer to the pair just in time to see a flustered Lucy snatch her hand back from Major Barton's.

"John," she implored breathlessly, "demonstrate your affection for your own flesh and blood by convincing the major that I do not wish to be entered in this race."

"Since it would assuredly fall to my lot to break the news of your untimely demise to our father, you may consider it done, love," John promised. "It is not that my sister is a poor horsewoman," he explained straight-faced to the expectant major. "You will note that she has a good seat and nice even hands when walking or troting, even at a brisk canter. Better minds than mine have attempted to describe what happens when her horse stretches into a gallop. You and I might feel that a gallop is actually a more comfortable ride—"

"Astride perhaps!"

John ignored this indignant interjection from his sister. "In short, sir, her control falls to pieces, she loses her heart and invariably her seat, so I must regretfully decline permission for her to enter the race."

"Thank you . . . I think! Talk about exceeding one's commission!" Lucy's smoldering glance was meant to wither both gentlemen as she gathered up her reins and moved nearer to the starting point, where the two contestants were in position awaiting Peter's signal.

An instant later they were off, Coralee on the larger horse taking the lead. As the flying figures receded farther from the group of spectators, the distance between the racers widened.

"Miss Fairmont seems to favor a neck-or-nothing style," said a low voice at her side that caused Lucy to start. In her absorption in the spectacle she had not realized the major had rejoined her.

"Gemma said she would cram him," she reported absently.

"Did Lady Gemma say how she would combat this tactic?"

"Why, yes, she—" Lucy stopped short, having no intention of divulging anything her friend had told her for the amusement of this superior male. She only hoped he had a large bet on Coralee!

"You were about to say?" he prompted gently, but Lucy's pretty mouth was firmly closed as she pretended not to have heard. Once again she was aware of his eyes on her but stubbornly kept hers on the small figures now in the far distance. She attributed his regard to determination to gain an answer to his question, completely unsuspecting that it might be pleasure in the picture she presented that kept the greater portion of his attention away from the contest. Her nicely curved figure was displayed to advantage in the strict tailoring of a well-fitting gray habit a few shades darker than her eyes. The narrow-brimmed hat of the same fabric meant that the only color about her was supplied by the rich chestnut of her hair and the flush of excitement on her pale clear skin. She raised a gloved hand to shield her eyes as the two riders rounded the far side of the lake and headed for the grove of trees.

"Gemma has narrowed the gap considerably. I think she'll catch up before they come out of the trees."

Lucy's prediction proved accurate, for the girl on the chestnut mare emerged from the trees and came pounding down the homestretch. In her excitement, Lucy didn't realize for a moment that something was wrong until a concerted movement around her drew her gaze from Gemma's approach.

"What is it? What has happened?" she asked as her brother, Lord Gresham, Captain Godwin, and Mr. Godwin moved past them toward the rider.

"Miss Fairmont hasn't come out of the trees," replied Major Barton. "It is so dark in there after staring into the sun that it's impossible to see what is happening." He tightened his grip on the reins as his horse snorted and strained forward in the wake of the exodus around them.

Gemma pulled her horse out of the gallop as four riders surged toward her and past her, then she wheeled and followed them back the way she had come.

"Please do not let concern for me keep you here," Lucy urged the major. "I'll follow you more slowly."

"Of what possible use is a one-armed rescuer? Besides, there are plenty of willing hands already on the scene. We'll go together."

Compassion flooded through her, but the intense bitterness in his tones kept Lucy silent as they headed their mounts toward the belt of trees at a trot.

When Gemma rode back into the grove just seconds after the men, it was to find her cousin on the ground being examined by Captain Godwin for injuries while the others sat in a concerned group at a little distance. She slipped off Fleurette and ran toward them.

"What happened? Are you hurt, Coralee?"

"It's no thanks to you that I am not dead," the blond girl cried, drawing an angry, sobbing breath as she sat up with Captain Godwin's aid and faced her cousin. "I told you I had lost my stirrup; I begged you to help me!" Coralee burst into tears and hid her face in the captain's coat.

Gemma broke the sudden silence that prickled along nerve ends. Her face white, she wrenched her eyes from the accusation she saw in Captain Godwin's and addressed her cousin in passionate protest. "What nonsense is this, Coralee? You did not call out to me, you know you did not!"

Coralee hunched a shoulder but still spoke into the captain's coat. "If a stupid race meant so much to you—"

"That's not true! You know it is not! I never heard you call me, and you were certainly not in any trouble when I passed you. I—"

"I feel it is of the first importance to ascertain that Miss Fairmont has sustained no serious injury," Mr. Delevan said quietly as Lady Gemma's voice escalated into shrillness. "Are you able to stand unaided, Miss Fairmont?"

In the few seconds that everyone's attention was concentrated on her cousin as she rose to her feet, clinging heavily to Captain Godwin and further assisted by Malcolm, Gemma strove for control of her emotions. She was trembling as she held out a misshapen hat to the other girl, but her voice was steady once more. "Tell the truth, Coralee. Did you call out to me to help you?"

Brown eyes compelled blue until Coralee closed hers and put a hand up to her brow. "My head is beginning to pound," she whispered.

"Later, Gemma; this can wait," said Captain Godwin brusquely. "We must get Coralee back to the house, where she can be attended to."

Gemma paid no heed. "Coralee?" she insisted with determined quietness, still looking full at her cousin.

"I am sorry, Gemma," began the younger girl, and Gemma's small taut figure relaxed, only to stiffen up at the next words. "I didn't mean to imply that you refused to help me. Perhaps my words were blown back by the wind so you could not hear me."

"There, that's all settled," said Captain Godwin heartily, evidently unaware that there wasn't a leaf stirring in the still wood. "Now let's see about mounting you." He looked around, avoiding Gemma's eyes.

"Take Fleurette," she said dully. "White Star has

run off." She turned her back on her cousin's sweetly
uttered thanks and made a project of brushing the dirt
from the hat she still held while its owner was carefully
lifted into the saddle by Captain Godwin. Coralee had
nothing to do but maintain her position as he and his
brother flanked the mare, leading her directly through
the woods up to the house.

Lord Gresham, who had remained silent throughout
the previous scene, rode back to meet the major and
Miss Delevan as they were entering the grove. "No real
damage done," he called out. "My cousin was tossed
but seems to be unhurt. She is being taken back to the
house. We might as well head for the stables ourselves."

Lucy ventured a look behind him as he indicated the
direction for them to take. "Is Gemma with her?"

"Your brother will see to it that Gemma gets back,"
replied Peter, and perforce the other two followed his
lead.

Standing alone among the looming trees, Gemma
watched her cousin being tenderly conveyed home by
the man she herself had waited for for two years.
Obviously his concern was all for the beautiful victim of
the accident, for he did not look back to see how she
might be faring without a mount. Her grip on the
sapphire hat tightened to knuckle-whitening intensity. A
second later she nearly jumped out of her skin as a
cheerful voice behind her said, "I think we've given
them enough of a start. Come."

The enormity of the disaster that had befallen in the
last five minutes had so overwhelmed Gemma that she
was experiencing a sensation of being lost in the center
of a storm, alone and at the mercy of rampaging
elements all around her. The sudden appearance of a
devil from the nether regions could not have been more
of a shock that the presence of Mr. Delevan at her side
holding down his hand to her from Blackbeard's back.

"I . . . What did you say?" She blinked at him uncertainly.

"I said they have enough of a start on us now. Shall
we follow?"

She seemed to notice his hand for the first time and, recognizing its intent, pulled back sharply. "I thank you, sir, but I shall walk back." She swept up the skirts of her habit over one arm and set off apace.

He dismounted at once and was by her side in two strides. "Very well, we'll walk back." His tone was equable and he did not offer further conversation, being perfectly cognizant of the fact that Lady Gemma was in no mood to welcome any human companionship.

Putting a visible check on her temper, she stopped and said with careful civility, "I don't wish to detain you, sir. Please ride on. I shall be quite all right."

"You are not quite all right and I shall not ride on unless you come with me," he replied, concentrating his sympathetic attention on her rigidly controlled countenance.

She stamped her foot, a gesture that was wasted on the soft ground of the wood. "Must I spell it out for you, sir? I prefer to be alone."

"I am aware of that, but it won't do you any good to be alone just now. All that bottled-up wrath needs an outlet before it chokes you. You must know by now that it will be perfectly safe to spill it over me."

A brittle laugh answered him as she plowed forward for another half-dozen paces, eyes straight ahead. "You are too kind, sir, but quite mistaken. Why should I need an outlet for wrath that exists only in your mind?"

"Because," he returned with great gentleness, "you would like to twist your cousin's throat the way you are twisting her hat, and it would not do the least good."

She stumbled over a tree root and would have gone sprawling had not Mr. Delevan caught her up in one arm. Mild blue eyes gazed into overbright brown ones. "Shall we ride?" he suggested once more. When she made no answer, he released her and remounted Blackbeard. This time she took the hand he extended to her and landed herself across the saddle in front of him. He eased back to settle her more comfortably against his chest and they moved off at a walking pace. Quite

deliberately she tossed the velvet hat into the under-
growth.

Nothing was said on either side for the next few
moments, but Mr. Delevan was conscious of the rigidity
with which his passenger held herself and he sought for
some way to aid her. No inspiration had come to him
when Gemma ended the silence abruptly.

"*She lied*!" she muttered fiercely.

"I know."

"I would like to *strangle* her!"

"I know."

"Can't you say anything more to the point than 'I
know'?" she snapped in exasperation.

"Why don't you just cry it out?"

"I *never* cry!" denied an indignant Gemma, who then
surprised herself very much indeed by doing just that.
She wept copiously and noisily like an abandoned child,
but fortunately for the sake of Mr. Delevan's sorely
tried sensibilities, the storm was as brief as it was
violent and before he had actually admitted to himself that one
more minute would find him wrapping his arms around
her in an ill-timed embrace that would ruin his chances
forever, she was grasping thankfully at the handkerchief
he offered and mopping up her face.

They rode on for some time with no more sound than
Blackbeard's muted hoofbeats and an occasional
hiccupping sigh from Gemma. Her slight weight was
relaxed against him now and he had steeled himself to
endure the pleasurable torment for another few
moments when she stirred in his grasp and sat straighter
again. She slewed around to search his countenance.

"Mr. Delevan?"

"Yes?"

"When I said Coralee lied, you said you knew. How
did you know?"

"No one who is at all acquainted with you would
believe you capable of denying a cry for help; therefore,
Miss Fairmont lied."

"But the only person who counts *does* believe her,"

she wailed, banging her small gloved fist down in frustration on top of the hand holding her about the waist.

He flinched and for an instant tightened his grip on her waist but made no reply.

"He did believe her, I could see he did," she insisted as though he had contradicted her.

Silence greeted this also. After a time Gemma twisted around again to peer up at her escort. His eyes were directed at a point beyond her shoulder, but something about the set of his features got through her absorption in her own pain. "Ohhh," she breathed in horror. "Pray forgive me, sir! I did not mean that . . . I mean—"

"It's all right, little one," he soothed, cutting into her stumbling apology. 'Shall I set you down by the side entrance so you may head for your rooms without attracting attention?"

"Yes, please," she whispered, seeming to shrink into herself. Mercifully, they were already rounding the side of the house, and less than a minute later she was sliding down from the big horse. Bravely she forced herself to look up at her escort while she thanked him for his services in a small voice.

He listened and disclaimed with his customary politeness, but the infectious smile was missing, and Gemma felt as if she had been set at a far distance. She flashed him an unhappy glance and shivered as she entered the house. He had said it was all right, but suddenly she doubted whether anything would ever be all right again.

9

So intent was the artist on the painting taking shape before her that it would have required a much noisier approach than faint footfalls on grass to warn her of another presence than her own in the vicinity. The man strolling forward took full advantage of the opportunity thus afforded him to study her at his leisure. Simply dressed in a green-dotted white muslin that left an expanse of slender arms bare, she had stationed herself within the leafy spread of an enormous elm tree. To the man coming closer, it seemed almost beyond recall when he had last observed an individual so at one with his setting or so at peace as this girl.

She leaned forward to paint in a small detail, and the sunlight was caught in that abundance of chestnut-brown hair, highlighting rich veins of red. The presence of a large straw bonnet of the variety designed to shield a woman's complexion from the effects of the sun told its tale to one trained to observe details. The hat had been cast off and weighted down with a stone to secure its safety when its owner had positioned herself in the shade of the elm, but the sun had advanced considerably since then, leaving the artist now almost totally exposed to its slanting rays as the afternoon waned. Every now and then a vagrant breeze rippled the pale-green ribbon drifting over the brim of the abandoned hat. A sister breeze blew a strand of hair across the artist's mouth, but apart from an ineffectual tossing of her head, she ignored it in her determination to achieve the result she sought. Both hands held brushes, which she exchanged from time to time until, satisfied at last, she sat back and viewed her efforts through narrowed eyes as one hand, still holding a brush, absently reached for the loose strand of hair.

The alien eyes watching the artist had been held by that tress of hair caressing her lips until a delayed sense of guilt at having invaded her privacy and set her at a disadvantage caused a surge of dark color to rush up under his swarthy skin. He stepped forward into the field of her peripheral vision.

"Good afternoon, Miss Delevan. Forgive the inter—"

"Ohhh," she gasped, and spun toward him with the result that the brush in her raised hand swiped a streak of brown across one cheek. An apologetic exclamation on the gentleman's part was brushed aside by the lady. "No, no, it was quite my own fault, sir. You could not be expected to advertise your arrival with a flourish of trumpets."

For a second he watched the scrubbing motions she was making with the palm of her hand on her face before he directed a quick glance over her painting paraphernalia. Selecting the cleanest container of water, he dipped his handkerchief and presented it to her silently.

"Thank you." She scrubbed, to better effect this time, then turned her cheek toward him.

He answered the question in the smoky-gray eyes. "Much better. There is just one smudge remaining near your chin. Yes, that's fine. Thank you." He received the handkerchief from her hands, noting with interest her total lack of coquetry and mentally acknowledging the effort it had cost him to refrain from offering to do the cleaning job himself. There was no doubt in his mind that her sun-warmed skin would feel like silk under his fingers. Abruptly, he wadded the handkerchief and stuffed it into a pocket in his gray coat. He had slammed the door on that kind of thinking after Toulouse. The last thing in the world he'd be likely to do would be to leave a false impression of his intentions in the mind of any marriageable female.

He had been staring unseeingly at the little Greek temple that was the artist's subject, and now, looking down, he discovered she had already returned to her task, underlining just how little account she took of his presence or absence from the scene. Wry amusement directed at his own conceit twisted his lips momentarily, but his voice was smooth as he explained that he had been detailed by their hostess to tell her that tea was being served. He did not bother to mention that he had beaten several other gentlemen to the punch when the duchess had announced that someone must be sent to find Miss Delevan.

"Oh, dear, I should return immediately, of course," she said with reluctance, "but another five or ten minutes would see the completion of this picture, and who knows when I shall have the light precisely the same again. Do you think, Major Barton, you might present my apologies and assure the others I shall be along presently?"

"There is no need to feel compelled to go racing up there only to participate in a daily ritual," he replied shortly. "And I wish you would not call me that."

He had her attention now. "Not call you what?" she asked, pausing to look at him in puzzlement, her brush suspended in midair.

"Major Barton. I have sold out. I am finished with the army, or rather, the army is finished with me."

She took no account of his gruff tones. "What shall I call you, then?" she inquired coolly as she returned her attention to the painting in her lap. "Lord Oliver?"

"Can you not manage plain Oliver?" he replied, to his own surprise and hers.

"I fear that if I were to address you simply as Oliver on an acquaintance of less than a fortnight I should be setting myself up for some deserved censure, so Lord Oliver it must be," she decided after a tiny pause.

For a long moment the rustlings of nature were the only sounds audible as the artist continued her painting and Lord Oliver continued his study of the artist.

"There!" declared Miss Delevan at last, laying aside her brush and holding her work out at arm's length while she examined it critically. "I feel that though I have not succeeded perfectly in capturing my impression, yet any additional touches will serve only to detract from what I have achieved.''

Wondering what had become of maidenly modesty since the days when his sisters had been taught to deprecate their own work as an inflexible tenet of ladylike decorum, Lord Oliver stretched out a hand for the painting and appraised it thoroughly while the artist busied herself with putting away her equipment.

"You must know by now that your drafting abilities are far beyond the ordinary run of a young lady's drawings," he said at last, glancing over to where she stood observing him quietly. "You have a real sense of the structure and solidity of architectural shapes, and yet the effect on this clear day is a rather romantic airiness."

A slow smile spread over her still features and the clear eyes held real warmth. "Thank you," she said simply as she handed over the box of paints for him to carry in exchange for the damp painting. "Actually, watercolor is not my favorite medium," she confessed as they started walking slowly back across the lawns. "I really prefer to take my time with oils."

As the walls of the hall appeared through the shrubbery, they were engaged in a slightly acrimonious but stimulating debate on the respective attributes of their favorite artists.

Lord Oliver stopped in his tracks. "Miss Delevan, may I ask you something?"

"Yes, of course," she replied, and waited.

"I do not wish to pry into what doesn't concern me, but did something happen yesterday after that abortive race, something more than Miss Fairmont's fall?"

For a moment Lucy was at a complete loss. The interlude of painting had been so satisfying, followed by the stimulation of pitting her wits against a sharp mind, that she had lost sight of the main reason she had decamped on a painting expedition in the first place. "What makes you think something might have happened?" she asked to gain time.

"Well, your evasiveness would have told me if I had not already noticed a bit of an atmosphere in the saloon just now. Yesterday it was perfectly understandable that we should not remain for tea in the wake of concern for Miss Fairmont's possible injuries, but today I received the distinct impression that all is not well between the cousins. You need not tell me anything that you would regard as a disloyalty; in fact, tell me to mind my own business if you like."

Lucy had been thinking rapidly since the beginning of this speech. In a way it was a relief to learn the Godwins had not reported the scene that had taken place in the wood. How she would like to believe it was because they had set it down to Coralee's jealous spite! She might not have learned of the incident herself had she not been waiting in Gemma's bedchamber for a report of Coralee's fall when Gemma arrived back at the hall. One look at her friend's red-rimmed eyes and trembling figure had sent Lucy flying for the bottle of sal volatile, and only the most desperate pleading on Gemma's part had kept her from summoning her maid at once. It had taken a threat of informing the duchess of her daughter's condition to induce Gemma to disclose the reasons for her pitiful state. Once started, however, she had even referred tearfully to the hurt she must have inflicted on Lucy's brother in repayment for his kindness and belief in her. On this head Lucy hoped she had been able to convince the younger girl that John would not despise her forever, but on the other count she had been powerless to offer any consolation that was acceptable to the sufferer. Lucy had not seen the accusation in George's eyes, had not heard the coldness in his voice, had not witnessed his tender concern for Coralee.

Knowing that nothing less than a full confession from Coralee could completely eradicate the impression the captain had received, and not being so naive as to cherish the least hope of obtaining such a confession, Lucy had decided there was nothing to be gained by a prolonged discussion. She had supported Gemma's spirits to the extent she was able, and had spent her best efforts trying to convince her friend that the affair would blow over, that if George loved her, he would not allow anyone to make mischief between them. Her efforts would have been more effective had she been able to convince herself that George Godwin did indeed love his childhood friend, but in this task she had been unsuccessful from the start. She feared Gemma was heading for heartbreak if her heart was set on having the captain. She was gripping her bottom lip in her teeth as she relived the scene with Gemma and at first was not aware that Lord Oliver was speakng again.

"I did not intend to drive you into the silence forever," he said with a keen glance from dark eyes. "Shall we go inside?"

"No, not yet," she replied, desirous all at once of obtaining a disinterested opinion. "Perhaps I should not be telling you this, but you have already been exposed to the consequences." Quickly she related the scene as told to her, leaving out only the conversation between John and Gemma on the way back to the house.

His face revealed nothing of his thoughts, but then it never did, and his first reaction was disappointing to say the least.

"You are so sure your friend is telling the truth? In the heat of the contest could she not have shut her ears to a cry from her cousin and been ashamed to admit to it later?"

"Unthinkable!" declared Lucy. "Apart from the fact that she is incapable of such an act in the first place, that race never meant the snap of her fingers to Gemma; she never doubted she would win it. It was Miss Fairmont who was so keen on proving something."

"Your loyalty does you credit, but it really boils down to the unsupported word of one girl against the other, does it not? There is not sufficient evidence to judge of who is telling the truth."

"I would agree if it were a hypothetical example with nothing known about the character of either person, but such is not the case, is it?" countered Lucy. "My brother and I believe Gemma, and Gemma herself is convinced that Captain Godwin believes Miss Fairmont's version of the accident."

"And whom does Malcolm Godwin believe? Or Lord Gresham?"

"I do not know."

"Nor really care. Would I be presuming too much if I were to postulate that the reason Lady Gemma appears pale and quiet today and is carefully avoiding her cousin's company—all of which, by the by, was evident to an unbiased observer within five minutes of setting foot on the premises—is because the opinion of one person—and one person only—is crucial to her happiness?" Lucy was silent, and he said quickly, "Forgive me, it was unfair to expect you to answer that."

"No," she said with a grudging honesty. "Gemma has not admitted it in so many words, but I have received the strong impression that she is in love with Captain Godwin and that it is no sudden thing."

Lord Oliver answered the unspoken question in her searching eyes. "George has never confided the state of his affections to me, but again as an unbiased observer, I would have to say that he seems taken with Miss Fairmont's charms at the moment."

"I have thought so too," conceded Lucy, "but neither of us is in a position to say that Gemma had not good reason to suppose that his affections were hers before he returned."

"But believing this," he persisted, "and seeing his reaction to Miss Fairmont, would it be impossible to conjecture her being so desirous of regaining his admiration that she might allow herself not to hear her cousin's call for help in order to win that race?"

"Totally impossible for someone of Gemma's makeup," stated Lucy in flat tones. "It is infinitely more conceivable that Miss Fairmont, upon seeing herself about to lose in a bid for admiration, came up with a scheme to ensure sympathy to herself and opprobrium for her rival."

"You are very severe. You must dislike Miss Fairmont very much."

Lucy sent him an icy glare. "You are quite mistaken, sir. It is no more necessary for me to dislike Miss Fairmont to speculate upon her motives than it is for you to dislike Gemma to put forth your conjectures. For one thing, if Gemma had succumbed to such an ignoble urge, she would be sure to be found out when Miss Fairmont had her say, while Miss Fairmont, with all the advantages of being the accuser, had little to lose, since the race was already lost and Gemma could never prove her innocence."

"It seems we are at point non plus, and tea awaits. I am willing to admit that I like Lady Gemma," he advanced in a provocative vein. "Are you equally willing to claim that you do not dislike Miss Fairmont?"

"I do not dislike Miss Fairmont," stated Lucy, disliking her antagonist's vaunted impartiality very much indeed but striving for a cool exterior that would defeat his penetrating glance. "I am willing to allow her every virtue not incompatible with an extraordinary degree of beauty."

"Ah? And what might be the virtues that *are* incompatible with great beauty?" he inquired with real interest.

"Humility, for one," she shot back. "The inclination to share the stage with others upon occasion, for another. A generous spirit and an acceptance of the fact that beauty does not automatically entitle one to first choice of all life's prizes."

He digested this for a moment, then asked slyly, "Is truthfulness incompatible with beauty?"

"Theoretically speaking, no—practically speaking, upon occasion," intoned Lucy, refusing to be backed into any corner of his devising.

"We have reached an impasse," pronounced Lord Oliver solemnly. "Shall we join the others?"

Lucy demurred on the reasonable grounds that she must first put away her painting gear and wash her hands, but she was ruthlessly overruled when she attempted to part from Lord Oliver at the top of the stairs. He handed the paint box to a footman, possessed himself of the painting, which he said would provide a welcome diversion, and firmly steered her toward the saloon, grimy hands and all, despite her frantic protests that she had absolutely no intention of submitting her amateur effort for universal judgment.

"Why this sudden excess of maidenly modesty?" he wondered aloud. "You had no scruples about letting me examine your work a few moments ago."

"That was different!"

"How so? Was my judgment likely to be kinder?"

"No, of course not," she protested, feeling out of her depth, "but you were standing right there, and there was only *one* of you. It was different!"

Lord Oliver, seeing the agitation in those generally calm eyes, took pity on her embarrassment to the extent that he halted outside the drawing room for a moment. Carefully shifting the now dry painting to a position under his stiff left arm, he took her hand in his and raised it to his lips. Intense dark gray eyes never left her startled light ones as he pressed a deliberate kiss on the backs of slim, paint-streaked fingers, nor when he lifted his mouth an inch to say softly:

"Trust me that our entrance with your painting will be the tonic that will lift this dreadful gathering out of the doldrums."

Before Lucy's dazed intelligence could summon up a reply, he had pressed another brief kiss on her fingers and ushered her through the door.

In the blue saloon matters proceeded exactly as Lord Oliver intended. He apologized for their tardiness, explained to the audience at large that he had taken it upon himself to insist that Miss Delevan stay to finish a painting he knew would give them all pleasure and had further overriden the natural modesty of the young lady to bring it along for their enjoyment. He produced the watercolor sketch with a flourish and led the ensuing chorus of praise, sparking a discussion of landscape painting in general.

A bemused Lucy sought a seat beside her school friend and endeavoured to efface herself within the shortest possible time. Very little of what was said in praise of her painting actually registered in her mind, and she could only trust that her own murmured responses were not total gibberish and expressed a proper appreciation for the compliments paid her work. The one fact that was impressed upon her, thanks to a speaking look from Lord Oliver, was that Miss Fairmont's voice was most often and most flatteringly raised on behalf of the painting. His slightly elevated eyebrow seemed to say, "So much for beauty's being unwilling to share the stage."

"Have you ever seen such authority and strength in a female's painting before, George?" Coralee demanded of the gentleman sitting next to her on the sofa. "I vow I would not dare to show my own poor efforts in company with Miss Delevan's."

"To be sure, Miss Delevan's work is most accomplished," replied Captain Godwin, bestowing his warm smile on the embarrassed Lucy for a moment before turning to Coralee to protest, "but you've absolutely no call to diminish your own considerable talent. Recollect that I was privileged to see those charming flower sketches you did last week. They showed great flair, did they not, Gemma?"

"What? Oh, yes, Coralee is quite clever at . . . sketching."

From behind the screen of her long lashes, Lucy's eyes clouded with compassion as she observed that Gemma's stony composure was betrayed in part by the white knuckled grip of her fingers on the teacup she raised to her lips. She had avoided looking directly at her cousin for as long as Lucy had been in the room, but she had not been able to prevent a quick glance at Captain Godwin as his dark head bent attentively toward Coralee's gold curls.

With the infusion of new life into the tea party, Lord Oliver gradually made his way to a seat near Lady Gemma, whom he succeeded in engaging in quiet conversation for the remaining quarter-hour that the gentlemen from the manor spent at the hall. Good manners alone enabled the dark-haired girl to conceal her initial surprise at being thus distinguished by a man who, in the course of a dozen or so meetings, had displayed no interest whatever in singling out any of the young ladies for his passing attention.

After the departure of the guests, the party broke up, with the members of the household going their separate ways until just before dinner. Lucy was even more relieved than Gemma to be able to escape to solitude and time for private reflection, for she had been woefully conscious that, with her paint-stained hands and wind-ruffled hair, she had been a scruffy object unfit for her hostess's drawing room. Despite the acknowledged necessity for a thorough wash, she dawdled over her toilette, her languid movements at great variance with the seething ferment in her mind.

The subject of her disordered thoughts was the inexplicable behavior of one large, formerly aloof, and generally cold gentleman of recent acquaintance. Staring down at her knuckles, immersed in soapy water, she conceded that his bullying tactics designed to hustle her into the tea party, though startling at the time, were compatible with his nature as revealed up to that point. But whatever had possessed him to kiss her hand in such a . . . such an intimate fashion? Her cheeks grew hot at the mere recollection of those unreadable dark eyes that had held hers captive while his warm mouth caressed her fingers. Heaven only knew to what extent she might have betrayed herself at the time!

Her fingers stilled their movements in the water and she stared, appalled, at her flushed reflection in the mirror over the washbasin. He would have attributed any reaction to shocked surprise, of course, which it was! Hastily she withdrew her hands and used the water as much to cool down her cheeks as to wash them.

His action toward herself had not been the entire sum of his uncharacteristic behavior either. After seemingly taking Coralee's part—or at least refusing to accept that Gemma must have told the truth—he had deliberately sought out the latter and devoted himself to her entertainment for the duration of the visit. Was he trying to decide whether she was, in fact, guilty as charged by her cousin? Did it even matter to him beyond an intellectual exercise? Lucy had been furious at his treating the story as such before they joined the others, but at least that was more consistent with the image of aloofness he had projected up to this point. His determination to relieve the tension in the saloon and the successful carrying out of his hastily improvised plan to achieve this end spoke to his quick-thinking mind but was diametrically opposed to his previous behavior.

Lucy was jerked out of a fascinating speculation about Lord Oliver's future conduct toward the inhabitants of the hall by the arrival of a note from her hostess requesting the favor of a short interview before Lucy went down to dinner. A glance at the clock jolted her into action, and by scrambling into her clothes and doing no more to her hair than confining it with a ribbon after a quick brushing, she was able to present herself at the duchess's door ten minutes before the dinner bell.

10

Lucy was admitted by Miss Penderbury, the duchess's long-time dresser, who immediately returned to her mistress, whose hair she was in the process of arranging for the evening.

"Do sit down, Lucy," said the duchess with a smile, and the girl sank onto a sea-blue velvet chair near the dressing table. While her grace complimented her guest on her appearance, Lucy was watching the dresser's clever fingers brushing the raven locks, which contained no trace of gray. Tonight her grace was wearing a gown of a deep-rose silk that was flattering to her rich coloring and petite figure. Almost, one was deceived into believing her as young as her daughter. Lucy returned the compliment with alacrity and they chatted about fabrics for a minute or two while Miss Penderbury fussed over the exact placement of two diamond-studded hair ornaments. The duchess bore this indecision with patience for another minute, then said briskly, "That is perfect, Penderbury, thank you. That will be all for now. Miss Delevan will help me drape my shawl, won't you, my dear?"

"Of course, ma'am," said Lucy, responding to the hint of mischief in the other's smile and averting her eyes from the suspicious glare of the dresser, who, without uttering a word, managed to convey her disapproval of any curtailment of her mistress's routine. Lucy made a hasty comment on the hair clips to cover the dignified exit of the abigail.

"She terrifies me, but she is a positive genius with my unmanageable hair," confided the duchess in a stage whisper as the door closed behind Miss Penderbury.

Lucy smiled in sympathy and waited for her hostess

to state the reason for the summons. She seemed to be in no hurry to come to the point, though it now lacked only five minutes until dinnertime.

"I was very much impressed with the quality of your watercolor sketch, my dear child, and apart from its obvious technical merit, you seemed to have expressed some of my own feeling for that charming little temple."

Lucy glowed with pleasure. "You must allow me to make you a present of it, your grace."

"Oh, Lucy, I did not bring you here to beg for your painting. What must you think of me!"

Her young friend smiled. "Why, what could I think but that you are a woman of refined artistic discrimination. Please," she repeated as her hostess chuckled softly, "it would give me great pleasure if you would accept it."

"Well, then, it will give me equal pleasure to possess it. Thank you, Lucy." The temporary animation that had taken years from the duchess's face and highlighted the resemblance to her daughter faded suddenly, and she half-turned her face away to fidget with some mother-of-pearl-backed brushes on the dressing table. The silence was becoming a bit uncomfortable for her guest when she squared her shoulders and placed her fluttering fingers in her lap.

"Lucy, why did you pick today to go off on a painting expedition?" Without waiting for a reply, she went on, "Am I correct in supposing that this is the first time you have done so during your visit?"

"Why, yes, ma'am. I have made some sketches in the gardens, but this was the first day I thought I might spare two or three hours to paint." As she strove to speak matter-of-factly, Lucy was miserably conscious of being subjected to a prolonged examination from fine dark eyes.

"I still cannot help wondering whether you went off by yourself today because you were desirous of painting or to escape the atmosphere of this place." When this invitation produced no comment from the young girl, who was no longer meeting her eyes, her grace leaned toward her and said earnestly, "Lucy, what happened yesterday afternoon? A mere fall from a horse could never account for Gemma's mood today, especially since it was Coralee who fell. Either my daughter is very unhappy or she is in a black rage, which she is at pains to conceal. But concealment is foreign to Gemma's nature, which is frank and open to a fault. And not the most insensitive creature alive could remain as insensible as Coralee would have us believe she is to the way Gemma is avoiding her. It is too ludicrous!"

"Your grace," said Lucy gently, hoping to curb the agitation that was visibly causing her hostess's breathing rate to increase, "have you asked Gemma what happened yesterday?"

"She wouldn't tell me." Swift contrition leapt into the dark eyes. "Oh, Lucy, forgive me, my dear child. My concern to try to do something to alleviate this awkward situation must be my excuse for placing you in such a horrid position. Naturally you feel you cannot betray a confidence." She jumped up from the dressing-table bench and began pulling out drawers, presumably searching for a scarf. Tact and sympathy kept Lucy from drawing her attention to the rose shawl reposing on the corner of the bed. When she had located a gauzy white length spangled with silver, the duchess straightened and presented a tightly controlled countenance to her guest.

Shall we go down together?"

"Let me help you with that, ma'am." Lucy took the scarf and arranged it around her hostess's shoulders, wishing that it were in her power to arrange the evening ahead of them to her grace's satisfaction. "It will most likely blow over in a day or two," she predicted in a desire to ease the worry that was gnawing at the duchess. "Gemma is not one to bear a grudge."

"Thank you, Lucy. I hope you are correct. You have confirmed what I already suspected: that Coralee has wounded Gemma in some way. Well, what can't be cured must be endured, after all." She raised her head to a proud angle and flashed a gallant smile at the tall girl by her side. "Meanwhile, shall you and I try to charm this gathering tonight with our own inimitable wit, sparkle, and intelligence?"

Whatever may have been the true spirit behind this confident, almost swaggering statement from the generally retiring duchess, her challenge proved doubly successful, initially in bolstering Lucy's determination not to fail her gallant hostess, and finally, in its result.

Certainly the dinner-table conversation was vastly easier than might have been expected, and it would not be overstating the case to attribute this to the concerted efforts of these two ladies, with the unobtrusive assistance of Mr. Delevan, whose social sense never failed. If the more observant among those present noted that Lady Gemma's twin dimples remained in hiding, at least she was careful to maintain enough of a share in the conversation to avoid drawing unwelcome attention to herself.

When the gentlemen rejoined the ladies after a brief interval in the dining room, the duchess was ready with a suggestion that Coralee, who prided herself on her cardplaying, might like to challenge her uncle to a game or two of piquet while the rest of the company played speculation or some such round game; or, if that program did not appeal and the gentlemen were determined to desert the ladies for billiards, then the latter would entertain one another by reading aloud while they sewed. Having cleverly established an atmosphere of free choice, she retired from the short discussion that followed.

Her son being the only gentleman ranged on the side of billiards and her niece fearful of being abandoned to the dreariness of exclusively female society, the question was quickly resolved in favor of piquet and parlor games. The long anxious day finally ended on a note of improvement, though nearly everyone was more than willing to retire at an earlier hour than usual. The duchess, by instructing Stansmere to bring in the tea tray a full half-hour ahead of schedule, had been instrumental in this decision too.

Thanks in part to the duchess's adroit manipulations, no open breach or even an articulated drawing up of sides ever took place, but there was one consequence of the racing incident she was powerless to prevent. After breakfast the following morning the duke requested an interview with his daughter in his study. His bland manner gave no hint of the nature of the upcoming conversation, but a well-developed sense of self-preservation prompted Gemma to present a guarded countenance to her parent when she joined him in his sanctum.

The duke wasted no time on amenities. "I do not know the cause or nature of your silly quarrel with your cousin, young woman, nor do I wish to," he began, "but you are to remember that she is your guest and cease this ridiculous sending-to-Coventry behavior that has succeeded in setting the whole household by its ears. Is that clear?"

No flicker of emotion crossed his daughter's face as she returned his stare. "Very clear," she replied softly. "Did my cousin complain of my behavior?"

"Your attitude was plain for all to see, but do not think your cousin has squeaked beef on you or tried to lay all the blame for the quarrel in your dish. When I asked her last night if something had happened, she admitted you two had had a falling out but made it clear that she bore you no ill will for your share in the misunderstanding."

"Generous of her," murmured Gemma with a tiny smile.

"Yes, it is, and I expect you to do no less!"

Again that queer little smile trembled on her lips. "But it is so much easier for the victor to be generous than the vanquished, do you not agree?"

If Gemma hoped by this enigmatic reply to incite

some curiosity on the part of her father to probe the history of the so-called quarrel, she was doomed to disappointment. Boredom was the only emotion evident in the duke's voice. "At the risk of sounding redundant, may I repeat that I take no interest whatever in feminine dagger-drawing, but I will not have my house made uncomfortable for my guests. I trust I shall have no occasion to remind you of this again." Light-blue eyes challenged dark-brown ones that did not waver.

"Is there anything else you wished to say to me, Papa?" inquired Gemma politely.

"Nothing at the moment."

The duke stood behind his desk and watched his daughter's petite figure go quietly out of the room. Not until she had closed the door behind her did he seat himself and reach for his ledgers.

His Grace of Carlyle was not quite finished with announcements for the day, however, as the members of the household discovered at lunchtime. They had all enjoyed a cold repast that was crowned by a delectable fresh-fruit tart when the duke delayed his son's imminent departure from the table.

"Stay a minute please, Gresham." His grace was at his most benevolent as he circled the table with a broad smile. "I was about to announce to everyone that, since we have among us a young lady who will celebrate her eighteenth birthday in a fortnight, her aunt and I have decided to hold a waltzing ball in her honor so that we may all rejoice with her on this happy occasion."

Lucy, who sat beside the duchess, noticed that the fork in the latter's hand paused midway to her mouth, then slowly descended to her plate, but her main attention was concentrated on Gemma, though covertly. There was nothing to be seen in that quarter, however. The duke's daughter, after the briefest glance in her father's direction at the beginning of his speech, continued to eat her way through a generous portion of the tart.

Coralee, who had been staring wide-eyed at her uncle,

found her tongue at last. "Oh, Uncle Ernest, thank you," she squealed ecstatically; then, overwhelmed by the inadequacy of the response, she jumped out of her chair and cast her arms about the duke's neck, almost upsetting his balance in his chair as she hugged him exuberantly. "Thank you, thank you, Uncle!"

"There, there, puss," he said fondly, setting her upright as he disentangled her arms from about his neck. "If you promise you won't strangle me, I'll tell you that the gown I owe you had best be a ball gown, something to catch the eyes of all the young bucks in the county."

"Oh, *famous*!" Coralee clasped her hands together to contain her delight. "Can we go to Bath today?"

"It is too late to dash off to Bath today, my child," put in Lady Sophronia repressively. "Besides, the weather looks threatening again. We'll discuss it later with your aunt."

"Yes, of course, Mama," submitted Coralee, subsiding back into her chair.

"And I suppose you have nothing to wear either, Daughter?" queried the duke, smiling at his offspring.

"Oh, yes, Papa. I have the white dress we bought for the Ellman twins' ball in May, which I have worn only once." Gemma returned her eyes to her plate, where the tart had almost disappeared.

The duchess spoke for the first time. "You will need new gloves, Gemma, and your silver-beaded evening reticule is not quite right for that gown. Lucy may require something also. Have you a ball dress with you, my dear?"

"Yes, thank you, ma'am. When John's valet arrived last week, he brought some of my things with him. I had not expected such a social summer when I arrived, so had not packed as much as I would need."

"Can't take the rackety pace, Lucy?" put in the duke slyly.

"Oh, I'll stay the course, sir, never fear," she promised, experimenting with one of Coralee's provocative flicks of long eyelashes.

"I have every confidence that you will, and that you'll break a few hearts along the way too," her host returned gallantly.

When the ladies meandered toward the blue saloon later in the afternoon, the upcoming ball was, quite naturally, the chief topic of conversation. It was the first opportunity to pursue it also. The duchess had been closeted with her husband for an hour after lunch, and Lady Gemma had excused herself to run an errand for her mother to one of the tenant cottages. Nothing less than a natural disaster was allowed to interfere with Lady Sophronia's afternoon rest, and she had demanded her daughter's attendance.

Lucy, with no demands on her and the sky too unpromising to chance another painting session, decided to put in some practice time at the pianoforte. After a thoroughly enjoyable two hours she retired to her room to change her plain cambric dress for one of her favorite light muslins in a becoming shade of lavender. She spent rather a long time fussing over her hair which wasn't behaving as well as it might, for it seemed imperative to atone for the untidy appearance she had presented at tea the previous day. By the time she was satisfied that her shining curls were confined in place and her dress was neat and uncreased, she was the last of the women to enter the saloon.

"You look charmingly, my dear," said her grace, smiling at the girl who came over to sit beside her.

"After yesterday, ma'am, anything would be an improvement."

"Oh, I wouldn't say quite that," demurred the duchess. "Yesterday you were most attractively rumpled and deliciously flustered but none the less appealing than this cool, pristine Lucy of today. A woman should have as many facets as a jewel."

"Like Cleopatra's infinite variety, Mama?"

"Do not mock Shakespeare, dearest. He knew it is a decided advantage in a female to be able to keep the gentlemen intrigued and unsure of what next she will be or do."

"It strikes me as a lot of posing," declared Lady Sophronia. "One must remain true to oneself above everything."

"Cannot one be true to oneself and still have infinite variety, aunt? How disappointing. I think I should like to be mysterious and enigmatic."

"Whereas generally you are as transparent as glass." Coralee laughed and forestalled any comeback from her cousin by turning to Lucy to inform her that they had decided to go shopping in Bath on the following day.

Stansmere appeared in the doorway at that moment to announce the gentlemen from the manor. The male residents of the hall arrived shortly thereafter to swell the ranks as the tea tray and sherry were brought in. As might be expected, the visitors received the news of the scheduled waltzing ball with pleasure.

"Well, that should prove the highlight of the summer season," said Captain Godwin, beaming at the duchess. "You will have all the local hostesses gnashing their teeth in chagrin, ma'am."

"Do you know, we have never waltzed together, George!" Gemma, having impulsively articulated her thoughts, looked a little conscious as all eyes turned toward her, but Captain Godwin was equal to the occasion.

"A situation we shall certainly remedy a fortnight hence, this provincial island having at last succumbed to the wicked temptations of the Continent." His smiling glance passed on to the golden-haired girl gazing at him with inviting pursed lips. "And may I be the first to solicit the guest of honor as my partner for supper on the occasion of her birthday ball?"

"I think you would take advantage of your advance knowledge to steal a march on the other gentlemen in the neighborhood, sir, but it is far too early to commit myself," declared Coralee, tossing her curls. "Imagine if we were to quarrel before the ball. It would quite take away our appetites to be compelled to endure each other's company at supper. No, you may ask me again on the day of the ball if you like."

"You may depend upon it," replied George, accepting her decision with a courtly bow.

Lucy, noting the flash of dismay that had leapt into Gemma's eyes before she bent her head to retie her sash, introduced a new topic by mentioning the proposed shopping expedition to Bath. The gentlemen revealed that they too had made plans to go into Bath on the morrow.

At this juncture John addressed his hostess privately. After a short conversation, she announced that the shopping party was to be entertained by him at lunch at the York House after their morning exertions.

"I'll be delighted to include you both," said John to Malcolm and George. "And Major Barton, of course, if you are all free."

Malcolm thought they were already committed to an early luncheon appointment, but George promised to try to stop at the York while the party from Monteith Hall was there.

"I dare not speak for Major Barton, though. He is undergoing a course of the hot baths in the hope that they will be of benefit to his arm. The treatments started today, which is why he is not here with us."

The elder ladies were moved to express their hopes that the famous waters would do the trick in restoring the use of his arm.

"Yes, poor man. It seems impossible to believe that all that apparent strength should be dormant," said Gemma in ready sympathy. "This paralysis cannot be permanent."

Lucy flashed her friend a quick smile for expressing her own views so unselfconsciously. She had grown rather silent in the last few minutes, glad that there were enough people on hand so as not to require a great effort from her to maintain the flow of conversation. The truth was that the party had gone rather flat for her from the second she had realized that only two gentlemen from the manor had called. With the honesty that characterized her self-dealings she admitted that she had been eager to see Lord Oliver today. With something less than her usual honesty she attributed her own sense of loss at his absence to disappointment that she would not now be in a position to observe whether he continued to advance in friendliness toward them all or regretted his lapse of yesterday and reverted to his former coldness.

A moment's consideration produced the unwelcome thought that perhaps his absence today was just that—an indication that he regretted his behavior of yesterday. She stared down at her fingers holding the teacup, the same fingers that he had kissed so deliberately, and had to be spoken to twice by her brother before her attention was caught. Aside from that one brief instance, no one present would have gleaned any hint from her agreeable manner that Lucy was applying a strict control over herself to conceal an inner perturbation and a growing desire to achieve some privacy in which to discard the smile that was becoming a trial to maintain.

Fortunately, a severe mental chastisement for indulging in girlish fantasies delivered by the sensible mature Lucy to the silly gooseish creature staring back at her from the mirror was nearly completely effective in banishing these fantasies. She enjoyed a good dinner and a peaceful evening of music and reading as much as anyone else in the family. If her sleep was all the sweeter for the hope that tomorrow might bring another meeting with the aloof but fascinating major, such a hope was kept well below the surface of her awareness and had not the least influence on the unusual pains she took with her appearance the following morning.

11

The sun shone down brightly the next morning and the gentlemen who had ridden out early reported that it bade fair to be a warm day. Miss Fairmont was regaling Miss Delevan with a description of the perfect gem of a parasol she intended to carry to Bath when word reached the breakfast table that Lady Sophronia had fallen victim to the only influence in her well-regulated life that she was unable to control by positive thinking: an attack of the migraine.

"Oh, that is too bad! Poor Aunt," said Gemma when Coralee seemed to be bereft of words. "Pray convey our warmest sympathy to her ladyship, Stansmere, and tell her we shall put off our shopping trip until she feels more the thing."

"Not go to Bath," exclaimed Coralee, finding her voice in a hurry. "Why should we postpone the trip when my aunt may go with us in Mama's stead?"

"I regret that won't be possible today, Coralee," replied her cousin. "Mama has an engagement with Lady Godwin this afternoon. If my aunt is still unwell tomorrow, I feel sure Mama will agree to take us."

"But my ball is scarcely a fortnight away. If we delay our shopping forever, there will be no time to have a gown made."

"I am persuaded Miss Weems could make you up a ball dress in a sennight if she knew the time were short. Do not disturb yourself on that account."

"I don't *wish* to have Miss Weems make me one of her démodé dresses even if she makes it overnight," declared Coralee, flushing angrily. "I plan to have my dress made by that new Frenchwoman in New Bond Street, Mademoiselle Analise. Will you excuse me please, Uncle? I am going to talk to Mama.'' With that she pushed back her chair before Stansmere could assist her, and ran out of the room.

Gemma turned limpid eyes on her father. "I fear poor Coralee is greatly disappointed.''

Peter let out a rude crack of laughter but closed his mouth at a look from his parent.

There was nothing in his daughter's words or tones to object to, but the duke's eyes narrowed and he said shortly, "So I see," before returning his attention to his breakfast.

Gemma did the same, and it was for Lucy to initiate a light conversation about the newest blooms in the gardens. They were running out of things to say about the flowers when Coralee came back into the room, a sunny smile on her lips in place of the sulky frown with which she had departed a few moments before. She turned the smile on Lucy first.

"Mama says she has a great respect for Miss Delevan's taste and would trust her to oversee the shopping trip if my uncle will permit us to go into town under Mr. Delevan's escort. You could have no possible objection to such an arrangement, Uncle, could you?" She focused confident blue eyes on the duke's features and smiled brilliantly.

"If Mr. Delevan is willing to take on the task of bear-leading a parcel of females on a shopping expedition, you have my permission," conceded her uncle.

It was now John's turn to bask in the sunshine of Coralee's smile. He forestalled the pretty plea trembling on her lips by stating at once that he would be honored to provide the young ladies with an escort in Bath.

During Coralee's fervent expression of gratitude, Gemma's glance skimmed his for a mere instant and he recognized that she as well as her cousin attributed his acceptance to the heady effect of the latter's charm. Since it was not part of his plan to try to persuade her otherwise at the present, he merely smiled kindly into slightly contemptuous eyes.

The duchess, when appraised of the situation, was not

best pleased to have the young women jauntering about Bath with only a masculine escort, but since the new arrangement had already won official sanction, she refrained from voicing an opinion that would seem to criticize her husband or sister-in-law.

The existence of a seat in the carriage did not influence John to alter his original intention of riding into Bath. Coralee did indeed attempt to change his mind, but her powers of persuasion proved inadequate to the task. In the most apologetic manner he confessed to a tendency to feel sick in a closed carriage. Lucy was privately amused to perceive that Gemma's countenance registered disbelief, and her cousin looked faintly scandalized at this disclosure. The subject was dropped immediately and the girls had the carriage to themselves for the hour-long trek to Bath.

Both Lucy and Gemma had spent several years at a Queen's Square seminary, and Coralee had passed much of her childhood at Monteith Hall, so a trip to Bath was no novelty for any of the girls. The talk en route consisted of a nearly complete review of the last three issues of *La Belle Assemblée*, offered by Coralee. Frankly bored after ten minutes, Gemma directed her attention to the passing scenery, leaving it to Lucy to supply the occasional cues to keep Coralee prattling happily along. It said much for the essential sweetness of Lucy's nature and the early training in good manners imparted by her mother that the girls arrived in New Bond Street with their mutual cordiality unimpaired.

Mr. Delevan delivered his passengers to the establishment of Mlle Analise and went off to see to the stabling of his horse. It was agreed that he should meet them at the modiste's in an hour's time, which, he was helpfully assured, would give him ample opportunity to see the abbey and take a peek in at the Pump Room.

Thus relieved of the responsibility for their escort's entertainment, the ladies proceeded to the business at hand. It had been decided in the carriage that Miss Fairmont was to have a white ball gown made. At the outset she had begged Miss Delevan's advice on color, which

that young lady had been reluctant to offer, feeling that
this should be Miss Fairmont's choice for the happiest
result. When pressed repeatedly for an opinion, she had
finally ventured to suggest that blue must always be very
complimentary to one of Miss Fairmont's coloring, only
to be told instantly by the latter that she was tired of
blue, perhaps she would have white this time, and what
did Miss Delevan think of white? Catching on to the
way Miss Fairmont's mind operated, Miss Delevan
thought white an excellent choice, and was thereafter
perfectly willing to put forth upon request suggestions
as to sleeve style and skirt detail for the purpose of being
overruled by the younger girl.

With a customer who knew her own mind as well as
Miss Fairmont, the business of selecting a design and
fabric was accomplished in fairly short order. Mlle
Analise, after one look at the beautiful young woman
desiring one of her creations, was all compliance and
eagerness to be of service. Such a marvelous advertise-
ment for the productions of her designing genius did not
come along every day. In Miss Fairmont she discovered
the perfectly proportioned figure to show off her
dresses—though she could wish the young lady a
fraction taller—combined with a beauty that would
draw all eyes to her person. Her loveliest fabrics were set
before this desirable client once the ladies had been
made comfortable in a room that could pass for a small
drawing room. Mlle Analise made a sketch from her
client's description of what she envisioned after her own
tentative designs had been rejected by that decided
young lady. When this was approved by all, Miss Fairmont was led to a small inner room to have her measure-
ments taken while the other two amused themselves by
glancing through some of the modiste's designs and
admiring the fabrics brought in by two young seam-
stresses from the near of the establishment. The entire
business was concluded with no reference to anything so
mundane as cost, though the dressmaker made doubly
sure that the account was to be sent to the Duke of
Carlyle at Monteith Hall.

It was no concern of Lucy's how Coralee spent the duke's money, and Gemma was determined to remain ignorant of the entire transaction. Lucy, who had an allowance fit for a queen, would not have dreamed of making such a purchase without full knowledge of the cost; indeed, she was by nature a thrifty shopper and rather prided herself on her eye for a bargain. She was therefore secretly rather appalled by the nonchalant attitude displayed by the duke's niece. Gemma had been taught by her mother to live within her very moderate allowance and was well aware that the duke frowned on requests for additional funds however valid the reason or pressing the emergency. This was not the first time she had been shopping with her cousin, so she was well acquainted with Coralee's general extravagance and her ingrained habit of buying things on impulse that she took a violent fancy to in the shops and that were largely consigned to the back of her wardrobe or the bottom of her drawers thereafter, sometimes without ever being worn at all. There was never any point in trying to argue her out of the purchase at the time, however, for she was as willful as she was extravagant, and any hint of opposition only increased her determination to possess the item in question. Lady Sophronia could afford to indulge her daughter's whims, knowing she could put a stop to her prodigality whenever she chose to put her foot down. What would happen should Coralee ever marry a man of modest means or any man who could not exert control over her was, thankfully, a nightmarish possibility that need not be considered seriously in view of her breeding and the material and personal assets she brought to the marriage mart.

"That went very quickly, I must say," approved Gemma as they closed the door of the dressmaker's behind them. "We have nearly twenty minutes before meeting Mr. Delevan."

"Perhaps we might be able to find you a pretty reticule in that little shop around the corner," Lucy suggested, directing their steps forward.

Coralee was in favor of this plan also, since she

wanted to buy a new reticule to go with the commissioned ball gown. "We can easily be back here by the time Mr. Delevan arrives."

It was not much more than fifteen minutes past the appointed hour when Mr. Delevan, waiting patiently outside Mlle Analise's door, espied his bevy of beauties strolling slowly toward him. He was able to appreciate the striking picture they made and assess the number of admiring glances directed their way by other passersby, since the girls were engrossed in an animated conversation and were impervious to their effect on others. As he approached his charges, pleasantly aware of the envy of other men at his good fortune, Lady Gemma spotted him first and quickened her steps.

"Pray forgive us, sir, for keeping you waiting. I fear we must be shockingly late."

"Not a bit of it. I am entirely at your disposal." He offered her his arm and included the other two in his welcoming smile. "My groom made arrangements yesterday with the proprietor of the York House to serve us luncheon at half after twelve. We are in good time, and anything we cannot accomplish before then may be done after lunch."

"Oh, marvelous," gushed Coralee, attaching herself to his other arm, "because my cousin and your sister have yet to purchase long gloves for the ball."

Her spontaneous little gesture in taking their escort's arm would have left Lucy to walk alone, but Gemma dropped back immediately to join her friend as the party proceeded to the glovers.

It lacked fifteen minutes to the appointed hour for lunch when they emerged from the glovemaker's shop. With his customary good nature, Mr. Delevan had made himself the repository for all the packages so far acquired. The hotel was nearby on George Street at the top of Milsom, so they would be in good time for lunch.

John and Gemma were somewhat ahead of the pace of the other two. The duke's daughter had felt very awkward in the company of her friend's brother just after he had brought her home on his horse following the racing incident, so miserably ashamed was she of her unthinking remark in response to his expression of belief in her honesty. On the following day she had spent as much time and effort trying to avoid being in his company as her cousin's, but for very different reasons . . . and with opposite results. It gave her a grim satisfaction to evade and ignore Coralee, but when she succeeded in putting distance between herself and Mr. Delevan, her misery only increased. In a remarkably short space of time he had become almost as comfortable a friend as Lucy. She wouldn't have believed that any other trouble could weigh her down when the anguish of knowing George had not believed her was so acute, but such was the case. From her hasty words he must have thought she counted his friendship and good opinion as nothing beside George's, and it wasn't so! True, she had apologized immediately and she would be glad to apologize again, but no apology could wipe out the callously inflicted wound. In her sore state she felt she had thrown away something precious. And then after tea, when she was on her way to her room to change for dinner, Mr. Delevan had appeared at her side as she headed wearily for the old wing.

"Lady Gemma, may I have a word with you?" he had asked in a quiet voice.

Speechlessly she had nodded, but after a fleeting look into serious blue eyes, hers remained glued to the carpet.

"What have I done to offend you? Why are you avoiding me?"

Her first reaction was to deny it, but such honesty compelled a like return. "It isn't you," she had blurted out. "It is I who have offended—what I said yesterday about no one's opinion counting but George's—it was a *terrible* thing to say and it wasn't true! You said it was all right, but it isn't, and I don't know how to make it right. I—"

Two fingers lightly pressed against her lips had brought this tirade to a halt and brought unhappy brown eyes up to meet smiling blue ones.

"You've just made it right. Knowing that you were

bothered by it is like being assured that we are friends, as I had believed. Am I correct?''

"Oh, yes," she breathed as the fingers were removed. The cloud of worry cleared from her eyes and she smiled shyly. Then he had done a surprising thing. One of those restraining fingers had gently touched each cheek in turn.

"I was afraid they were gone forever," he had said softly to mystify her, then had added briskly, "Now, no more avoiding me?"

She shook her head.

"Good." He had turned and headed for his own wing without another word, but the brief estrangement between them was over.

Now, on a sunny day in Bath, walking by Mr. Delevan's side, Gemma broke the companionable silence to ask, "What did you think of the abbey?"

"I liked it, and not just the whimsical angels going up the ladders to heaven either. The fan vaulting inside is magnificent, and so is the setting . . . Well, not magnificent, but just right, nestled by the river as it is. I was so interested in strolling around the grounds that I never did get to the Pump Room. Another day perhaps."

"There will be other opportunities to come into Bath. All the world passes through the Pump Room sooner or later."

"Have you ever drunk the water?" he inquired curiously.

"I'm never sick." Her smile was saucy, and his eyes as always sought out the dimples.

"That's begging the question. Have you?"

"Once, one gulp." She shuddered theatrically. "If medicine must taste horrid to be efficacious, the waters of Bath should be a universal panacea."

"You have just talked me out of sampling them."

"Oh, no! All visitors to Bath drink the waters. It would be a sacrilege to refuse. Think of your liver, think of your gallbladder!"

Sudden mischief sparked in electric blue eyes. "Very well. I'll drink half a glass if you'll finish it."

"Unfair!" She laughed. "I have had my dose." She glanced back to check on the progress of Lucy and Coralee, and at that moment a street urchin darted out of a doorway. When Gemma turned forward again, she caromed into the running child and was instantly down on the pavement.

"Lucy!" John spun about and thrust the assorted packages into the arms of his sister, who had come dashing up. The urchin was already half a block away. He bent over the kneeling figure and assisted her to her feet but became aware almost at once that she was putting no weight on her left leg. Her face was ashen and the velvety eyes were full of pain.

"Lean on me," he commanded urgently, and took most of her weight as she complied readily. "Is it your ankle?"

She nodded, biting her lip to keep back a moan. "It will be fine presently. Just let me stand still a moment."

Lucy and Coralee had divided up the parcels and were watching her anxiously while the other pedestrians split like a river going around an island in its center. They were beginning to attract attention. One or two men stopped to stare curiously at the pretty girl leaning heavily on a masculine arm.

"Look, Lucy, you and Miss Fairmont go on to the hotel. It's only another block. If necessary, I'll carry Lady Gemma."

"You'll do nothing of the kind," hissed the accident victim in horrified protest. "I'll be able to walk in a minute. Do go on, girls. We'll follow directly."

"Lady Gemma is right. There's nothing you can do. We'll take it very slowly."

Reluctantly, Lucy allowed Coralee to pull her forward. Gemma put her injured foot down and cautiously leaned a little weight on it, though John's arm was still taking the major strain.

"Shall I carry you? What do you care what a lot of strangers think? It's only a short distance in any case," he persisted, eyeing her colorless cheeks with concern.

"All the more reason to do it myself," she said

between gritted teeth. She did manage the feat with the support of John's strong right arm. It was uphill all the way and her progress was slow and painful, but she was depending less on the supporting arm when they finally entered the hotel. Still, it was impossible to conceal her relief when at last she subsided into a chair in the room their host had hired for the luncheon.

"Shall I call for cold cloths for your ankle, Gemma?" asked Lucy, hovering over her friend.

"It will be fine after a rest. Your brother can tell you that I was walking much better at the end. I do hope lunch is ready. I'm starving."

John took the hint and went to see about their order. The York House had upheld its reputation, and they enjoyed a bountiful meal planned around a roasted chicken brought to the table for their host to carve. The girls were especially pleased with some tender early asparagus served with a delicious lemon-flavored sauce. Lucy, eyeing the array of jellies and tarts with which the meal ended, knew that her brother, who preferred fruit and cheese, had tried to cater to what he imagined were feminine tastes.

The light conversation ranged from details of their shopping experiences to a list of all the places John must see if he were to claim that he had indeed visited Bath. Gemma and Lucy solemnly reminded him that a pilgrimage to Queen's Square to gaze at Miss Climpton's Seminary, which had had the privilege of educating them, was an inescapable obligation for a loving brother and friend.

Coralee was amused. "A shrine, in fact. Do not fail to treat it with proper reverence."

John took out a pocketbook and made a note. "Anything else?" he inquired, pencil poised.

Lucy and Coralee giggled and Gemma smiled, but the dimples were barely visible. He had kept an unobtrusive watch on her throughout the luncheon and was nearly persuaded that her ankle, far from being forgotten as one would expect of a momentary wrenching, was causing her increasing discomfort. Despite earlier claims, her appetite had definitely waned, for she had merely made a pretense of eating. Her hands were frequently in motion and a look of strain had come into her face. He glanced around the table and concluded that a suggestion of leaving in another five minutes would not be too pointed. Meanwhile, he would send a servant with a message for the coachman.

The door that opened to admit the servant also admitted Malcolm and George Godwin, very pleased with themselves for arriving in time to share a glass of wine and plan the afternoon's activities. At that moment John wished them both at Jericho.

"It is the most perfect summer day imaginable," said Captain Godwin with enthusiasm. "We thought a walk through the Sydney Gardens would be a pleasant program for the next hour or so." He smiled around the table but failed to notice that two of the faces that looked back did not share his enthusiasm. "The owner of a spectacular parasol such as that one"—he nodded toward the pink-and-white-striped confection of ruffles that reposed against a chair—"must wish to parade it before as many of the town's elegant ladies as possible." This time the smile was just for Coralee.

"How did you know it was mine?" she asked, fluttering golden-brown lashes as she opened those beautiful eyes to their widest.

"Clairvoyance," he responded promptly, "not to mention an innate fashion sense that tells me that this particular parasol would not compliment Gemma's yellow gown or Miss Delevan's blue and white."

Gemma broke in on the captain's lighthearted nonsense. "I am so sorry, George, the Sydney Gardens must be lovely at this season, but I stupidly twisted my ankle on our way here and I fear I could not quite manage the walk today."

"Not even if you were to take my arm and lean on me the whole time?" The captain's caressing smile was aimed full strength at Gemma now.

She swallowed once and shook her head. "I am sorry."

"Do not be such a baby, Gemma. You managed to walk here on the ankle," her cousin said impatiently.

Lucy pushed back her chair. "Gemma, let me see

your foot!'' Ignoring the surprised looks of the others
and Gemma's protests, she grasped the back of her
friend's chair and wrenched it away from the table
unceremoniously, kneeling down beside her.

"Good Lord, Gemma, why didn't you say something
earlier? This ankle should have been bound the moment
we arrived. You must be in agony.''

John had risen almost as soon as Lucy, and as he
stood looking at the puffed-up ankle, his expression was
as nearly grim as anyone had ever seen it. Fortunately,
the sufferer had surreptitiously untied the strings to her
sandal during luncheon, but he was in total agreement
with his sister's diagnosis. Brushing aside Lady
Gemma's embarrassed protests that it could wait until
she got home, he was about to ring for a waiter when
Malcolm volunteered to go out at once for a bandage.
John nodded his thanks. When the waiter came in a
moment later to clear the table, he ordered cold cloths
and brandy for Lady Gemma and stood over her like an
avenging angel until she had swallowed a modest
amount of the loathsome stuff from sheer inability to
hold out against his determination.

At this point Lucy took over from her brother,
ordering that Gemma be moved to the one upholstered
chair in the room and her feet raised to another chair.
Bypassing the question of permission, John lifted her
and accomplished the transfer expeditiously though not
without additional pain to the patient and, therefore, to
himself. By this time the cold cloths had arrived. Lucy
applied them immediately. It was too late to prevent
swelling, of course, but in conjunction with raising the
injured foot, now shoeless, they helped to ease the
constant discomfort that had turned the past hour into
an endurance trial for Gemma.

When Malcolm returned a few minutes later, Gemma
was able to smile at him and thank him for his kindness.
Lucy, all business, interrupted to advise her friend to let
John wrap the ankle as he was more skilled then most at
achieving the desired support with the least discomfort
to the patient. Again John hadn't waited upon per-

mission. He had already dragged a chair from the table over to the spot and was unrolling the bandage, which he proceeded to wrap most securely and neatly about the injured foot.

Miss Fairmont and Captain Godwin, after suitable expressions of shocked sympathy, had been relegated to the fringes of the action during this time, in the unenviable position common to witnesses of accidents whose good intentions could find no method of expression.

Now Coralee spoke solicitously, "Poor Gemma has had a trying time. I should not think it advisable to subject her to the jolting of the carriage until after she has rested. Could we not hire a bedchamber where she may lie down for an hour or two? The rest of us could pass the time walking in the gardens so that she might have complete privacy, unless she should wish Miss Delevan to stay with her."

This suggestion did not find favor with Lucy, who had assumed the direction of the affair. Looking at her friend's downcast eyes and pallor, she gave it as her firm opinion that the sooner Gemma was home, the better it would be. John, who was speaking with a waiter at the door, looked around and announced that the carriage had arrived. Captain Godwin, acting with the speed of a soldier accustomed to making quick decisions, bent over and picked up his old friend in his arms.

"I'll take great care not to jolt your foot," he promised with a tender smile.

After a rather searching look at his concerned face, Gemma closed her eyes and relaxed against him. Malcolm Godwin held open the door, and after scooping up all their possessions, the others trailed in procession out to the waiting carriage, where Gemma was established as comfortably as possible. John had lingered inside for a moment to beg the loan of a couple of the hotel's pillows, which he handed up to his sister to arrange as best she might to cushion the ride for the injured ankle. The carriage door was closed and the driver given the signal to start.

12

As anyone who knew her could have predicted, the next few days proved exceedingly difficult for Lady Gemma, but perhaps even more so for her family, whose combined efforts to see that she did not delay her recovery by imprudent behavior were scarcely appreciated by the recipient and were disregarded whenever possible—that is to say, whenever the eye of authority was temporarily removed. One of her active nature would always chafe at any physical restriction, and for the next four days it was impossible to fit a shoe on her swollen foot. Of necessity she was confined to a sofa, but she refused to be confined to her room. After breakfast in her bedchamber she was carried to her mother's sitting room by her brother or one of the footmen, and there she remained for much of the day, sewing with the women or reading when the rest of the feminine population was elsewhere. A tray was brought into the room at lunchtime, and she was carried to the blue saloon at teatime. To her fell the task of writing the invitations for the waltzing ball, but she was glad of any task that would shorten the hours of confinement.

Not that she remained as confined as the doctor ordered by any means. On the third day after the accident she appeared in the small dining parlor for lunch, having hopped from the sitting room with the assistance of a nervous footman.

"Hallo, everyone," said a breathless but triumphant Lady Gemma as she thankfully dropped onto the chair Mr. Delevan jumped up to pull out for her. "I hope we are having something nice for lunch. I'm starving."

She turned to thank her escort, ignoring the looks of consternation that had spread over the faces of most of those gathered around the table, but now a chorus of protest arose.

"Dearest, you should not!"

The duchess's soft expostulation was nearly drowned out by her niece, who warned, "You are likely to get a permanently thick ankle."

"Most unwise of you, niece," pronounced Lady Sophronia.

The reluctant invalid assumed a meekly penitent air that fooled no one, and proceeded to consume her usual sustaining meal in company. When her father granted Mr. Delevan permission to carry her back to the room she was beginning to regard as her prison, she ventured no more than a token protest, but the trek was accomplished in mutinous silence on the lady's part and patient resignation on the gentleman's. This was possible because he well knew that Gemma's forgiving nature would make any slight forfeiture of her regard merely temporary. In this instance he was rapidly reinstated into her good graces by being the prime mover in a plan to establish her under the trees in a shaded part of the garden the next day. Any change of scene was welcome, of course, but one of the first things he had noted about the duke's daughter was her preference for the outdoors.

Visitors proved to be the salvation of that trying period when Gemma was confined to a couch. Mrs. Biddleford and her two eldest daughters called to commiserate with Gemma on the fourth day after the Bath trip, to find her comfortably established on a day bed that had been moved into a shady area near the rose garden. Only Lucy, sketchbook in hand, was keeping her company at the time, but the advent of callers brought the other ladies outside and kept Stansmere and his minions busy carrying extra chairs to the garden. Eventually the Godwin brothers arrived, accompanied by Lady Godwin, and the result was a sizable al fresco party that doubtless increased the work of the servants threefold.

John, noting the smiling face of a very junior housemaid enlisted to fetch and carry during the impromptu party, wondered if anyone else realized, as he had recently, the extent to which Gemma was held in affection by the staff employed in her father's house. Ever since she had been carried into the house with her bandaged foot dangling over his arms and her brown eyes dulled by the pain she refused to acknowledge verbally, the footmen and maids had fallen all over themselves to offer her assistance, and the chef had been sending up special treats to tempt an appetite that never needed tempting. John had been in the duchess's sitting room on two occasions in the past two days when a maid had popped her head in to see if there was something she might do for the young mistress. Watching her now as she smiled and chatted with the Misses Biddleford—pleasant-enough girls, though one had an irritating laugh—he marveled that she should remain so unconscious of that quality that drew people to her. It was one of her strongest attractions, at least for him, though certainly not the only one.

Lady Gemma gave a little bounce in her chaise and winced as her untimely enthusiasm resulted in a twinge in the ankle. The smile was back in a second, but Captain Godwin leaned forward solicitously.

"Did that hurt very much? Shall I call for some extra cushions to elevate the foot?"

"Of course not, George. It was nothing but a momentary twinge from moving too quickly. I am fine really."

"You must take great care not to aggravate the injury as it heals. We cannot have you sitting among the dowagers at the waltzing ball."

Nothing disturbed the calm friendliness of John's expression, but his face was not in accord with his thoughts at that moment. The injury to Lady Gemma had produced an increase in attentiveness on the part of her old friend that was causing her silent suitor no little trepidation.

From the beginning of their acquaintance John had known that his must be a game of waiting if there was to be any chance at all for him to win her affections. Lady Gemma believed herself in love with Captain Godwin and was set on opposing her father's plans for her future. On the point of retiring from the fray, John had taken heart from the captain's correct and charming manner on greeting the girl who had been faithfully awaiting his return for two years. He was convinced no man in love could have suppressed all sign of tenderness, of desire, at the moment of meeting that shyly revealing glance. The presence of Miss Fairmont, with her provocative beauty and dedicated coquetry, had nourished his hopes of seeing the old attachment wither away painlessly. The incident after the horse race, though unpalatable and regrettable, might have served to hasten the process. But perhaps he had indulged optimism too far.

Miss Fairmont's narrow-eyed glance at her cousin and Captain Godwin indulging in a brief tête-à-tête confirmed his own impression that there had been a shift in the balance of the captain's attentions. He was ever the consummate ladies' man, John acknowledged with some rancor, skilled in leaving each female with the notion that she was especially attractive to him. Coralee Fairmont with her inviting ways had been the prime beneficiary of this talented performance up to now, but the emphasis had shifted to Gemma Monteith these last few days. Captain Godwin brought her little gifts of fruit and flowers daily and the latest novels from the lending libraries in Bath to help her while away the tedium of her incarceration. And there was no denying that Lady Gemma was blooming under the influence of his attentions. This much was plain for anyone to see.

What was less clear was the reason for the shift in the captain's favors. Had his infatuation with Miss Fairmont run its course in such a short span? Had Lady Gemma's accident and subsequent stoic bearing shown him suddenly where his true affection lay? Was he just being kind in trying to cheer up an old friend, or was he perhaps trying to make Miss Fairmont jealous by his attentions to her cousin? The imputation of this last unworthy motive to the captain gave John no satisfaction, but though he struggled with his own demon of jealousy, he couldn't entirely dismiss it, for he did not believe that Captain Godwin was in love with Gemma now, whatever might have been his feeling for her in the past. His interest in Miss Fairmont, though disguised at present, was intense and had not waned. He did nothing so crude or obvious as to ignore her; he simply refrained from competing for her favors while she perfected her flirtatious technique on his brother Malcolm or John himself. John had found that the method that served him best in his own tightrope walk was to go along with Miss Fairmont's flirting in the playful manner of an adult indulging a precocious child. Malcolm Godwin, though an obvious admirer of the fair Coralee, was of a retiring nature and seemed more comfortable in the company of Lady Gemma, a preference that he was demonstrating at the moment, much to the chagrin of one of the Biddlesford girls, the one with the cackling laugh.

The whole complexity of relationships between the sexes being played out here at Monteith Hall this summer would, he imagined, be fraught with piquancy for an emotionally distant onlooker such as the absent Major Barton, but he was too deeply involved himself to appreciate the evolving pattern or derive any true enjoyment from the pulsing of its separate strands, unless the strand that was Lady Gemma should pulse unhesitatingly in his direction. It had been clear from the start that his knowledge of her prior attachment prevented him from taking the initiative in his own quest, but there was nothing to gainsay his seeking to consolidate his present position whenever opportunity offered. If he were restricted to the blunt sword of an insidious accretion of platonic feelings . . . Well, even blunt swords were formidable weapons if used forcefully, and platonic feelings had been known on occasion to convert to something warmer.

Consequently, John was not slow to act when a situation conducive to such consolidation presented itself the next day.

Lady Sophronia informed her daughter at lunch that she had had a syrup for the relief of a persistent catarrh brewed in the still room for Nanny Higgins, and that she would be obliged if Coralee would deliver it with her compliments that afternoon to the old nurse, who lived in a cottage at the edge of the village.

"I'm afraid that won't be possible today, Mama. George and Malcolm have arranged to take Miss Delevan and me riding this afternoon."

"You may ride in the direction of the village as well as not," replied Lady Sophronia.

"Unfortunately, we plan to ride in the opposite direction to the village. George has promised to show us the new foal that was born at the manor the other night." Coralee glanced over at her cousin. "Gemma cannot ride yet. Why can she not take the syrup to Nanny?"

"If Gemma cannot ride yet, she certainly can't walk that distance." Lady Sophronia frowned at her daughter.

"I don't propose to walk," said Gemma, entering the discussion at the first opportunity. "If you wish Nanny to have the syrup today, Aunt, I will take the gig—that way the wretched ankle need not be subjected to the strain of walking or riding."

"If I may be permitted to accompany you," put in John with a smile, "I will answer to Lady Sophronia that you do not endanger your recovery in any way."

Gemma wrinkled her straight little nose adorably. "I don't need a driver or a guard dog, but I shall be glad of the company," she finished, softening the effect of her first statement.

Coralee turned her beautiful eyes half-accusingly on

John. "Did I not hear you tell George that you'd like to see the foal also, Mr. Delevan?"

"Yes, but I didn't say when I'd ride over to the manor. Perhaps in two or three days Lady Gemma will be able to take Fleurette out again. The foal will have enough admirers today with you and Lucy cooing over it." John's tranquil smile brought a minimal response from Coralee, who was always averse to seeing a member of her court slip away.

The sprightly bay mare harnessed to the gig seemed to be as ready to enjoy an outing as Lady Gemma was. She tossed her head and nuzzled the hand patting her smooth nose.

"What a perfect day, and what a delight to be locomoting on my own, even if my foot will only fit in Coralee's old sandal," enthused the radiant girl, accepting John's help in ascending the seat with a care to the foot in question.

"Are you always this uplifted when performing a good deed?" he asked, quizzing her with wicked blue eyes.

"This is not a good deed, this is blessed freedom! I shall drive," she stated firmly in case he should have other ideas. "You signed on this cruise as a passenger, sir. You needn't fear I'll spill you into a ditch, though. I have been told that I am a competent whip."

Small capable hands gathered in the reins and accepted the whip from the patient groom who had brought the gig around to the side entrance. She thanked him and off they moved toward the avenue leading to the main gates on the lane. John angled himself so he could watch the delicately made girl beside him handle the reins as though it were second nature to her.

They took the turn in style and headed at a steady pace down the lane in the direction of the village. Only the profile beneath a chip-straw hat was visible to him as she concentrated on her driving, but he had no complaints to make. One feathered brow, a charming nose that just escaped an upward tilt, inviting rosy lips, a firm rounded chin that didn't reveal the cleft from this angle, and one deliciously curved earlobe beneath dark ringlets added up to an enchanting vision, the contemplation of which filled him with sheer joy.

She turned and caught him staring. Both brows arced upward. "You cannot really fear I'll overturn us in a gig," she exclaimed.

"Of course not."

The feathery arcs descended to a straight line as she frowned. "Oh. Well, you were staring at me so intently as if wondering whether you were safe."

"The danger is not that you'll overturn me."

"Oh? What is the danger, then?" she asked innocently—too innocently.

He could see the dimple in her cheek struggling to surface and felt his pulse quicken in anticipation. So far she had shown no disposition to flirt with him, or with anyone, for that matter. He said, whether to disconcert her or test her he could not be sure, "The danger is not to my limbs but to my heart."

She pursed her lips together and nodded wisely. "I have heard of people dying of fright. Their hearts just stop beating."

The minx! "You are a very difficult girl to flirt with," he complained mildly.

She gave him one of her direct looks. "Do you wish to flirt with me?"

"No, not really," he replied upon consideration, returning her look with an unusually serious one of his own. "I'd just like us to be happy together today."

"We always are," was the startling response, but before he could search her face for any deeper meaning, she had returned her attention to the horse, and her next remark was on a neutral subject.

The lovely summer day and the exclusive company of the most entrancing girl in the world combined to produce a sense of well-being and contentment in John. He would have been satisfied never to reach their desination, but all too soon they pulled up before a tiny slate-roofed cottage set behind a rather weedy collection of flowers lining the dilapidated fence that had a gap but no gate leading onto a flagged path. John jumped down and tied up the mare, devoutly hoping no frisky movement on her part would pull down the whole fence. Turning back, he was just in time to prevent his companion from jumping down from the gig unassisted. She looked guilty at his exclamation.

"I forgot about the foot; it feels so much better," she offered in extenuation of this injudicious move.

"If you wish to dance at this ball next week, you will control your unfortunate and unnatural inclination to do everything for yourself and permit others to wait upon you," he advised sternly as he lifted her down from the seat, marveling anew as he did so at the delicate smallness that could contain such boundless energy and vitality. His hands spanned her waist perfectly and he loosed them with reluctance.

"What is so unnatural about wishing to do things for myself?"

"Females are raised to expect men to assist them—that is, females of your class," he amended hastily as a strapping young woman carrying two heavy pails of water entered the cottage across the street.

"Pooh! What does such a female do, pray, when there is no man around? Sit there unmoving like a log until rescue comes? What a ridiculous waste of time! I am not so feeble," she declared with perfect truth, reaching back into the gig for the basket before he could retrieve it for her.

"Shall I wait for you here?" he asked as she started up the path.

"If you would not mind coming inside for a minute, Nanny will love meeting you. She has been very lonely since her brother died. She kept house for him here after we left the nursery and doesn't wish to leave the cottage now, but it gets lonely for her sometimes, though the neighbors are good to her."

It was very dim coming inside from the bright sunlight, and his eyes were a time adjusting to the gloom, but Gemma went unerringly forward to the shawl-wrapped figure stirring in the chair. John felt he had never encountered anyone as old as the wizened form that greeted them from a rocking chair near the fireplace.

"Is that you, my love, come to see old Nanny? I heard tell you had an accident in Bath and couldn't walk a step," the old woman said in robust tones that, coming from such a shrunken figure, startled Mr. Delevan. It told him something about the speed and efficiency of village gossip as well.

"It was nothing, Nanny, merely a sprained ankle that's all better now," explained Gemma, leaning down to kiss a withered cheek. "I have brought a syrup for your cough from Aunt Sophronia." She placed the basket in Nanny's lap.

A rumble of laughter shook the black-clad form, ending in a hacking cough. When she retrieved her voice, the old lady said, "Eh, she was ever a one for brewing possets and cures, her ladyship was, but thank her kindly for me, my love. She was a good girl, Lady Sophronia was, never gave me a moment's worry, not like Master Ernest, now. I well remember how he would—"

"I have brought someone to meet you, Nanny," said Gemma, cutting off the old nurse's reminiscences of the duke before they should prove embarrassing. John stepped forward. "This is Mr. Delevan, who is visiting us this summer."

John made his best bow and found himself being studied by two bright dark eyes, sunken in their sockets but decidedly alert for all that. "I am very pleased to meet you, Nanny Higgins," he said, returning her gaze with interest.

"You won't get 'round me with that sauce, young man. Why would anyone want to meet an old worricrow like me?"

Not in the least disconcerted by this attack on his

veracity, John replied, "I am happy to know any friend of Lady Gemma's, ma'am, and I understand you to be her oldest friend."

The crone looked rather pleased by this refusal to knuckle under. "Hrummmph, you've a mighty smooth tongue, I'll say that for you. Isn't your sister staying at the hall too?"

"Yes, Nanny," confirmed her former nurseling. "Lucy would have come with me today but she was engaged to ride with Coralee and the Godwins."

"And why are you not out riding too? Why do you waste time on a useless old woman?"

"I can't get a boot on my foot yet, and you've never complained about my visiting you before. Don't you like me to come?" teased Gemma gently.

One clawlike hand waved away this irrelevance. "So that pert piece is up at the hall too, is she? And still determined to take anything that belongs to you for her own, I'll be bound."

Neither of her listeners was in any doubt as to where this slighting reference was aimed.

"Coralee and I get along fine now, Nanny," said Lady Gemma.

"Then she must have altered for the better since last I saw her." Shrewd snapping eyes captured Mr. Delevan's. "Has she?"

"Miss Fairmont is a very amiable young woman," he replied smoothly.

"I hear she has turned into a diamond of the first water. Is that true?" probed the old woman.

"I believe you would have to agree with common opinion that holds Miss Fairmont to be a beautiful young lady." Mr. Delevan was at his blandest. The woman studying him was clearly dissatisfied.

"Do *you* share this common opinion?"

"Yes, certainly I do."

His inquisitor changed tactics. "I have heard that Coralee's beauty casts Gemma here into the shade. Is that also true?"

"Nanny!" protested the girl. "You are embarrassing Mr. Delevan!"

John relented. Smiling into the intent eyes fixed unwaveringly on his face, he said simply, "No one could ever cast Lady Gemma into the shade, Nanny Higgins."

He was rewarded with a toothless smile. The little figure in the rocker relaxed against the backrest and set the chair in motion again. In the silence that greeted John's declaration, she opened the basket on her lap. "Oh, grapes! Thank you, my love, they're beautiful."

"They were always your favorites," babbled Gemma, eager to get the conversation on another track. "These are the first of the season from Papa's succession house. Shall I put these things on the table for you?"

"Yes, do." The old woman gave up the basket and closed her eyes, thereby intensifying the image of great age. One forgot it for a time when she was speaking and those lively eyes were interrogating her audience.

Gemma came back and stooped to kiss her once more. "I hope we haven't tired you too much, Nanny. Will Flossie be in later with your supper?"

"Yes, she's a good girl, Flossie."

"I'll bring Lucy to see you next time, shall I?" asked Gemma, preparing to depart.

"If you like, and you may bring your young man again too."

Almost to the door, Gemma stopped so suddenly John nearly bumped into her. Avoiding his laughing eyes, she corrected Nanny Higgins firmly. "Mr. Delevan is *not* my young man, Nanny. He is my father's guest."

A raspy chuckle floated over to them from the creaking chair. "Does *he* know that?" inquired Nanny Higgins.

She was allowed the last word as Gemma was making a dignified exit. John turned for a farewell smile in his champion's direction before following his hostess out into the sunshine once more. He was careful to school his features to impassivity, and after a quick look, Gemma decided not to pursue so awkward a subject even if it meant allowing him to come away with mistaken ideas.

John was about to hand her up into the gig when a tiny child lurched across the street crying, "Lady! Lady!"

His companion waited to admire the unsteady progress, then bent down to scoop the child up into her arms. "Hallo, sweetheart, have you a kiss for me today?" A smacking kiss was delivered to her cheek as two tiny arms wrapped themselves around her neck.

Lady Gemma turned so her escort could see the slightly grimy but sparkling face of the little girl. "This is Hannah. Her mother, Flossie, used to be my maid until she married Tim Evans. They live in that cottage on the other side of the street, and Hannah should not have come across by herself. You know that, Hannah," reminded Gemma, holding the child off for a moment to look sternly at her.

"I saw Lady," piped up the unrepentant imp.

"Yes, I know, but next time you call to me and I'll come to see you. Do you understand, Hannah?"

A vigorous nod of red curls attested to the fact that Hannah understood.

"Will you say good afternoon to Mr. Delevan, Hannah?" The red curls were presented to John as the child sought the safety of Lady Gemma's neck in a rush of shyness. "If you hide like a silly baby, Mr. Delevan will think you do not like him and he will feel hurt. You don't wish to hurt his feelings, do you?" The curls vibrated again with a negative shake. "Then come say hallo," coaxed Lady Gemma.

Two green eyes peeked shyly at him as Hannah compromised with a smile to return his greeting. Lady Gemma shifted her burden slightly and Mr. Delevan took the child from her before either party could protest.

"She's too heavy for you at present. You must rest

your foot. Hannah won't mind if I carry her home to her mother, will you, Hannah?''

Fortunately, since the little girl showed every inclination to protest the abduction, her mother appeared in the doorway at that moment and came hurrying across the street to them.

Flossie Evans dropped a curtsy to Mr. Delevan on being presented by her former mistress, and she relieved him of her squirming daughter. They exchanged a few civilities while John helped Gemma mount into the gig to get her off her feet. Unlike Nanny Higgins, who took full advantage of her venerable years to speak her mind, Mrs. Evans made no reference to Mr. Delevan as Lady Gemma's young man, but her thorough inspection of his person left him in no doubt that she'd recognize him the next time he crossed her path. He bore the scrutiny with his usual calm demeanor and bade the woman a civil farewell in due course.

As they headed back toward the hall at a spanking pace, Gemma glanced over to her passenger to thank him for accompanying her on her errand.

"No need to thank me; it was my pleasure.''

"Thank you, you are very obliging, but I daresay this has been the most boring afternoon you have thus far spent in Wiltshire.''

"Then you would be wrong,'' John said quietly. "I have not been at all bored. In fact, I cannot conceive of being bored in your company.''

She was slightly shaken by the unmistakable sincerity in his tones but strove to keep the atmosphere light. "Vastly prettily spoken, sir, thank you. I promise that our next outing will be more to your taste.''

She changed the subject to some impersonal topic and he willingly followed her lead for the remainder of the short ride home. When he had assisted her down at the entrance to the old wing, so she could retire to put off her bonnet and gloves before tea, however, he reverted to their earlier conversation. As she thanked him for taking charge of the gig, he fixed her eyes with a speaking look and said softly, "I meant every word I said, little one."

"Th-thank you," she stammered with downcast eyes, and fled into the house.

John whistled softly and cheerfully as he returned the gig to the stables. Today marked the first occasion on which he had had Gemma to himself for more than a few moments, and he congratulated himself that she had been content to have it so. At no time this afternoon had he felt that he was merely a substitute for George Godwin. On the other hand, he reminded the impatient lover who inhabited his placid form as he made his slow way back to the main house, Gemma's spirits, depressed since that horse race, had been much improved of late, and he could not claim any credit for the transformation. He could only hope that this upswing was not entirely due to the increasing devotion of her captain. Although his confidence was not of a very high order, it would not do to despair entirely.

There were two irrefutable facts in the hazy situation in which he found himself. One was that Captain Godwin did not love Gemma, and the other was that the duke would not countenance a marriage were the captain to seek his consent to pay his addresses. Neither of these factors furthered his own suit, of course, and much as he desired Gemma for his wife, he would not be a party to any coercion. She must come to him willingly.

By the time he entered the house all inclination to whistle had left him.

13

At dinner that evening, the conversation touched as usual on the activities engaged in by various members of the house party. Lady Sophronia subjected her niece to a catalog of questions on the exact state of Nanny Higgins' health and spirits, all of which Gemma responded to with exemplary patience before her ladyship dismissed her, thanking her almost as an afterthought for carrying out the errand of mercy.

Lucy in her turn was unexpectedly voluble on the subject of the Godwins' new foal. "He is the dearest, most perfect little creature imaginable," she announced to the company at large, going on to detail the foal's many outstanding attributes.

His Grace of Carlyle eyed the animated visage of his daughter's friend with masculine approval tinged with amusement. "I am relieved to discover that you can find something to admire in the equine species, after all, my dear Lucy, even though I apprehend the vital quality to be extreme smallness of stature."

Aware of being teased, Lucy pouted charmingly. "I protest, sir. You do me a disservice in equating my poor equestrian performance with a dislike of horses. In general, I find them to be amiable and useful beasts with, however, a disconcerting quirk in their otherwise equable natures that is reflected in a universal and wantonly malicious desire to rid themselves of my presence on their backs. I do not know why this should be so, for I vow I have fed them more sugar over the years than any three of you here combined."

"Not above stooping to bribery, eh?" inquired the duke over the good-natured laughter that greeted Lucy's plaint.

"Anything that would serve, sir," she admitted ruefully before addressing her brother. "John, you really must plan to see the foal soon while he is still such a delightful baby."

"There will be plenty of time to ride over to the manor when Lady Gemma can get her boot on again," he replied with a smile.

"Since it is my fault you were unable to see the foal today, Mr. Delevan, let me atone by driving you there tomorrow," offered Gemma, adding mischievously, "if you are now prepared to acknowledge publicly that I am a competent whip."

"Bribery from one, extortion from another," mused the duke aloud. "Typical female practices."

Despite the provocative nature of this remark, it was clear to all that the duke was in an uncommonly amiable temper, but John chose to take him at his word. "Lady Gemma knows she had no need to extort compliments on her driving skill, sir. I never had a moment's doubt that I was in the charge of a very capable whip today and I'll prove it by accepting her kind offer to drive me to see the foal tomorrow."

"Or you might prefer to ride over to the manor with the rest of us and let Gemma rest her poor ankle for another day," suggested Coralee, flicking long lashes at John.

"You seem to forget that I was out driving today, cousin."

"Oh, so you were. I trust you haven't stretched my sandal all out of shape."

John made good use of the breathing space afforded by the cool exchange between the cousins to have his answer ready when both glanced expectantly in his direction.

"If Lady Gemma's ankle has suffered no ill effects from today's outing, I flatter myself that, in accepting her kind offer to drive me to the manor, I shall be ensuring that for tomorrow at least she will spend her time restfully in a carriage and not on a horse."

"How very smug and virtuous you look, Mr. Delevan," said Lady Gemma, widening her eyes at him across the table.

The gentleman smiled but returned no answer, content to discern the presence of a telltale dimple in each cheek despite an otherwise creditable effort to maintain an expressionless mien.

Young Gresham was absent after dinner, having taken himself off on some private revels with friends. When the duke requested a few hands of whist on entering the room where the ladies were gathered, John took instant advantage of the fact that his sister was playing on the pianoforte to challenge Lady Gemma to a game of cribbage. Far from finding her the deplorable cardplayer described by her father, he had to exert himself to keep even in the games that followed. Success in cribbage might be largely dependent on the quality of the cards dealt, but after two hours of hotly contested play, John concluded that his worthy opponent, in addition to being slightly more favored with good cards, had an uncanny knack for knowing when not to pair up his seemingly innocent offerings, a knack that stood her in good stead in the pegging.

By the time the tea tray arrived he reckoned himself the most contented loser in creation, for he had been granted an uninterrupted interval with the most enchanting girl in the world. He found her sweetness, joie de vivre, and essential simplicity of nature endlessly entrancing.

Lucy had drifted over in the last half-hour to sit on the arm of her brother's chair and watch the proceedings, but hers was never an intrusive presence.

When the time came for the ladies to retire after a spirited replaying of the whist game over the teacups, John had to guard his expression from revealing too much when he bade Gemma good night. This quiet day spent in homely pursuits had been the most enjoyable of his stay so far by virtue of her companionship, but he could not afford to lose sight of her avowed devotion to

George Godwin. He no longer questioned that he had gained her friendship and goodwill, but none of that signified a corresponding lessening of her accustomed feeling for her childhood friend. He would not have chosen to become embroiled in a quest where success was measured in inches, but he accepted that the human heart rarely had the power of choice when it came to the direction of its affections; it was more often the victim of Cupid's errant darts than the seeker after love. Each small advance in her favor meant a rededication to patience. He sighed silently as his glance followed the retreating back of his unconscious little love, her arm linked with Lucy's as they ascended the staircase behind the other ladies.

As the girls parted outside Lucy's door, she made reference to the planned excursion to the manor the next day, again reiterating her delight in the appeal of the baby horse.

"I have never known you to be so captivated by an animal before, Lucy," said Gemma. "It must be that I think of you as essentially a city-bred person, and animals are so much less prevalent in a town as a part of daily life."

"Well, I admit that ordinarily I might have admired the foal and passed on had it not been evident that your cousin and Captain Godwin were conducting a quarrel at the time just a few feet away. One would not wish to appear to notice or be curious, of course, so Mr. Godwin and I lingered by the foal some minutes longer and found the little darling eager to be petted and talked to."

Gemma smiled in sympathy with her friend's enthusiasm but went to her bed pondering over what Coralee and George could have fallen out about. She considered Coralee inconsiderate and hard to get on with, but men seemed to find her universally charming. She acknowledged a rather mean hope that her cousin might take such lasting umbrage with George that he would wake up to her true nature, and fell promptly asleep.

The sky the next morning looked too lowering to chance a drive in an open vehicle. Gemma and John decided to postpone their proposed outing until after lunch to give the weather time to settle.

The ladies gathered in the duchess's cheerful sitting room about midmorning to assist her with some of the more practical sewing and mending. They worked together in a relaxed atmosphere punctuated by sporadic bursts of inconsequential chatter from the girls or improving discourses on various aspects of housekeeping provided by Lady Sophronia for the edification of the young. She had just imparted an instructive aside on the efficacy of boiling two or three snails in the barley water of a sufferer from night cough when the duchess noted her daughter's eye fixed on herself in an assessing fashion.

"What's amiss, dearest? You are staring so intently at me. Is my cap askew?"

"Nothing's amiss, Mama. To the contrary, I was just thinking how blooming you look today. Having company must agree with you. I could almost swear you have put on some flesh lately."

"I agree with Gemma that you are looking a deal stronger than when I first arrived, ma'am. It is most becoming," said Lucy with a smile.

A trifle conscious but pleased by their observations, the duchess agreed, "I believe I am feeling more robust lately. One of these days I shall astonish you all by coming down to breakfast."

"Did I not tell you how it would be, Emilia, if you faithfully took that new tonic I had made up for you?" Lady Sophronia complacently assumed the credit for the improvement in her hostess's health. "If there is one thing I pride myself on, it is my knowledge of the healing properties of plants. Nature provides a cure for every disease if mankind has but the wit to seek out her secrets. I have made a lifetime study of this fascinating branch of knowledge."

"Yes, I know you have," concurred the duchess, smiling serenely at her masterful sister-in-law. "It is most commendable and very useful." Having gratified her guest and being much too kind to reveal that she had never taken the tonic in question, she held up a shirt with a torn sleeve and addressed her daughter. "Peter asked me to mend this for him, but do you think this sleeve is long enough? There isn't much point in mending it if he will only pull it out again because it is too short."

"I'll find him, Mama, and see if it fits." Gemma seized the shirt as a heaven-sent opportunity to avoid listening to any more tidbits from her aunt's inexhaustible supply of recommendations for conducting every aspect of life. As she headed for the door before anyone could dissuade her, she made an impudent little face at Lucy, who dropped her eyes swiftly to her own stitching and concealed a smile.

Gemma ran her brother to earth in the billiards room, where he and Mr. Delevan were involved in a serious contest. The latter looked up with a welcoming smile at her entrance, but Peter's concentration was too single-minded to admit of interruption. She stood quietly enjoying the match until her brother muffed a shot and threw down his cue in disgust.

"That's five straight games you've beaten me." He rolled his shoulders to ease their tension, grumbling, "All I've got out of this morning's exercise is a stiff back."

"You were much more competitive that last game," John said.

Peter grinned. "That's what all the sharpers say to their pigeons," he replied good-humoredly. His eye fell on his sister. "Perhaps Gemma can give you some of what you've been handing out to me all morning."

"I just came to show you this shirt, Peter," she inserted hastily. "Mama isn't going to mend it if it doesn't fit you properly."

"That's one of my favorite shirts. Of course it fits me. Here." He relieved her of the shirt and thrust his cue stick into her hands. "You take over here and I'll bring this back to Mama."

As Gemma stood looking undecided, John gently urged, "If you have nothing more important to do at the moment, I'd enjoy another game."

A vision of Lady Sophronia prosing on to her captive audience flitted before her mental vision and weighted the scales in favor of pleasure before duty. Gemma capitulated without further struggle.

The match that ensued was close fought by two players of nearly equal ability, but in the end Gemma was forced to concede her opponent's superiority.

"Why is it that I can never seem to beat you?" she sighed. "I beat Papa about one game in three and George more than half the time. George and Papa both beat you occasionally, I collect, so why cannot I? It isn't logical."

"We have played very few matches thus far, a situation I am most willing to correct. Behold me eternally at your service."

Gemma grinned up into his smiling eyes. "Aha! Do I detect a Captain Sharp as my brother warned?"

"Do you really wish to beat me so badly?"

This time Gemma could not sustain the intimate light in bright-blue eyes that seemed always to drag her into a dangerous alliance before she knew what she was about. Her eyes fell. "No, not really," she confessed, then rallied. "And do not be thinking I wish you to throw a game to me out of misguided chivalry either. I should hate that," she replied fiercely. "And I should know if you were to do it too."

"Heaven forbid." He raised his right hand solemnly. "I have to look to my laurels in one area at least. Remember you beat me at cribbage last night."

"Oh, cribbage, a child's game!"

"Ah, here you are, Gemma."

"George, good morning!" Gemma beamed at the smiling man in the doorway.

"Just barely morning. While you two gladiators have been contending, lunchtime has arrived. The duchess has invited me to join you."

"Splendid. Is Malcolm with you?"

"Not today. Have I interrupted your game?" This was addressed to Mr. Delevan, who had acknowledged the captain's nod with his pleasant smile before knocking a stray ball across the table.

"No, we had just finished."

"Did you win?"

This to Lady Gemma, who wrinkled her pert nose at him and flung a challenging smile at Mr. Delevan before replying, "No, that pleasure is still in the future."

"Speaking of future pleasures, I've come to drive you to Little Menda this afternoon. The Biddlesford girls sent a request by way of Malcolm that you all come to tea today. I've just received my new sporting curricule from the carriage maker, and you must have the honor of being the first to ride in it."

"Oh, George, I should have enjoyed that immensely, but Mr. Delevan and I have already made plans to drive over to the manor to see the new foal this afternoon."

"That's no problem. You may easily put off visiting the foal for another day. Delevan won't mind a post-ponement, will you, old chap?" The captain smiled affably at the man standing by the billiards table.

Gemma glanced uncertainly at John. No trace of dis-pleasure marred his pleasant countenance as he said with quiet deliberation, "I am willing to defer to Lady Gemma's wishes in this as in most matters."

"That's settled, then," declared the captain, turning his charming smile on his old friend, who was still looking at Mr. Delevan. "The others may ride over to Little Menda with Mal, and I shall drive you and your ankle in style."

"Wait, George. Mr. Delevan has kindly deferred to my wishes, but it must always be my wish to honor previous commitments. I would not be thought a flighty piece whose promises mean nothing."

"Don't be a little idiot, Gemma. Why should Delevan think any such thing? It is a matter of very little moment, after all."

"So it is," she replied cheerfully. "Thank you for asking me to be the first to ride in your new curricule,

George. Another time I should love to try it out.''

"You won't change your mind, then?''

She shook her head. "I'm sorry, George.''

"Then there is nothing more to be said.'' The captain bowed stiffly and stalked out of the room.

John, who had been idly knocking balls around the table during this last exchange, was standing, cue stick in hand, to receive her glance when it returned from the doorway through which her George had stormed. He could not be positive, but thought he detected a hint of apology in the deep-brown eyes. "I fear Captain Godwin was a trifle miffed,'' he ventured.

She sighed. "Sometimes George behaves like a spoilt child.''

Sternly repressing an urge to stoke the fires of discontent, John refrained from adding so much as a coal, saying with cheery solicitude, Well, I am persuaded it will all blow over very quickly. As the captain said, it is a matter of little import.''

This earned him a grateful smile and a glimpse of her famous dimples. "Yes, George is not one to cherish a grudge. Shall we head for the breakfast parlor? I believe it is nearly time for lunch.''

John's subsequent observations at lunch did not bear out Gemma's assertions concerning her old friend's disinclination toward grudge-bearing. From where he sat, Captain Godwin's behavior looked to be a prime example of the childish tactic known as "getting even.'' Not once did he voluntarily address a remark to the girl he had just invited to drive with him, and when called on to respond to some conversational offerings of hers, he did so in the briefest terms possible short of outright rudeness. Any lingering doubts Lady Gemma might have as to whether or not her recent refusal had put him in a state of high dudgeon were set to rest by his pointed attentions to the other two young ladies present. Lucy accepted her share of the captain's charming overtures with her customary composure and no discernible desire to secure more of his attentions to herself. Coralee, on the other hand, had been noticeably cool to the captain initially, but she was never proof against subtle flattery, and by the end of the meal she had agreed to drive out with him to call on the Biddlesford girls that afternoon. Lucy had earlier declined to make one of the party, explaining sweetly that, knowing Gemma and her brother planned to go to the manor, she had promised herself a few hours of painting.

Peering across the table, John was relieved to see Gemma calmly eating her usual hearty meal with an enjoyment apparently unimpaired by any regrets that her action in the billiards room had resulted in throwing her cousin and Godwin together. It had been manifest from his covert observation of his love during the meal that her attention had been largely concentrated on Godwin. She had appeared to be studying him and listening carefully to his conversation. John hoped he wasn't just grasping at straws to postulate that, for the first time since he had known her, Gemma was bringing her intellect to bear on her judgment of the man she had long been in the habit of loving. Certainly she seemed unusually thoughtful—but not, he trusted, unhappily so.

The gravity of her manner at lunch disppeared entirely on their expedition to the manor to see the foal. She was relaxed and happy in his company, that much was clear, and her laughter bubbled over on numerous occasions. John's conceit of himself was not of such a high order that he dared describe Gemma as completely contented with only his society, but he went to bed that night more hopeful that at any time during his visit that the girlish infatuation with her romantic soldier was running its course, helped along by the revealing light of reality.

That waltzing ball was now only a few days off. Before going to sleep, John allowed himself a few moments to savor the heady prospect of having Gemma in his arms. There would be some way to get her all to himself during the evening; he'd manage to evade the chaperones if only for five minutes. A lot could happen in five minutes.

14

By the time the blue-and-gold summer day had faded
to a scented pale-mauve twilight on the date of the
waltzing ball, the best that could be said for that much-
planned-for and happily anticipated event was that it
represented an anticlimax. Depending on whose opinion
was elicited after the dance, with the single exception of
Miss Fairmont's, the descriptive terms employed would
have been a deal more pejorative.

The days before the dance sped by, crowded as they
were with the necessary preparations for entertaining
upward of eighty people in a style that would reflect
credit on the duke's establishment. Beyond arranging
the flowers on the day of the ball, a chore that Lucy and
Gemma had undertaken to perform, the young people
were not directly concerned with these preparations.
The duke's resident staff, under the able direction of
Mrs. Benedict and augmented by daily help from the
village, was quite capable of accomplishing the
scrubbing and polishing and airing out that was judged
essential in an unobtrusive manner that did not reduce
the daily routine of the inhabitants of the hall to a
shambles during the interval.

Stansmere and the chef were closeted regularly with
the duchess regarding the menu, drinks, and extra
supplies of glassware and plate to be retrieved from
their various storage places and washed. Lady
Sophronia continually gave her brother and sister-in-
law the benefit of her advice and experience in entertaining on a large scale, an activity that had been her
delight when the indulgent Mr. Fairmont was alive. The
stables were being reorganized to accommodate a score
or more of strange carriages and their attendant drivers.

There remained to the young ladies only their own appearance on the night in question with which to concern themselves, but since Miss Fairmont was having a gown made, another trip to Bath was planned for the necessary fitting. This time the girls made the excursion under the aegis of Lady Sophronia, who was pleased to award her endorsement to her daughter's choice of ball gown. Lucy felt constrained to decline her share of her ladyship's praise, aware that her own contributions to the selection of design and fabric had been of a negative rather than positive value.

Lady Gemma's injured ankle had improved to the point where she could wear her own footgear and go about her regular routine, provided she did not remain on her feet for unreasonably long periods. At the instigation of Lady Sophronia they visited the Pump Room after leaving the showroom of Mlle Analise, and later attended the noon service at the abbey. After a luncheon at the White Hart, which, since it overlooked the Pump room, was deemed the most proper choice for saving Lady Gemma's foot, there remained only one or two small commissions to execute before driving home.

It was when they had purchased a selection of sweetmeats at Molland's, a confectioner's on Milsom Street, that the small party of ladies ran into Lord Oliver Barton on their way to meet their carriage.

The residents of Monteith Hall had not been privileged to receive a visit from Lord Oliver since he had embarked on his course of hot baths nearly a fortnight before. If the truth were known, only one of the four ladies to whom he now offered a civil greeting had felt the lack of his company, and she would have died rather than acknowledge either that life had seemed strangely flat just lately or that her heart, beneath a madly becoming dress of crisp pink-and-white-striped cotton, had set up an increased tempo the instant her quick eyes' discerned his tall remote figure moving purposefully among the strollers.

No one watching Miss Lucinda Delevan returning

Lord Oliver's salutation with a polite good afternoon and a small social smile could have guessed that she was desperately hoping for some tiny sign from those penetrating dark eyes that would distinguish her from her companions, or that, not finding any sign that even the most optimistic or romantic temperament could seize upon to nourish fledgling hopes, something delicate and tremulous had expired within her spirit. She did not droop physically, her proud carriage still epitomized the intrinsic grace of a young queen that she projected unconsciously, but she felt as though she were progressively shriveling up inside as she listened to Lady Sophronia questioning Lord Oliver on the results of his treatment. She was unaware that her smoky eyes darkened with pity at Lord Oliver's brisk dismissal of the subject.

"There has been no change."

Since he did not venture a glance in her direction after that first greeting, she was not called upon to perform the additional task of disguising her compassion. Unlike the other young men who passed through the hall that summer, Lord Oliver was not in the least intimidated by Lady Sophronia's regal presence or commanding manner, and he never experienced the least difficulty in extricating himself from unwanted conversation. This talent he now displayed, bidding them a curt adieu in terms that were unfailingly correct, no matter how suspect his manner might be.

There were few subjects on which Lady Gemma and her cousin agreed, but now they united in wholeheartedly abusing Lord Oliver as a brusque, insufferably uncivil man whose company gave no pleasure. With difficulty Lucy maintained a self-protective silence under this attack, but aid came from an unexpected quarter as Lady Sophronia spoke up in her decided way.

"Nonsense, girls. Why should you get upon your high ropes only because a man refuses to pander to your conceit of yourselves as irresistible drawing cards? Can you not see that the unfortunate man is wretchedly unhappy? That's what makes him as cross as crabs most of the time.''

Lucy cast their duenna a grateful look that the recipient did not see, since she was dealing graciously at the time with the tenderhearted Gemma's stammered apology for her uncharitable assessment of Lord Oliver. On that subject Coralee preserved an unconvinced silence and soon changed the direction of their discourse.

Lucy sat back in her corner of the well-cushioned carriage, letting the conversation wash over her unheeded for much of the drive home. Once having acknowledged the lowness of her own spirits, she berated herself for allowing the brief encounter just now to dampen them out of all proportion to its importance. After all, had she not already concluded from Lord Oliver's nonappearance over the last week or two that he regretted having taken her a little way into his friendship and was taking this method to ensure that he did not raise any false hopes in an impressionable young woman? It was the action of a decent man, and she honored him for it, she insisted to that romantic little fool inside her head who had permitted herself to dream on the flimsiest possible grounds.

It would have been ridiculous in the extreme to imagine that the son of a marquess—moreover, one whose title went back to the early Stuarts—would ever consider taking for a bride the daughter of a banker, and one, moreover, whose fortune had been amassed largely by a grandfather in trade. The sooner she squashed these ill-omened yearnings, the sooner she would revert to her cool, unimpressionable self and the sooner she would be happy again. She sensibly refused to listen to the insistent small voice that reminded her that she had not really been happy before, but merely . . . waiting. By dint of constant dwelling on the unsuitability of the match, the lack of common experience, and the probable incompatibility of their tastes and temperaments, she was nearly able to persuade herself by the time they reached the hall that she was grateful to Lord Oliver for showing no disposition to pursue a suit that must only result in unhappiness for both parties. She felt that her lawyer brother would applaud the logical and convincing case she had made out, and refused to admit that one ardent look from Lord Oliver could demolish it instantly.

If Lucy was a bit quieter than usual during the days immediately preceding the ball, it went unnoticed in the happy bustle of final arrangements. Certainly she put forth as much effort and skill as Lady Gemma in seeing to the dozen or so floral arrangements that were made up to decorate the reception rooms and ballroom for the occasion. From the cutting of the flowers early in the morning, while still bedewed and before the hot sun forced them open, to the temporary placement of the vases in a shaded corner convenient for the maids to respray them at intervals during the afternoon, it was a task that consumed hours. For once, neither girl was averse to a short rest after lunch in imitation of the elder ladies.

After an hour of so, Lucy became restless and, as much to discourage unproductive daydreams as for any artistic motivation, decided to take up her painting materials and go off to make another sketch of the Grecian temple, this time for her father. She met no one on her way out except Stansmere, whom she acquainted with her plan in case her presence should be required by any member of the household.

It was another in a succession of mild clear days and promised to continue propitious for the evening. She made her way slowly toward the little temple, savoring the perfumes released by a light breeze as she progressed through the rose garden. Today she walked on past the giant elm that had shaded her previous painting session, circling around until she found another angle that pleased her on the far side of the building. In a matter of minutes she was settled in the shade of some huge rhododendrons that flanked the grove, busily sketching away, her unquiet mind temporarily emptied of any thoughts that did not have to do with capturing the scene before her on paper.

Miss Fairmont was alone in the blue saloon when Captain Godwin and Lord Oliver were admitted by Stansmere. She favored them with a delightful smile and exclaimed merrily, "Just in time to save me from expiring of boredom. I have been here nearly fifteen minutes without seeing a living soul. Where is everyone, Stansmere?"

The butler, who had been about to retreat, stopped in the doorway. "Her grace will be down presently and her ladyship is writing letters in the morning room. I do not know Lady Gemma's present whereabouts, but Miss Delevan went out some time ago to sketch the Greek temple. I regret that I am uninformed as to where my Lord Gresham or Mr. Delevan may be at present. His grace is, I trust, on his way home from Bath."

"Thank you, Stansmere," said Miss Fairmont, and when the butler had shut the door, she laughed up at her callers, "Well, Stansmere has his fingers on the pulse as usual, but I thought I detected faint annoyance that Gemma, Peter, and Mr. Delevan have all given him the slip. No doubt Gemma is with Mr. Delevan somewhere in the gardens. They share an interest in flowers, or so they would have us believe." Encountering Lord Oliver's narrowed look, she suggested gaily, "Shall we wander down toward the temple and disturb genius at work? If no one interrupts her artistic concentration poor Lucy will very likely miss her tea again."

She smiled a challenge at Lord Oliver, who replied repressively, "I believe I'll take a turn in the gardens in the hope of coming across Delevan."

He stood unwinking while Captain Godwin expressed an interest in rounding up Miss Delevan for her tea, and accompanied the others to the terrace door, where they separated, Miss Fairmont and Captain Godwin ambling toward the temple and Lord Oliver making his way into the cutting garden, which, had he any eye for blooms, would have struck him as rather depleted after the raid on it that morning by the flower arrangers.

However, since he had no interest in flowers at any time and very little concern at that moment in locating Mr. Delevan, it was as good a place as any in which to ask himself for the tenth time in the last half-hour what he was doing here at all. Why had he succumbed to an irrational impulse that could have no other consequence except to provide a setting for more self-torment? Surely it was carrying masochism too far to wish to gaze anew on the forbidden object. He kicked viciously at a stray pebble that had invaded the grassy path between the beds. If he had kept away for nearly a fortnight, why could he not have continued such a sensible policy, especially since he was obliged to be present at this infernal dance tonight? The answer was, of course, that seeing Miss Delevan in Bath the other day had played havoc with his good intentions.

At first it had been easy to stay away; he had the perfect excuse provided by the course of hot baths he had allowed the Godwins to talk him into undergoing. Though setting no store by the wonderful healing properties claimed for the treatment by its supporters, he had promised himself that he would resume his visits to Monteith Hall if the arm showed signs of responding. Once he had accepted that the waters were not going to have any effect on the paralysis, it was a simple matter to continue to avoid the hall. After all, there was now every reason to shun Lucy's company; she was outside his reach forever, and the sooner he departed the manor permanently, the better for his peace of mind.

And here he stood today, imbecile that he was, skulking about in a damned garden like a moonsick calf. Suddenly he raised his head, thinking he heard voices beyond the hedge in the rose garden. He opened his lips, but instead of making his presence known and joining the others for an insipid half-hour, he closed his mouth again and retreated around the hedge.

Lord Oliver's long legs rapidly ate up the distance to

the elm tree. He could see at once that Lucy was nowhere near the spot where he had found her before. He stood gazing at the temple for a moment wondering how he could have missed seeing three people heading toward the house, unless he had spent a lot longer in the garden than he had thought. He began an aimless circuit of the building and was rewarded a few minutes later by the sight of his quarry painting away in splendid isolation. At this point a prudent man would have reversed his footsteps before being discovered, and later sent someone else to bring the artist back to the house. Lord Oliver, prudence cast to the winds, stepped forward and was recognized by Miss Delevan.

He had the curious impression that there had been a glad welcoming light in her eyes at the instant of recognition that was replaced immediately by a shuttered politeness. Her words were light and conventional.

"How do you do, sir? Have you come once again to remind me that tea is served? I'll come at once." The hand holding the paintbrush went directly to empty the water pan and she began a swift gathering up of her materials. This time when he reached for her work, she did not stop to observe him but was quite ready to leave when he raised his eyes from the contemplation of her painting.

He spoke for the first time and she could not miss the hint of dryness. "There is no occasion to go tearing off at battle speed, Miss Delevan. There was no one in the blue saloon when I came down here. Miss Fairmont and George headed in this direction before me. Have you not seen them?"

"Why, no. Perhaps they returned to the house when they didn't find me under the elm tree. Shall we follow?"

He did not bother to reply to this. Something about her obvious haste to be gone aroused a little demon of opposition in his breast. Fixing his eyes on the graceful little building ahead, he remarked, "I have never been inside the temple. Is it attractive?"

"There is a rather good mural of mosaicwork on one
wall, Paris presenting the apple to Venus. There are no
furnishings except some curved stone benches."

He sauntered off in the direction of one of the two
open sides of the temple, and after a brief hesitation
during which Lucy realized it would appear blatantly
uncivil to go back to the house without him, she
followed in his wake. When a backward glance
confirmed that she was behind him, Lord Oliver waited
for her and they approached the shallow flight of steps
in a rather charged silence. At the first step he put an
automatic hand under her elbow to guide her. They had
only ascended two or three when he felt her jerk to a
stop. Glancing down in slight surprise, he noted her
white staring face and the way she bit fiercely on her
bottom lip, and he turned back to see what had so
affected her.

A second later he was piloting her back down the
steps at a much faster pace. Numbly she allowed him to
set the pace until they had rounded the temple and were
approaching the elm tree, when she stopped just as
suddenly and shook off his hold on her arm, clutching
at his sleeve in her turn.

"Please," slow down, sir. I think that is Gemma
ahead of us with John. Do you think they saw them
too?"

Lord Oliver peered around the giant elm at the figures
disappearing over the crest of the hill. "Judging by the
time it took us to get this far, I should say the chances
are excellent that the audience for that little tableau
numbered four instead of two."

He set off again up the slope, and Lucy trailed behind
with reluctant steps. She found him patiently waiting
when she reached the crest before starting the second
gentle ascent to the gardens and terraces. So far neither
had made any comment on the cause of the mass exodus
from the temple, but now Lord Oliver said with some
impatience, "We were quite *de trop*, I agree, but it
certainly doesn't rate such profound shock or deep
dudgeon or whatever it is that is making you look like

you've seen a ghost." When this produced no response, he added nastily, "Unless, of course, you are another of George's conquests and your hopes too are now blasted."

"You must know that I am not," she retorted with pardonable asperity.

"Why must I? Why should you be any different than a hundred other females? I assure you, George always mows them down in squads wherever he goes."

"If it amuses you to assume that I am one of the victims of Captain Godwin's practiced charms, then you are free to do so," replied Lucy, gritting her teeth, "but I was not thinking of myself at all." She stopped abruptly and closed her lips, but Lord Oliver brushed aside this belated attempt at circumspection, showing no reluctance to step in where angels might fear to tread.

"Look, Lady Gemma is no fool. I refuse to believe that she has not seen which way the wind was blowing before now."

Lucy's troubled countenance did not lighten at this blunt summing up of the situation. She sighed deeply. "Recognizing something with one's intellect is a far cry from having one's worst fears confirmed before one's eyes."

He shuffled his feet, looking uncomfortable for the first time in their acquaintance. "It was only a kiss, when all's said and done. Not every kiss leads to the altar, you know."

Enormous gray eyes searched his face. "Do you think that would make a difference to Gemma's feelings?"

"No." He turned from her and stared down toward the temple. After a moment he spoke over his shoulder. "But neither do I think that Lady Gemma will be inconsolable for long. Your brother will see to that."

"My brother?" she echoed blankly. "Do you mean John?"

"Who else?"

Lucy was so occupied in coping with the shock of his words that she failed to notice he was regarding her with a half-tender, half-amused light in his eyes, and by the time her absent faculties returned, he was carefully expressionless again.

"What a fool I've been! But it is always so difficult to tell what John is thinking. His manners are perfect and he is an absolute clam, a combination that defeats inquisitive little sisters." Lucy's former dejection had vanished miraculously. She was on tiptoe with excitement. "I confess I have not noticed any languishing after Gemma on John's part, but naturally John would not languish," she said laughingly. "He is protective of her, but so am I. Gemma falls into one scrape after another, you see." She continued to muse aloud, almost unaware of her listener. "And then, he does flirt with Coralee." A touch of anxiety dimmed the animation in her face and she clasped her hands together in an unconsciously pleading gesture. "You are sure?"

"He is playing his cards very close to his vest, but yes, as sure as one may be in these matters. And everyone flirts with Miss Fairmont, even Malcolm Godwin in his quiet way. It means nothing."

"You don't flirt with her," stated Lucy, and then wished she had censored the thought before it reached her unruly tongue as all signs of human interest faded away and the lines of his face hardened again, congealing into the indifferent mask with which he faced the world.

"It is different with me," he said repressively.

"How, different?"

Lord Oliver experienced a dizzying rush of fury to his brain and had to throttle an impulse to hurt the girl staring up at him expectantly. Did she think to torture him? Was that her idea of amusement? He'd enjoy seizing those shapely shoulders only half-covered by the wide neckline of her gown and shaking her until she begged for mercy—and even that act was beyond a man with one arm! He clenched his fist and his teeth, setting a muscle twitching in his jaw.

She was repeating, "How is it different with you?"

Goaded beyond bearing, he took his revenge in

words. "So you insist on having me spell it out for you? Because, Miss Delevan, a one-armed man is in another category entirely. Along with hunchbacks and idiots, he is removed from the field of competition. Do you now understand?"

Wide shocked eyes locked with his, but instead of reacting with fear to the clear danger in his black gaze, she blazed up at him. "*You utter fool*! One would think that shot had pierced your brain instead of your arm! You have another one, have you not? Self-pity is what I have no patience with; it is cowardly and destructive. I beg you will excuse me, sir. I find I do not wish any tea today." She seized her paint box from under his rigid arm and sped away.

Lord Oliver was left standing outside the garden hedge staring after Miss Delevan's retreating figure, his mind a swirling mass of conflicting impressions. For a second he felt rather as if a pet dog had turned savage and bitten him. Part of his mind was recalling how magnificent she had appeared, tall and stately, with those luminous eyes flashing, but the image was soon swamped by an upsurge of the blackest rage he had ever known. How *dared* this girl who had never lost anything in her life, this pampered daughter of a wealthy man, accuse him of cowardice! Had a man said what she had just said he'd be measuring his length on the ground right now!

Lord Oliver's long legs almost outdistanced his furious rantings, for before he realized his intention he was rounding the corner with the stables dead ahead. He made a stern effort to mask his fury enough to avoid provoking the groom's interest when he asked for his horse. His reputation for being unapproachable came in handy and spared any necessity of exchanging common-places. A faint gleam of sardonic amusement came into his eyes as the man scurried to obey the order. Pleasant sociable persons like John Delevan must find it the very devil when they were out of sorts to get away from people without wounding sensibilities and ruffling feelings. How glad he was that he wasn't a pleasant sociable person.

Lord Oliver would have had less cause for self-congratulation on that score had he been aware that impatience and suppressed rage radiated from him like heat from a flaming brand and caused the stable boy to exclaim to the groom as he rode out of the yard, "I wonder what put 'is nibs in such a rare tweak? A proper 'ellion 'e is!"

This piece of impertinence earned him a sharp rebuke from the groom, who though secretly sharing his inferior's opinion, had no intention of confessing the same.

Had she but known it, Miss Fairmont's sly suggestion that her cousin and Mr. Delevan might be found in the gardens together had been quite correct.

Casting a critical eye over her handiwork when she came downstairs, Lady Gemma had decided that two of the arrangements would benefit from the addition of several flowers. Accordingly, she gathered up shears and cutting basket and headed back to the cutting garden to make further depradations in the worthy cause of the hall's beautification for the ball. John discovered her there some minutes later—accidentally, as far as Gemma was concerned, a misapprehension that he permitted to stand as he greeted her in simulated surprise.

"I was under the impression that the floral arrangements were all complete," he commented idly, enjoying the picture she presented in a green-sprigged white muslin dress that drifted and floated as she bent to cut suitable blooms.

"Some of them looked a little sparse, but an extra spray or two will do the trick. Can you reach that stalk of delphinium over there, Mr. Delevan?"

Obligingly he cut at her direction, but when she would have taken the stalks, he put his hands behind his back and asked gravely, "Do you think you can bring yourself to use my Christian name? Are we well-enough-acquainted yet?"

Her face as serious as his, she tipped her head to one side and gazed at him consideringly. "Is this a case of extortion, sir? Am I not to receive the flowers unless I accede to your request?''

To her surprise a faint flush spread over Mr. Delevan's cheeks and he handed the flowers back to her at once. ''I would not dream of coercing you in anything, little one. Any favor granted, any pleas accepted must be by your own desire.''

Brown velvet eyes widened as she accepted the flowers mechanically and laid them in the basket. ''You must know I was only teasing you,'' she protested, not comprehending his intensity. ''I think of you as John. I cannot think why I haven't called you that before, except that you have never requested me to do so.''

Cursing himself for a coward and a clumsy fool, John strove for a light touch. ''That favor is usually granted at the lady's discretion.''

''Oh?'' Mischief flashed into her face as the dimples were given full play. ''I have the most wretched memory, for I really cannot recall granting you permission to call me by that silly 'little one' you affect upon occasion.''

He put up a hand in a fencer's gesture. ''*Touché.* I plead guilty to presumption. Would you like that tall spike of larkspur over there?''

Lady Gemma thanked him prettily and they proceeded to complete her errand in perfect amity, descending from the cutting garden into the rose garden to select a couple of pink beauties for accents.

Entering the house a few minutes later, she called to the butler, who was crossing the hall. ''Stansmere, do you know where Miss Delevan might be?''

''Yes, my lady. She is painting at the Greek temple.''

''Thank you.'' She inquired of the man at her side, ''Would you care to wander down and fetch Lucy back for tea, John, while I pop these flowers into the arrangements?''

He pretended to consider, then countered with a suggestion of his own. ''If yours isn't to be a terribly time-consuming task, we could walk down to the temple together when it is done.''

''Very well. I shall be quick about it.'' She led the way

to the shaded room where the vases were stored and replenished them with deft fingers, accepting John's praise with no false modesty as they headed back outdoors.

"Yes, I am rather good at this; I enjoy it so. Flowers give such pleasure."

They strolled down toward the decorative building that so fascinated Lucy, not talking much but enjoying the late summer afternoon. The earlier breeze had died down and an expectant silence hung over the world, undisturbed by birdsong or the buzz and whirr of insects at the moment. They were practically at the temple before it dawned on them that Lucy was nowhere in sight.

"Perhaps she's on the other side of the building," suggested John. "Can we walk right through it?"

"Yes, it's open on two sides."

They were already ascending the shallow steps when John became aware suddenly that the temple was tenanted at the moment. His step faltered and he wheeled instinctively to shield Gemma, but one glance at her stricken face told him it was too late. The interior of the temple was dim compared with the sunny brilliance outside, but not so dim that it had been possible to mistake the sight of the blond girl in the embrace of the dark-haired man for anything other than what it was.

Betrayal—that is how she will see it, he thought numbly as he took her elbow to guide her back down the steps. For a second she resisted, and his eyes, which he had averted from her face, either in compassion for her suffering or because he couldn't bear the story it might tell on his own account, flew back to discover a totally composed mask so unlike Gemma's expressive countenance that his heart contracted and he hastily averted his gaze once more.

He was persuaded they had not made any noise in their approach to the steps. It was vital to get Gemma away from here before they were discovered by the pair inside. In her shocked state Gemma could not be relied on to produce the casual inconsequential chatter that would enable them to carry the thing off. This time his tug at her elbow met with automatic compliance, and in another thirty seconds they had passed the big elm.

Not until they were halfway up the slope did he again look at the girl beside him. He was surprised to find her arm still in his light grasp as she plodded along like an automaton, eyes straight ahead. The silence between them threatened to become permanent, but all John's natural ease in social situations had deserted him. He could think of no conventional phrases to bring comfort to Gemma and was terrified to utter even one of the words of love and desire burning in his brain and struggling for release by his tongue. She was in no mood to hear them, would resent them most like, and he would only succeed in queering his own pitch. Patience was his game, his only weapon, he reminded himself grimly, unaware until she winced and removed her arm from his grip, that his fierce efforts at restraint had tightened his muscles and resulted in a bruising pressure on her elbow.

"I-I beg your pardon," he stuttered. "Gemma, my dear, I—"

"No, don't say anything," she warned in flat tones, "not one word," as his lips parted again. "There is nothing whatsoever that needs to be said."

He searched her face for some sign of emotion and found nothing save impatience to be released from his scrutiny. She turned away from him without a word of farewell as they reached the hedge surrounding the rose garden, and he was left with no recourse except to respect her desire for privacy.

He remained standing outside the garden for a long moment, unable to conceive what his next action should be, until he finally decided to seek the solitude of his own room before Miss Fairmont and Captain Godwin should end their tryst and discover him here. He was in no condition at present to welcome an exchange of pleasantries with that pretty pair, even though, too deeply embedded to be acknowledged by his better self, there existed a feeling of gratitude toward them for resolving a situation that had held him in impotent suspension for a seeming eternity.

15

"Come in, girls, and let us see you in all your glory."

The duchess, magnificent in burgundy silk and diamonds, with a delicate tiara gleaming against raven locks, rose from her chair and glided over to examine her daughter and Lucy at close range. Except that Lucy was a trifle pale and Gemma's smile was less spontaneous than usual, not the most carping critic could have found fault with their appearance. Her Grace of Carlyle beamed maternally and impartially on both as they twirled slowly to allow a comprehensive view of their finery.

"Absolutely enchanting, girls. Lucy, that mauve silk is devastating with your beautiful hair. It's rather a shame you cannot keep the silver-spangled shawl on while you are dancing because it's the perfect final touch. Gemma, the white sarcenet was definitely one of our happiest purchases, and I am in agreement with Miss Weems that the yellow ribbons at the shoulder are just the detail that was lacking last time. They'll float when you dance, and speaking of dancing, is the ankle comfortable?"

"It is fine, thank you, Mama."

"Where is Coralee? I was under the impression that you three had planned to come in together to dazzle our old eyes," remarked the duke.

"I believe she intends to make an Entrance," replied his daughter somewhat dryly.

If that was Coralee's intention, she was certainly successful, thought the duchess a moment later when her niece entered the saloon. Even one who had grown used to the girl's beauty had to admit that tonight she fairly took one's breath away. She could only nod agreement as the duke told his niece that she looked like a fairy princess. Small wonder her proud mother had tears shimmering in her eyes.

From the top of her head, with its burnished gold hair swept up high and pinned in a mass of curls that were surrounded by a wreath of artificial rosebuds, to the tips of her pale-pink dancing slippers, Coralee was a vision to behold. Everyone agreed that the white silk open dress worn over a blush pink slip with a scalloped and embroidered hem was a great success. The scalloping was repeated in the low-cut bodice and down the edges of the overdress. It was a gown for a fairy princess, and Coralee's perfection of face and form did it full justice. She had never been in better looks or spirits; indeed, her beauty was enhanced by a glow of excitement and triumph that drew all eyes. Not the most doting parent in the world could deny that the others, very pretty girls both, were like farthing candles compared with the sun that was Coralee Fairmont. Fortunately for the self-assurance of the other two young ladies, daily familiarity had bred, if not contempt, then a casual acceptance of Coralee's looks on the part of her cousin Peter and Mr. Delevan, neither of whom was disposed to ignore the claims of the others to a share of the masculine attention.

Dinner was a rather hurried meal and, it must be reported, one that none of the younger generation save Lord Gresham partook of very extensively. This was quite naturally attributed to the excitement and antici-pation produced by the imminence of the ball, and was looked on indulgently by their seniors. Gemma's and Lucy's innate good manners assured that it would have taken a very keen eye to detect that neither girl was really in spirits. Mr. Delevan did indeed note to his sorrow that Lady Gemma was taking pains to avoid crossing glances with himself, but such is the optimism of young love that he still cherished hopes of seeing her vivacity revive in his company under the happy influ-ence of music and dancing.

In the event, half of his wish came true. A disinterested onlooker that night would have had no
hesitation in declaring that Lady Gemma was in high
force. If Coralee Fairmont was the undisputed belle of
the ball, her cousin ran her a close second as the most-
sought-after young lady present.

John would have been delighted at this transformation had he been granted his fair portion of her time
and attention. One waltz early in the evening—
moreover, a waltz during which his partner, though a
pliable delight in his arms, had only bright nothings to
offer by way of conversation—was his entire share of
her company. Thereafter, he could not come within
talking distance of his contrary little love. She had
refused his invitation to be his partner at supper on the
suspect grounds of a prior commitment to Malcolm
Godwin. Since John had asked her before the first
guests arrived, he strongly suspected her of prevaricat-
ing, which the subsequent sight of her going into supper
on Mr. Godwin's arm did nothing to diminish. She
scattered her favors impartially during the evening, but
if one gentleman could be said to have benefited more
than any other, that one was Malcolm, a fact not lost
upon the elder Biddlesford girl. John had the doubtful
pleasure of dancing with this rather awkward young
woman at a time when Gemma was whirling expertly
around the floor in the arms of the fortunate Malcolm.
Miss Biddlesford's lack of natural grace on the dance
floor was compounded by her obvious attempts to keep
these others in view at all times, a habit not likely to
endear her to her own partner, who was already wincing
mentally at each shrill laugh she emitted. To his ever-
lasting credit, Mr. Delevan did his duty by Miss Biddlesford and, in the course of the evening, by several other
young ladies in need of a partner.

This selflessness won him the commendation of the
duchess, who was a considerate and conscientious
hostess. He had been previously unaware of how high
he already stood in her regard, for she had taken the

utmost pains all summer to do nothing that could be construed as meddling by her autocratic husband or her strong-minded daughter. As he looked back on the ball, the rueful truth was that his dances with the charming duchess marked its highlight, for her gentle approval enveloped him in a warmth that delayed for a time the onset of the chill that was creeping into his bones.

And if his own troubles were not sufficient to occupy his mind, there was the problem of Lucy. His sister was enacting the part of contented guest in competent fashion; she had her share of good partners and managed to look graceful even when going around the floor in the arms of a poor dancer, but her underlying unhappiness hit him like a sudden blow from behind when he partnered her just before supper.

"Thank you, dear brother," she whispered fervently on being rescued from the persistent attentions of a stolid young man with a lot to say on the subject of scientific farming, but once on the floor she fell silent.

John was in no humor to attempt conversational brilliance either, but when they had circled the floor twice with only three monosyllables from Lucy in response to idle observations on his part, he subjected her to a closer examination. Despite the heat produced by hundreds of candles and dozens of warm bodies revolving about the ballroom, the slight pallor noted by the duchess earlier still prevented his sister from being in her best looks. The simple lines of her gown showed off her magnificent figure and that mauve shade flattered her coloring; her hair was most becomingly arranged and glowed with red lights whenever she passed near the candles; but the gray eyes looked absent and she smiled with effort when he complimented her on her performance in the dance. Brotherly concern prompted his next remark.

"You are not enjoying yourself tonight. What is wrong, my dear?"

She did not attempt to deny his observation, but neither was she forthcoming. "It is an inappropriate place to choose to indulge a fit of the dismals, is it not?" She achieved a movement of her lips that might be called a smile. "Never mind, I shall try to do better."

"Lucy, what is it? Is there something I can do?" he persisted, unwilling to leave matters as they were if any action on his part could restore her spirits.

She shook her head. "No, nothing. There isn't even anything I can do—at least, there is but I am not going to be given the opportunity."

As John digested this, a twinkle appeared in his eyes. "In case you are laboring under the impression that you have just explained something to me, let me hasten to disabuse you of that notion. I remain completely in the dark."

At that she looked up and gave him a natural smile. "No, I know. The truth is that I've done something terrible. But a party is not the time to be making confessions. I'll tell you about it tomorrow."

"Shall I take you in to supper?" John asked in haste as the music ended.

"I am promised to Mr. Accrington, a friend of Mr. Godwin's. Gemma asked us to join them. Why do not you come too?"

"I'll try," he promised as Mr. Accrington came up just then to collect his partner.

In the end John found himself engaged with a party of very young men and girls that included Lord Gresham and some of his cronies as well as the younger Biddlesford girl, who was a decided improvement over her sister even if she had little to say for herself. The most vital contribution he made was to exert a restraining influence on some of the choicer spirits in the group to keep the general hilarity from disturbing those around them. He had thus interpreted a message from the duchess's dark eyes entreating his assistance when she spotted her son's noisy crowd arriving *en masse* at the long buffet table in the supper room. Actually there was not an ounce of harm in any of them, and it was a pleasure to witness people diverting themselves happily with no thought to tomorrow's problems.

John had ample time to observe that Gemma and Lucy contrived to leave the impression of greatly enjoying the company of their escorts. Like Captain Godwin and Coralee, they were continually surrounded by admirers. Of Lord Oliver he caught no glimpse during the whole time he remained in the supper room. Since he didn't dance and wasn't of a gregarious nature, an evening such as this must be decidedly boring for the former soldier. The last time John had seen him was when he had noticed his broad shoulders vanishing into the card room before the second waltz.

The refreshments were up to the high standard he had come to expect from the duke's kitchen. The young people devoured ham and cold meats, lobster patties, salads, and ices as if they had been fasting for days, and then went back into the ballroom refreshed and eager to expend more energy on the daring German dance that had taken the country by storm.

John made one more attempt to secure a dance with Gemma. As she left the supper room on the arm of Mr. Godwin, he planted himself squarely in her path. This graceless maneuver was necessitated by her persistent refusal to meet his eyes all evening.

"I trust you have saved me the second dance I requested early in the evening, Gemma. When is it to be?" A bland smile masked the fact that his assumed confidence was as false as her start of surprise at finding him in front of her.

"Why, Mr. Delevan—I mean, John," she amended hastily as his brows rose at this form of address, "how you startled me, popping up like a genie. I am so sorry, but the remaining dances are already promised." As he continued to look at her gravely, she mounted a feeble defense. "It has been such a busy evening, has it not? The time has simply flown by. Not seeing you in the ballroom earlier, I fancy I must have assumed you had grown tired of dancing and had joined the party in the card room. I am so sorry."

The brittle tone and meaningless social smile that accompanied this lie would have confirmed his fears that his beloved was intentionally avoiding him, if confirmation had been wanting. There was nothing to do but accept his dismissal with what grace he could muster.

"I am more than sorry to be deprived of the great pleasure of waltzing with you," he said quietly, taking some small measure of comfort from the brief flicker of what he was going to call shame that appeared in her eyes as he bowed.

He turned aside and his glance met that of his hostess, whose expression revealed that she had witnessed her daughter's rejection of him and was both surprised and disturbed. He managed a reassuring smile for her before taking himself off to the card room, feeling he had contributed his full share to the success of Miss Fairmont's ball.

Breakfast was poorly attended the morning after the ball. With the exception of Lucy, all the ladies elected to remain in their rooms to recruit their strength. The duke was in his usual place and facetiously congratulated the Delevans on their stamina. What conversation there was centered naturally on last night's successful event. His guests were quite sincere in offering their thanks for the splendid entertainment provided, and their host was quite honestly gratified to accept it.

When his sister had finished her second cup of coffee, John suggested a walk in the gardens, to which she readily acquiesced.

They strolled in companionable silence for a few moments while he tried to make an assessment of her mood. It was evident that she had taken pains with her appearance this morning. She was wearing a crisp dress of a cheery deep pink and her abundant chestnut locks were neatly confined by a ribbon of the same color. He suspected that in any lighter color she would look a trifle washed out, and now that they were alone, the un-

happy look was back in her eyes as she wandered
aimlessly among the rose bushes.

"Isn't it time you opened the budget and told me
what's wrong, dear?" he asked, plunging right to the
heart of the matter. "Last night you said you had done
something terrible, which I confess has had me in a
puzzle because you don't do terrible things as a rule.
Are you certain you are not merely feeling mopish over
some trifling misunderstanding?"

"It isn't a trifle, John, and there was no misunderstanding. I called Lord Oliver a coward, and now
he won't even speak to me—at least, he bowed and said
good evening, but he didn't even look at me. He never
came near me all evening, so how could I apologize? I
cannot write him a note; it would not be at all the thing,
would it? So what am I to do?"

Beyond a slight widening of his eyes, her brother
remained his placid self during this impassioned out-
pouring, but she had succeeded in surprising him.
Somehow he had not connected a man with her unhappiness, and if he had suspected such a thing, Lord
Oliver would have been his last choice. She was standing
before him with her hands gripped together, gazing up
at him imploringly. To gain time while he gathered his
wits about him, he took her arm and led her to a
wrought-iron bench, pushing her gently down onto it
when she simply stood there.

"Don't you think you had best tell me the circumstances under which you called Lord Oliver a
coward?" he asked when he had seated himself beside
her.

About to launch into her tale, Lucy was brought up
short by the recollection that she and Lord Oliver had
been discussing John's feelings for Gemma at the time.
Her brother had never given her any hints on this
subject and she could not bring herself to broach it. She
was scrambling around in her brain trying to decide how
to avoid mentioning John when he reminded her, "I
can't help if I don't know the whole story, love."

"I . . . we were talking about someone flirting with Coralee Fairmont, and Lord Oliver said it meant nothing, that everyone flirted with her." She paused and John waited patiently. "I reminded him that *he* didn't flirt with her, and he said that was different."

John nodded encouragingly when she looked at him.

"I asked why it was different for him and he became angry. At first he didn't say anything, just looked thunderous, but I persisted, and he said, all soft and menacing with that black scowl of his, that he was in a different category, that like hunchbacks and idiots, he was out of the competition."

Her voice had risen in pitch with the telling, and now she raised questioning eyes to John, whose lips had tightened, but he maintained a waiting silence. Lucy continued with a rush, "I was so stunned, *appalled* that he could feel that way, and then I became angry too, angrier than I can ever remember being. I . . . I told him he acted as if the bullet had hit his brain, not his arm. But . . . but that wasn't the really terrible thing." A film of tears shimmered in her eyes, and John took her hand in a comforting clasp. "I reminded him that he had another arm and said I thought self-pity was cowardly."

When she did not go on after a moment or so, John prompted gently, "What did Lord Oliver reply to this accusation?"

"He didn't say anything. I did not give him a chance to reply. I ran into the house."

"How disconcertingly feminine of you, my dear," murmured her brother. Had it not been for Lucy's very real distress, he'd have laughed outright at a vision of Oliver Barton of the acidulous tongue being left with no object upon which to vent his fury. He stared frowningly at their clasped hands. There could be but one explanation for such torment, of course, but he'd been too wrapped up in his own delicate affair to notice that his little sister was falling in love with the misanthropic major.

"What should I do, John? Should I write him a note of apology?" Lucy ventured in a timid voice, breaking into his thoughts.

He fixed her with a penetrating stare. "You are in love with Lord Oliver, are you not?"

"Yes, but that is beside the point."

"I beg to differ with you. It is very much to the point. Does he return your regard?"

"Of course not! It would be a dreadful mésalliance. Why, his family is almost as old as the Monteiths, and I . . . we are—" She broke off as it struck her of a sudden that John's birth was as far removed from Gemma's as hers was from Lord Oliver's.

"We are very newly arrived?" he finished for her. "Encroaching perhaps, to dream of allying ourselves with the nobility? That would matter to some, but I have not found Major Barton to be at all high in the instep. I don't think the question of pedigree is one with which he would concern himself if he were in love."

"Well, he isn't in love," she enunciated flatly.

John could not add to her sufferings by agreeing that he had seen no sign of a developing *tendre* on Lord Oliver's part. He had taken Lucy's hand upon his knee and now he sat there in musing silence playing idly with her fingers while he sought to recall the most recent occasions on which he had met Lord Oliver. They had not been frequent of late. The man had been occupied with the series of hot baths and had not called at the hall in some time. He and Gresham had ridden with the men from the manor on occasion, but he could not recall the last time he had seen Barton here, apart from last night, of course. Or, wait, had it not been the day Lucy had gone off painting and Lord Oliver had escorted her back for tea? They had been quite late, he remembered, and Lucy had been a bit disheveled in appearance. He had noted in passing that the generally taciturn major had been quite garrulous that day, taking charge of the limping conversation. It had been immediately afterward that they had heard of his treatment, and until last night he had kept away from the hall.

A thought struck him and he raised his head. "When came you to have this unfortunate conversation with Lord Oliver?"

"Yesterday afternoon."

"Was Lord Oliver here yesterday? I did not see him."

"Why, yes, he came with Captain Godwin. Did you not have tea with them?" Lucy was looking puzzled.

John's eyes were veiled by half-closed lids. "I had no tea at all yesterday. There were things I wished to see to before the dance."

Lucy did not pursue the subject. "Would it be improper of me to send him a written apology?"

"Do you wish to apologize for what you said?" queried her brother, regarding her curiously.

"Of course I do! I had no right to say such a terrible thing to him."

"Apart from breaking the rules of civility, was it the truth, or perhaps I should say did you believe what you said at the time?"

"Yes, I did. Don't *you* think self-pity is cowardly?"

"Yes," replied John, smiling gently at her, "but I can understand his feeling that he has no right to offer marriage in his circumstances. A man has his pride, my dear."

"But to renounce marriage for such a nonsensical pride is *stupid*," cried Lucy, aghast at such a display of masculine idiocy. "The arm would not matter in the least to a woman who loved him."

John looked into honest gray eyes and nodded. "He may come to realize that one day. We must hope for it for his sake. Meanwhile, I should not write to him just yet. No doubt he will be calling with the Godwins in a day or two and you will have an opportunity to make your apology in person."

Although Lucy meekly accepted her brother's advice, John was proved quite wrong in his prediction. Lord Oliver did not accompany the Godwins when they arrived for tea that afternoon, and when he did call three days later, he was alone and came for the sole purpose of taking his leave of the Monteith ménage.

The Godwin brothers found the young ladies sitting rather listlessly on the terrace when they arrived, victims of a post-party decline in spirits. Actually, it would better serve the cause of strict accuracy to state that two of the young ladies were victims of this *malaise*. Miss Fairmont had been in tearing spirits, but her attempts to generate a post-party discussion had met with discouraging resistance in the form of polite monosyllables from Lucy and stubborn silence from her cousin, who was uncharacteristically engrossed in a piece of needlework. Coralee greeted the gentlemen with pleasure not unmixed with relief.

The eager light in Lucy's eyes when Stansmere had announced the callers faded as the two men came forward. It was a case of self-discipline rather than inclination that prompted her participation in the conversation that ensued, and she greeted the appearance of her brother and Lord Gresham with heartfelt relief, grateful to be able to fade into the background. Though she did not volunteer any observations unsought, she was aware of the ebb and flow of talk and the shifting and reforming of conversational groups as the minutes passed. The senior members of the family drifted out for tea, which necessarily altered the emphasis but did not reverse some disturbing trends she had noticed.

The main target of Captain Godwin's charming attentions was Miss Fairmont. There was nothing particularly surprising about this. Except for a few days when Gemma was indisposed with her sprained ankle, he had always gravitated toward Coralee within the bounds of conduct acceptable in a gentleman paying calls. In fact, after what had passed between the two yesterday, Lucy would not have been astonished to hear an announcement of a betrothal. Captain Godwin could not be considered a splendid match for the well-connected young heiress, but somehow it had always seemed to Lucy inconceivable that Coralee should fail to get her own way in anything upon which she had set her heart.

The really disturbing observation she had made in the past hour concerned her dear friend Gemma, a girl whom Lucy had hitherto considered incapable of the provocative kind of behavior that was so typical of Coralee. Today, Gemma was conducting a flirtation in her cousin's style with the basically inarticulate but very willing Malcolm Godwin in full view of everyone. If that had not been sufficient to attract censorious attention, she was also subjecting Lucy's much-loved brother to a cavalier offhandedness that made her old friend long to box her ears. From her vantage point Lucy had noted the initial surprise and dismay on the gentle features of her hostess before that lady's habitual vagueness of expression was assumed to shield her from prying eyes.

His daughter's outrageous behavior had not been lost on the duke either. Only an obstinate refusal to meet his glance could have enabled Gemma to remain oblivious of her father's glowering disapproval. Even the essentially self-engrossed Coralee was conscious of a change in her cousin, and Lucy intercepted several speculative glances the blonde cast in her direction. As for John, his loving sister was proud of his cool grace and impeccable manners in such trying circumstances, but her heart ached for his pain. Her own nerves were at screaming pitch by the time the Godwins took their leave and she took advantage of the stir of farewells to escape to her own room.

Gemma was not so quick off the mark as Lucy, but knowing it was incumbent on her to put some distance between herself and her parents, she evaded them with a practiced maneuver and headed for her bedchamber by a circuitous route. She was more than a little astonished on opening her door to find her cousin installed in a round boudoir chair facing the door. She remained standing with one hand on the latch and no expression whatsoever on her face as she gazed at her unexpected caller.

After enduring several seconds of that unnerving scrutiny, Coralee said pettishly, "Aren't you going to close the door?"

"That depends. What do you want?"

"Merely to know what game you think you're playing, putting on that ridiculous exhibition with Malcolm Godwin."

"Is that any bread and butter of yours?"

Coralee shrugged. "No, but you must know there's no point to it. Uncle Ernest would never allow you to marry Malcolm, and you could lose your rich suitor if you keep this up."

"I repeat, what concern is it of yours?"

"None at all," Coralee replied airily, rising to her feet. "I merely thought to do you a good turn by warning you of what could happen if you persist in acting the fool."

"*Do me a good turn*?" echoed Gemma, stung into dropping her aloof pose. "When did you ever do anyone a good turn? It's my belief that you are simply annoyed to see one of your court desert you. You'll have to accustom yourself to receiving the attentions of only one man after you and George are married, you know."

Coralee looked back at her cousin without batting an eyelash. "I have no intention of marrying George Godwin," she stated calmly.

16

Quietly, carefully, Lady Gemma Monteith closed her bedroom door and turned to confront the girl watching her with a secretive little smile on her lovely face.

"Would you repeat what you just said?" she requested politely.

"Certainly. I said I have no intention of marrying George Godwin. Why should you imagine I'd throw myself away on the younger son of a mere country squire? I may not have a title now, but like you, I am the granddaughter of a duke, and with my dowry and my face I can look as high as I please for a husband."

Still carefully polite, Gemma asked, "Do you mean you are not in love with George?"

"How you do harp on George," mocked Coralee. "Yes, I do mean I am not in love with George."

"Then what were you doing kissing him in the little temple?" blurted her cousin.

For the first time Coralee looked disconcerted. "What can you mean?" she stalled.

"I saw you, and so did John Delevan, and since Lucy was painting on the other side of the temple, it is entirely possible that she saw you too."

Her cousin had recovered her countenance by now. "Well, if you must know," she replied with obvious reluctance, examining her fingernails closely, "George has asked me to marry him, but I wasn't sure at the time. Now I am sure."

Gemma expelled a pent-up breath. "You've been playing with his affections. You led him on with no intention of accepting him, probably just to spite me. I think you are despicable!"

Although the color in her cheeks heightened under the

scorn flashing from Gemma's dark eyes, Coralee's glance didn't waver. "You are terribly concerned about your precious George," she sneered. "What has he been doing but playing with *your* affections? You two were as good as promised two years ago but he offered for me barely a month after his return."

"If you cannot see the difference, I shan't waste my breath trying to explain it to you. Besides," added Gemma, yielding to the prompting of a baser self, "as you have just pointed out, you are the better business proposition."

This shaft went home with a vengeance.

"George Godwin is in love with me and you know it!" stormed her cousin, brushing past the smaller girl to pull open the door. On the threshold she paused. "But perhaps I'd prefer John Delevan, after all. He at least stands in no need of a wealthy bride."

On this threat she departed, leaving her cousin too shaken for the moment to appreciate that she had had the better of an altercation for the first time in a lifetime of antagonistic dealings with Coralee. She tottered over to her bed and slumped onto it, still finding it difficult to believe what had just transpired.

It was not that she had ever had any illusions about Coralee, but to realize that her cousin had deliberately enticed George for the sole purpose of spiting her and with no concern for his feelings gave her a sick shaky sensation in her stomach. She could only pray that her attraction for him was a blind infatuation rather than a deeply felt love, but whichever it turned out to be, he was going to be hurt when Coralee finally gave him her answer. It hurt to be rejected even if one's love had no more substance than a young girl's romantic dream as she had found to her cost just lately.

By the time her maid came in to help her dress for dinner, Gemma had dismissed the situation between George and Coralee from her mind in favor of brooding over her own heartache. She felt she had taken the only decision possible under the circumstances, but it was proving so much more difficult than she could have anticipated to renounce what she desperately desired. Not much more than twenty-four hours had passed since her path had become clear, and she had never been so unhappy in her life, not even when George's preference for her cousin had first become apparent. The pain of that had been real enough, but even at its most acute she had recognized the element of hurt pride involved in his choice of her abominable cousin over herself. She now knew it was infinitely more painful to refrain from seizing what was in one's grasp for selfless reasons than to be cheated out of something by an outside force.

It became manifest to all before the evening was fairly launched that the cousins were at outs again. Coralee spent the dinner hour exerting herself to charm Mr. Delevan under the smoldering eyes of Lady Gemma. John could have thrown his arms around young Peter's neck when the latter proposed a game of billiards after dinner in a timely rescue operation.

Miss Fairmont's sudden and inexplicable preference for his society became even more of an embarrassment on the following day.

"Persistence, thy name is woman," he muttered to himself as he slipped into the library on spotting a drift of blue coming down the stairs in midafternoon. Coralee had been wearing blue at lunch and he did not require a reminder of the fate of one who hesitates. It was always a pleasure to look at her, and he found her company amusing in regulated doses, but just lately he had come to appreciate all the sensations of the fox in the hunt. If Gemma had made the least attempt to enter the mysterious competition for his attention, he might have regarded himself as one of the favorites of fortune, but she continued to give him the cold shoulder while making her unfavorable opinion of her cousin's tactics quite evident. In fact, it must be acknowledged that his uncooperative little love was conducting herself in a manner strongly reminiscent of that of the fabled dog in

the manger. He could only hope these present un-
accountable patterns of behavior would become
intelligible in the fullness of time.

Meanwhile he had every intention of burying himself
in the library with a soothing book until teatime. He
even took the precaution of turning a large winged-back
chair away from the door so that he would not be visible
to anyone glancing in. It would be a simple-enough
matter to pretend he had dozed off should anyone
follow his or her voice all the way into the room. Perhaps they would be fortunate enough to receive a
number of callers later this afternoon. The larger the
crowd, the better from his point of view.

Unfortunately from several points of view, the afternoon brought only two visitors, Captain Godwin and
his brother. At another moment Lucy would have
enjoyed Miss Fairmont's dilemma as she endeavored to
keep two men in thrall without obviously favoring
either, but her own disappointment at not seeing Lord
Oliver had affected her sense of humor. The unwelcome
spectacle of Gemma again monopolizing Mr. Malcolm
Godwin's attentions also failed to touch a humorous
chord; in fact, it strengthened Lucy's determination to
get to the bottom of the strange reversals that had
occurred since the ball.

Accordingly, as the guests were taking their leave, she
slipped a hand under her friend's arm and steered her
over to the French doors and out onto the terrace.
"Come with me. We are going to have a little talk."

"What do you wish to talk about?"

"My brother, but it is my intention that you will talk
and I shall listen and learn."

"What can I teach you about your brother?" asked
Gemma with an uncertain little laugh.

"You can tell me what John has done to offend you
and forfeit your friendship," the other replied, refusing
to be diverted.

"*Nothing*! Of course John has done nothing to
offend me!"

Gemma was staring down at her pink sandal that was tracing the joints in the flagstone terrace, and now Lucy said compellingly, "Look at me, Gemma." When the younger girl had complied with discernible reluctance, she went on, "What has happened that has made you so cold toward John since the ball? What has he done?" Gray eyes searched brown ones that looked shamed and unhappy.

"Nothing. I told you."

"Then why are you flirting outrageously with Malcolm Godwin and treating John like a pariah?"

"Believe me, Lucy, it is for John's sake that I am doing it."

Lucy blinked at this earnest claim and paused to adjust her thinking. At last she ventured, "Do you think you could tell me how flirting with Mr. Godwin and treating John with coldness can be considered to be for his benefit? I confess I don't see it."

Gemma held her friend's gaze and said seriously, "If I tell you what I am about, you must promise me not to breathe a syllable of it to John or anyone. Do I have your solemn promise?"

"You have," agreed Lucy after a slight pause.

"I am hoping John will believe I have formed an attachment for Malcolm so he will not feel it is his duty to offer for me."

"His duty! What can you mean?"

Gemma searched her friend's uncomprehending face. "Did you not know that John came here for the express purpose of making me an offer? Our fathers arranged it in London."

Lucy stared. "I . . . I cannot . . . Are you certain of this?"

"My mother told me the day you arrived that Papa was determined I should marry John." She ran the tip of her tongue over her lips to moisten them and swallowed before continuing. "I had considered myself pledged to George, and I told John this the very next day. He was most understanding and promised not to

pursue the suit. You must have noticed that George
. . . that George is very taken with Coralee.'' Here the
small chin lifted to a determined angle as she finished
with a rush. ''Well, he has asked her to marry him. She
says she will refuse, but that doesn't make a particle of
difference. Can't you see that I must free John from any
obligation he may think he has to save my face by
offering for me?''

This amazing story had succeeded in robbing Lucy of
all power of expression, even of coherent thought for a
time. Her initial reaction had been to protest that her
brother would never have agreed to such a coldly
arranged marriage, but Gemma said she had actually
confronted John about it. She said he had been most
understanding. *Understanding!*

Lucy choked back an hysterical desire to laugh and
dropped limply onto the wrought-iron seat behind her.
Gemma's behavior over the last couple of days was now
explained, at least partially, she thought as her eyes
roved her friend's doleful countenance. She was clearly
unhappy, but was it at losing George or, as Lucy was
beginning to suspect, because of the role she had set
herself to play with respect to John? With an idea of
clearing up the mystery, she pursued the second of
Gemma's revelations.

''Did you say that George had offered for Coralee
and she intends to refuse him? Did she tell you this?''

''Yes, because I had already guessed—about the
offer, I mean.''

''So you did see them in the temple? I thought you
must have done.''

Gemma nodded. ''John and I had gone down to look
for you.''

''Did she also confide why she plans to refuse him?''

Sparks flew from soft brown eyes and scorn hardened
her voice as Gemma burst out, ''She said she has no
intention of throwing herself away on a second son. She
wants a brilliant match and a title. It was all a deliberate
plot to lure George away from me! Coralee has always

tried to take everything I ever valued for her own, but this is beyond anything, to tamper with a man's feelings!''

"It is the outside of enough," agreed Lucy dispassionately. "Poor George. I must tell you that your cousin is something quite exceptional in my experience. I'll back her to capture her titled prize too. Do you still want George?'' she inquired, fixing her friend with a rapier look that belied the casual tones.

"Good heavens, no," cried the dark-haired girl. "Would you, under the circumstances?"

"If I still loved him—after he had recovered from his broken heart, of course.''

A faint flush had mantled Gemma's cheeks and she answered in a rather defensive fashion. "Well, I don't still love him. I think now that I never did really, but it was exciting to be in love with a brave soldier going off into danger, and he is so handsome and persuasive. Since he has returned, I have discovered that it is almost a passion with him to attach every attractive female in the room, not that he means anything improper by it. He has a great deal of natural charm and genuinely likes feminine company, but I am persuaded this would be an uncomfortable trait in a husband," she finished with a quaint air of discovery.

Lucy preserved her countenance with difficulty. It would indeed be an uncomfortable trait in a husband! She shot a glance at her friend's brooding face. Was Gemma dwelling on what living with just such a trait had done to her own mother over the years? She hastened to give her thoughts a new direction.

"Why is Coralee now pursuing John? He hasn't a title and I do not think he could be described as a brilliant match.''

"She is doing it to spite me. She is nothing but a jealous cat.''

"Agreed, but how could it spite you?" Lucy asked in feigned innocence. "Does she know about our fathers' scheme?"

"I don't know. She may have guessed."

"Hmmmmm," Lucy murmured thoughtfully, and rose from the iron seat. She concentrated on shaking the creases out of her skirts as she went on, "*Are* you forming an attachment for Malcolm Godwin?"

"No, of course not. I explained that."

"It is my impression that John is rather unhappy over your treatment of him. And if Mr. Godwin should believe you to be serious, I should think Miss Biddlesford might be rather unhappy about it too, not to mention Mr. Godwin himself, if he should actually chance his luck with you."

For a moment Gemma looked almost haunted at these new problems, but her chin firmed and she repeated obstinately, "What I am doing is for the best. If John believes me to be falling in love with Malcolm, perhaps he will leave quite soon, then I may stop encouraging Malcolm and Letty Biddlesford need never know anything about it."

"Is that what you would like?" pursued her friend relentlessly.

"Yes." Gemma's tones were decided. "And remember, you have promised you will tell no one of this conversation."

Lucy was thinking of her promise with regret the next morning as she examined her brother across the writing table in the big library, where she had come to pen their weekly letter to their father. John was smiling at her as he dictated a message for their parent, but it was a mechanical effort and she looked in vain for the lurking twinkle that generally dwelled in his blue eyes. She knew in her heart that his placid exterior concealed a very real wound dealt him by her misguided friend. She might have overcome the inherent delicacy that would keep a younger sister from delving into her brother's affairs of the heart had it not been for that pernicious promise Gemma had extracted from her before she knew how senseless it was. She had devoted a good portion of a nearly sleepless night to the problem of Gemma and

John without coming up with any helpful contribution she might make, chained as she was by her pledge of silence.

The night's ratiocinations had produced theories, however, which she was nearly confident enough to call conclusions. It still strained her credulity that John had apparently agreed to a marriage with a girl he had never seen, but putting aside this stumbling block, the one fact that kept resurfacing was that her brother had remained in Wiltshire for over a month in the constant company of the girl who had warned him at the first opportunity that she was promised to another man. What reason other than love for Gemma could have induced him to remain for so long a period under such unpromising circumstances? The claims of civility could have been satisfied in a sennight or less. The pressures of work could have been advanced at any time to excuse his departure.

Lucy was within ames ace of taking her oath that John was in love; her convictions were not quite so firm with regard to Gemma's feelings. The duke's daughter was a tenderhearted girl who might think this the best method of staving off a proposal, if she feared he was in danger of falling in love with her. On the other hand, her present ridiculous behavior might be explained in quite another manner.

During the weeks of their visit Gemma and John had become as thick as thieves. If she had recently discovered that it was really John she loved, after all, might she not send him away if she feared his offer would be made only in the spirit in which the marriage had been arranged by their fathers? Would a girl seize the chance to marry the man she loved even if she knew her sentiments were not returned, or would pride step in and cause her to renounce the offer? Lucy simply could not decide. For herself the question would be easy to resolve—she could not bear the thought of being married to a man who did not love her, but she accepted that this was not the case with every female. Many girls expected to marry men their parents selected for them without troubling themselves overmuch with questions of feelings.

Not Gemma, though! Lucy's lips quirked as she recalled how quickly Gemma had warned John off in the beginning—the day after she met him, she had said. But that was not simply a case of refusing a man who did not love her but of believing herself already committed to someone who did.

It was no use; argument and counterargument revolved endlessly in her confused mind, and John was speaking to her again. He had wandered over to stare out of the window that faced the lake. Now he said over his shoulder, "I have been thinking that I should be getting back to my chambers soon. I have been away from my work a deal longer than I intended originally. Perhaps tomorrow or the next—"

"No," blurted his sister in her distress at this unexpected turn of events. "Not yet, you cannot go just yet, John." She rose from behind the table and took a step toward him.

"Why can I not?" he queried mildly. "What is there to keep me here?"

Afraid she had detected a faintly bitter tone under the smooth words, and bound to silence on the one subject that could influence him, Lucy bit her lip and stared at him in consternation. She opened her mouth and closed it, tried again, "Stay just a little longer, *please*, John. Things may not be what they seem at the moment."

"What do you mean by that? What things?"

"I . . . I can't tell you any more but—"

She was interrupted by a knock on the door. John called permission to enter and Lord Oliver walked into the room dressed for travel, with a lightweight driving coat of drab draped over the shoulders of his dark-blue coat. Spotless Hessians gleamed as he approached slowly, carrying a pair of York tan gloves.

"Stansmere told me I might find you both here and allowed me to announce myself. I trust I don't interrupt?"

John made the correct response, explaining about the letter-writing while Lucy sought to recover her countenance. Prompted by a premonition of disaster, she moved instinctively closer to her brother's reassuring presence.

"I came to take my leave of you," Lord Oliver continued in formal tones. "I shall be setting out for my parents' home in Hampshire within the hour."

With a supreme effort of will, Lucy kept the moan that fled her heart at this announcement from escaping through her lips, but her face was paper-white and she was incapable of speech or movement for the moment. All of her strength was committed to keeping herself upright and decently quiet.

Once again John came to the rescue, saying all that was proper to the occasion, expressing warm phrases of regret on behalf of both of them. He turned to her then, and his eyes were like steadying hands on her quivering spirit. She mustered up the composure to echo her brother's sentiments in a calm colorless voice containing the merest hint of huskiness. She was able to offer Lord Oliver a cold hand that did not tremble, and when he raised it to his lips instead of shaking it, she bore that unflinchingly too. However, after one glance into that formal mask when he had explained his errand, she had kept her own eyes down, never raising them above the level of his square chin lest they should betray the anguish that was taking possession of her soul.

There was an awkward moment when Lord Oliver released her hand and swept a low bow, but John was there proposing to walk with him to his phaeton. With senses dulled by pain, Lucy watched the man she loved walk out of her life forever, his height and massive shoulders almost dwarfing her brother's slim wiry figure beside him as they crossed the dozen feet of space to the entrance. Then the door was closed, closed on any opportunity to apologize for her cruel judgment on the day of the waltzing ball, closed on any future opportunity to tell him what was in her heart, closed

permanently, shutting off her future with a barely
audible click.

After a minute or two of gazing blindly at that door,
Lucy spun away and moved toward the same window
John had retreated to earlier. It didn't face the front of
the house; she had no intention of watching Lord
Oliver's phaeton disappear into the distance in the time-
honored fashion of romantic heroines. She didn't feel
like a heroine, she felt . . . empty.

By standing to the far left of the window she could
just glimpse a corner of the Greek temple, but it had no
power over her today. For a short time it had seemed to
exert a spell that brought a dark, difficult man close to
her in an exciting way she had not experienced before.
But now the spell was broken and he was gone, taking
the excitement with him.

She was staring into a future that resembled a vast
desert with nothing on the horizon to alter the sameness
when the library door opened again—her brother come
back to offer her what comfort he could. She kept her
sightless gaze directed out the window.

"He's gone, John," she said huskily. "I'll never see
him again."

"Yes, you will," replied a voice that was nothing like
John's. "Every day of your life, if you can bear the
thought."

For the space of several heartbeats Lucy's courage
failed. This could not be happening, she would turn
only to find her brother standing there. Her ears
strained but there was no sound in the large room except
her own harsh breathing. She whirled, almost colliding
with the man who had advanced soundlessly across the
thick Turkey carpet. Blazing dark eyes in a swarthy
face, now curiously pale, clashed with her wildly seeking
ones for an instant until his image wavered and
dissolved as the tears she had refused to shed when she
thought herself unloved cascaded down her cheeks.

"Ah no, sweetheart, don't," he groaned, before
abandoning words in favor of wrapping an arm like a

steel band around her shoulders and trapping her quivering lips with his own warm mouth. The pain and wonder of that bruising embrace mingled about equally, but Lucy welcomed both, in proof of which she managed to extend her pinioned arms around his back to assist him in eradicating all space between them. Neither drew back until driven by the need to draw breath. And now it was Lord Oliver who seemed incapable of speech. He contented himself with pressing light kisses all over her wet face while Lucy sought to reestablish a normal breathing rhythm. She wriggled an arm free and placed caressing fingertips on the jagged line where the French bullet had creased his cheek.

"Why did you come back, Oliver?" she whispered. "What made you change your mind?"

"These," he said, kissing first one eyelid and then the other before tipping up her chin to repeat the action on her lips. Raising his mouth so he could look into adoring gray eyes, he explained, "I had decided I was in no case to offer marriage to a woman, and until I met you it was not much of a sacrifice. All that changed when I fell headlong in love with you. It became a living purgatory and I realized I must get away from you, must leave temptation behind. Then I watched your face a few minutes ago when I said good-bye. You only looked at me for an instant, but your beautiful eyes were agonized as though I had dealt you a mortal blow. You called me a coward once before, my darling, but that was the moment when I really lost all my courage. I did not have the willpower to walk away and leave you for a whole man to love."

"No, don't say that," protested Lucy, vehement but breathless as she finally eluded the finger that had been pressed against her lips to keep her silent. "You know I could never love any other man. Do not frighten me like that." She threw her arms around his neck and pressed nearer to him.

"Shhhh, angel, don't tremble so," he soothed, gathering her closer once more. "Believe me, the die is now cast. I may have only one arm, but I know how to hold what is mine." Those jet eyes, alive with an intensity that would have terrified a lesser woman, were demanding a commitment that Lucy was only too happy to give. A twinkle reminiscent of her brother's illuminated the smoky-gray glance that held his steadily, but her voice was demure.

"I believe you, my lord, and should perhaps inform you that I too have a very possessive nature."

His teeth gleamed in a rare smile. "I am properly warned, ma'am." Before he swooped to kiss her again, Lucy noted with a little thrill of pleasure the radical difference happiness made in her future husband's stern aspect. Though only thirty, he had seemed infinitely older than John or Captain Godwin but she had just glimpsed a younger, almost boyish Oliver, and she gloried in the knowledge that it was her privilege to bring that look back to his face permanently.

He released her responsive mouth with reluctance after another mutually satisfying interval and brushed a hand over her hair to cup the back of her neck gently. "My lovely Delilah, you beguile me into forgetting the existence of time. Your brother and my groom will think me irredeemably caper-witted. I told them I had forgotten something."

"Oliver! You don't still mean to leave today?" Lucy was rocked out of her blissful state, and she gazed up at him in distress.

"I think I must, my love. I have already taken leave of my hosts. If we do not wish to have our affairs bruited about the countryside before your father and my parents have learned our news, I had best continue with my plans. I'll be back as soon as I am able, but I must see your father at once, and my parents are expecting me." His eyes roved her features hungrily as if fixing them in his memory as he added softly, "I don't know how I thought to find the strength to leave you forever when it is absolutely hellish to have to part even for a few days. Unless," he finished with sudden eagerness, "you were to come with me? Would you, Lucy?"

By now Lucy had had time to consider the situation, and she shook her head regretfully. "I could not go on such short notice. Gemma invited me for the whole summer, and the duke and duchess have been too kind to repay them in such a scrambling fashion. Besides, my brother's affairs are not in good order at present; if I stay, I might be able to help. But you will not be gone too long, will you, Oliver?"

"Not one moment longer than I must, my heart." He looked at her gravely without touching her and said with some hesitation, "Your father might not deem me a sound proposition for a son-in-law. Are you prepared for that?"

Lucy showed him a serene countenance in which clear gray eyes smiled confidently. "My father will accept that I know my own mind. He wishes me to have the same kind of true union he and my mother shared. Can you spare another few minutes so that I may write to him?"

On receiving her lover's fervent assurances that he would be glad to wait for anything that might help smooth his path with Mr. Delevan, she went back to the writing table and tore up the letter she had been laboring over.

Ten minutes later John entered the library to find his dreamy-eyed sister sitting at the writing table with her chin resting in one cupped palm and the other hand toying with a pen. She returned his smile but said nothing as he crossed to her and dropped a kiss onto one smooth cheek.

"I have just congratulated and bade Godspeed to my future brother-in-law, who, by the by, looks an entirely different person already. I am persuaded you two will suit admirably, my dear, if a brother's opinion counts for anything."

"Thank you, John. I mean to make him happy." She laughed out suddenly. "Poor Oliver is terrified that

Father will think him an unfit husband for me."

John grinned. "I hope you did not tell him that our esteemed parent was more likely to fall on his neck when he sends his card in if he guesses that Lord Oliver means to make you 'my lady.' " His smile faded. "Will you tell everyone here?"

Lucy hesitated. "Not just yet. I would prefer to wait until I have Oliver to support me."

"The duchess may guess your secret. She was returning to the house when I left Oliver just now, and she could not have failed to note the difference in him when he bade her farewell. She doesn't miss much for all her quiet ways and diffident manner."

"I should not mind the duchess knowing."

John's eyes fell on the torn scraps on the writing table and his eyebrows escalated. "Our letter to Father?" At Lucy's guilty nod he said resignedly, "I can see that I shall have to write, after all. Father will get nothing coherent out of you today."

He pulled her unresisting from the chair and took her place. "I shall give Barton a sterling character and forward my blessings on the match to help resolve any doubts Father might have that aren't covered by the title and fortune." He picked up the pen, and feeling herself dismissed, Lucy drifted out of the library and turned toward her room.

At the top of the stairs she met the duchess, whose smiling glance lingered on her young guest's features.

"You are looking very radiant this morning, my dear child."

The older woman's greeting could be taken as an invitation if she wished, but the duchess would never pry. Suddenly Lucy found it easy to share her good news even without the support of her betrothed. "Yes, ma'am," she said simply. "Lord Oliver Barton has just done me the honor of asking me to be his wife."

Her hands were taken in a warm clasp as the duchess reached up and kissed her. "I am so happy for you both! You will know how to lighten the shadows in his world. You are exactly what he needs." Two dimples appeared in her cheeks, heightening the resemblance to her daughter as she went on with a mischievous smile, "And he is exactly what you want, yes?"

"Yes, ma'am," confessed Lucy, blushing furiously.

"I should not tease you," said her hostess, patting her hand in contrition, "but I am so delighted to have something good come out of this summer."

A wistful look had invaded the deep-brown eyes, and Lucy said impulsively, "I shouldn't worry too much about Gemma, your grace."

The duchess bent a searching glance on the girl who was looking acutely uncomfortable at having brought up a topic she was not free to discuss, and with the delicacy of touch that was basic to her personality, she refrained from pursuing the subject. She merely said out of the blue, "I do so like your brother, Lucy," before inquiring if the news of her guest's betrothal was to remain secret for the moment.

"If you please, ma'am, just until Lord Oliver returns," Lucy replied gratefully.

The duchess nodded before starting down the staircase. "I'll see you at lunch, my child."

17

His Grace of Carlyle was seated at the desk in his study with the open estate ledgers in front of him. The most cursory glance, however, would inform that he was not engaged upon this mundane task. A frown had settled on his brow, and his lips were compressed into a straight line. His unfocused stare seemed to be directed at the empty chair of maroon leather on the far side of the desk, and it was obvious that no very pleasant topic occupied his thoughts at the moment.

Until a week or so ago his grace had had every reason to congratulate himself on the success of his arrangements. Matters had fallen out much as he had planned; affairs were nicely under control, marching toward the conclusion he intended. Since the waltzing ball, however, the threads in his all-but-completed pattern had started to unravel, forcing him to take a hand in the matter lest his vital design be destroyed. Careful observation had not secured enlightenment as to the causes behind the present crisis, but he knew where to lay the blame—squarely on his daughter's slim shoulders. His grace's lips thinned even more. Gemma's contrariness had always been the one stumbling block that it was imperative to remove from the path to his objective. He had foreseen the difficulty of gaining her cooperation from the inception of his scheme, but unfortunately, circumstances had left him with no alternative except to use her prospective marriage as the means to reestablish his financial position.

The duke was not attempting to avoid responsibility. He accepted that the estate was at rather low water at present almost entirely due to his own extravagance and bad management over a long period of time. His losses at cards and at the race meets had been sharply higher in the recent past, and one or two investments of a speculative nature had turned sour on him in the same period of time. With the clarity of hindsight he could now see that he had been overly generous to the succession of ladybirds who had engaged his interest over the years, but one owed something to one's consequence, after all, and he would not have it whispered in the clubs that Carlyle behaved in a scaly fashion to anyone under his protection.

Expenses always seemed to outrun income. There were repairs to be undertaken at the hall, his bailiff had been plaguing him to death to put some money into the farms, and before the year was out, Gresham would come into his majority with a concomitant increase in his allowance. It had gradually become unavoidable that the only avenue for getting the necessary revenue that did not entail unpleasant economies or diminishing the estate was through a beneficial marriage settlement on his daughter.

And he had pulled off a coup with ridiculous ease. The duke had long had his banking arrangements at the institution controlled by the senior Delevan and had come to know him well in a business way. To be fair, he'd seen no signs that the fellow was trying to worm his way into the inner circle. His interests seemed to be confined to making money, which he did very well indeed, and his family, about which he could be a bit of a bore, a trait that clearly marked him as a cit. The idea of aligning the families germinated on the occasion when Mr. Delevan referred to the friendship between their daughters for the third or fourth time; it germinated, matured, and exploded in the duke's brain within seconds of his becoming aware that the banker, far from being content with his enormous wealth, was possessed of audacious social ambitions centered in his children.

At this point the duke had thankfully turned away several respectable suitors . . . at his daughter's

request. He had scarcely embarked on a tactful
approach to forging a more personal friendship with
Delevan when he discovered the latter to be fully cognizant of his intent and perfectly willing to be open-
handed should the young people consent to the
match.

In fact, matters had marched merrily as a marriage
bell until now. Happily, both Delevan children had
turned out to be more than presentable, though he could
wish the brother a trifle less intellectual and a bit more
in the dashing style that attracted young girls. Knowing
his daughter's intransigence, he had refrained from
approaching her directly, although he had taken the precaution of acquainting her mother with his intention in
case her cooperation should be required. Once the scene
was set, he had taken great pains to remove himself
from the proceedings.

The unexpected return of George Godwin to the cast
had given him cause for momentary alarm, but the
presence of Coralee in the wings had been a godsend in
that respect. He hoped he knew how to value his own
daughter, certainly he had received confirmation
aplenty of her popularity since her come-out, but she
could not hope to compete with her beautiful cousin. He
knew he didn't have to worry about Mr. John Delevan's
being ensnared by the latter's beauty because there was
never a question of his niece's marrying anyone whose
birth did not equal her own. Coralee had been raised to
expect a brilliant match, and he had every confidence
that she would achieve it. Had young Delevan exhibited
the least inclination to dangle after her, the duke would
have speedily acquainted him with the facts, but the cub
knew on which side his bread was buttered and
appeared to set about fixing his interest with Gemma in
the right way. Coralee had needed no encouragement to
enslave George Godwin, putting an end to that old boy-
and-girl affair beteween him and Gemma.

So, what had gone awry? What was the chit playing
at, flirting with Malcolm Godwin? Couldn't she see she
had young Delevan eating out of her hand? Having

formed a good opinion of this gentleman's address from the start of their acquaintance, the duke had kept out of the business, but he was beginning to suspect he might have overrated Delevan's ability to handle a high-spirited girl like Gemma. And an even nastier rodent of suspicion had begun to gnaw at his complaisance. It was just conceivable that the banker's son had decided the game wasn't worth the candle. There was no lack of impoverished aristocrats with marriageable daughters in the land, as he must know. Certainly in the last week his efforts to charm Gemma out of the sullens had diminished to the vanishing point, though his manners as always were perfect. Too perfect!

"Doesn't the young cub have any red blood in his veins?" growled his grace into the room's silence. "With that ready tongue of his he should be able to make circles around that dummy Godwin with any female."

He took out his watch and saw that it was within two minutes of the hour he had named for an interview with young Delevan. It might be time to put all the cards on the table and see exactly how matters stood so he could give them a nudge in the right direction.

John arrived punctually and was waved to the leather chair facing the desk. Assessing light-blue eyes noted that he was, as usual, perfectly turned out with neatness and propriety. There was nothing dashing about his appearance, though he looked every inch the gentleman. His bearing too was above criticism. He combined an ease of manner with the attentive and respectful air proper to conversation with a man old enough to be his father. The very traits that had won the duke's approbation earlier in the summer had begun to irritate him of late. What right had the cub to look so well-contented when he was being beaten to the post by a nonstarter? Was he completely insensible of what was going on under his nose?

With a conscious effort his grace relaxed his mouth and smiled at the good-humored young man awaiting his pleasure.

"I thought it was about time we two had a talk, my boy."

"Did you, sir?"

Nothing to object to in words or delivery, but the duke's irritation increased imperceptibly at the lack of encouragement in the bright-blue eyes meeting his steadily. He glanced down at the pen in his hands. "You've no doubt wondered why I have never mentioned the subject before?"

As the older man raised his eyes, the younger was already speaking easily, "Why no, sir. I merely gave you credit for realizing that once I was on the scene, the matter was out of your hands and my father's and rested solely with Lady Gemma and myself."

The duke chose to ignore for the present the unwelcome sensation of having been put in his place. "Exactly so, and you managed to get upon the friendliest terms with my daughter with admirable dispatch. Would you agree, though, that recently you appear to have lost headway with Gemma?"

A rueful twist of John's lips pointed his reply. "I could scarcely deny it, could I?"

"What do you propose to do about the situation?"

After a pause John replied somewhat evasively, "I don't believe Lady Gemma has formed a *tendre* for Malcolm Godwin, if that is any comfort to you, sir."

"It is certainly welcome news but scarcely aids your cause," pointed out his host somewhat dryly. When his guest made no immediate response, he repeated his question. "What do you propose to do?"

"Nothing precipitate, your grace. The time is not right."

There was a slight relaxation in the posture of the older man at the relief of knowing young Delevan still meant to marry his obstinate daughter.

"Would it help if I had a little talk with her, underlined your qualifications, so to speak?"

"*Good God, no*! One word from you and I'd lose her forever!" John was startled out of his respectful stance.

Noting his host's narrowed, icy expression, he decided he might as well be hung for a sheep as a lamb, and reiterated, "One hint of coercion and Lady Gemma would retreat for good. You may forbid her to marry against your wishes while she is under age, but you delude yourself if you imagine she will ever marry at your command. And I'd never be able to convince her that I love her."

The last soberly delivered statement affected the duke enough so that he swallowed the anger aroused by the first part of this extraordinary speech, and looked searchingly at the interesting specimen across the desk from him.

"Do you mean me to understand that you are in love with Gemma?"

"Yes."

"How convenient. Accept my congratulations."

The hint of a sneer in the duke's murmur brought a surge of red into John's cheeks. "Perhaps," he began silkily, "I should explain to your grace that I did not come here with the intention of making Lady Gemma an offer."

"No?" One lifted eyebrow conveyed the duke's disbelief.

"No." This was uttered in a decisive tone. "I'm not sure I can explain exactly how Lucy and I feel about our father. He has not been himself since our mother's death, and we have been very concerned. This scheme of yours to marry me to Lady Gemma has brought him back with a vengeance." Another wry twist distorted John's mouth for a second. "Can you understand that I couldn't refuse even to look at the girl he had selected? I never intended to remain at the hall for more than a few days."

"But here you are," said the duke with spurious affability.

"Yes." The young man's eyes had the unfocused look of one examining something in the past. "She told me the second day that she was as good as promised to

George Godwin, but even then, it was too late for me to escape." His eyes fastened onto the man opposite and hardened in a way no one at Monteith Hall had ever been privileged to witness. "Please understand me, sir. I mean to have her heart, all of it, or none of her at all."

The duke's brows met in a heavy scowl. "Do you mean to tell me you hadn't the wit to wait longer than twenty-four hours to propose marriage to a girl you'd just met? No wonder she turned you down! I thought better of your intelligence than that."

"No, you misunderstood me, sir. I have never made Lady Gemma an offer."

Her father's head snapped up at that. There was a white line around his nostrils. "So, her mother told her! I might have known no woman could keep her tongue between her teeth."

Too late John realized that Gemma had not been meant to know of the arrangement. He said hastily, "I am persuaded her grace had good reason for her action. Her concern would have been entirely for Gemma's happiness."

The duke gave a laugh that didn't ring true, and shrugged. "At least you will have observed that Gemma is not like her mother," he remarked with an attempt at joviality. "She may have inherited her looks, but my daughter is full of spirit and knows how to keep her own counsel."

"I am desolated to have to contradict you, sir," came the gentle riposte, "but in everything that counts Gemma is very like her mother. She has inherited her grace's generous heart and her sweetness of disposition, and in time she will develop the same tact and graciousness that make her mother such an exceptional hostess." Prudence and good manners forbade him from adding that he would see to it that Gemma never developed her mother's languid air of melancholy that came from knowing herself undervalued by her husband. He rose from his chair and smiled pleasantly at his host, who was regarding him with a mixture of veiled hostility and speculation.

"If you will be patient a little longer, sir, I will do my utmost to convince Lady Gemma of my sincerity as soon as she has stopped running away from her fate."

"I wish you luck, my boy. Women are capricious creatures at best," said his host from the depths of his vast experience.

"Thank you, sir. I rather think I'll need all the luck I can find," replied John with a touching lack of confidence that made him suddenly human and went some way toward reconciling his prospective father-in-law to his choice, which he had been actively regretting for the last few minutes.

A suspicion of a vertical line between his brows was the only outward sign of his perturbed mental state when John emerged from the duke's study, but he was in fact torn between satisfaction at having unburdened himself to enumerate some long-unappreciated qualities of the duchess and her daughter, and self-blame for having violated his host's hospitality by so doing. It had been so much wasted breath in any case and highly presumptuous to hope to inculcate upon the duke an appreciation for what clearly held little value for a man of his worldly nature. However, there was finally some relief for the lover in him who had chafed to see the beloved object belittled, if not verbally at least by implication. He shook his head once, trying to shake off the mood of dissatisfaction that had descended on him. The scene with the duke was over and done with.

As John headed toward the rose garden in the faint hope of accidentally meeting his evasive love, he only wished it were possible to rid himself of a prickling sense of time running out that warred with an instinctive reluctance to rush Gemma. If he could trust his own observation, she had never felt herself really loved by her father, and she had been disappointed in the man in whom she had invested her first romantic fancies. It was understandable that she should be extremely wary of giving her heart away again, and she had shown herself uninterested in a marriage of convenience. He had been discouraged by her flirtation with Malcolm Godwin until it had been borne in upon his lacerated sensibilities that all this determined flirting was not making her happy. Her gaiety had a brittle quality these days, and the constant effort required to project an image of carefree happiness was taking its toll on her energy and spirits. If she would just lower her guard for an hour and stop avoiding him, he was in a mood to chance everything on one throw despite his sensible words to the duke just now. Lucy had confided that Lord Oliver wished to bring her to meet his family when her visit here could be brought to an end. Once his sister departed, there would be no excuse to prolong his own visit. Time was swiftly running out. He would not be surprised to see Barton back in Wiltshire in the next few days.

This prediction came true the very next afternoon. Lord Oliver walked into the library, where John was attending to some correspondence.

"I don't have any idea where Lucy may be at the moment," he admitted when they had shaken hands and exchanged a few remarks on Lord Oliver's journey and his cordial reception by Mr. Delevan.

"Stansmere said she and Lady Gemma had gone out for a ride. I thought perhaps you and I might go in search of them, if you can spare the time."

"Good idea. Give me five minutes to get my boots on," agreed John, heading for the door on the words.

Lucy and Gemma had ridden into the village on an errand and were taking a roundabout route back through the wooded area behind the village. The sun shone warmly down through the trees, and the girls were riding at a dawdling pace enjoying its benefit.

"It's so good to get away from the house for an hour," confessed Gemma. "This is so relaxing, ambling along on our own."

"I should imagine you'd find a mountain-climbing expedition relaxing compared with that continual charade you are acting out these days," said her friend, eyeing her frankly. "When are you going to have done with this nonsense?"

Gemma sighed. "It isn't nonsense, Lucy. I have no intention of entering into a marriage of convenience."

"Why should you believe it would be that? It's my opinion that John is head over heels in love with you if you'd just give him a chance to prove it."

An eager questioning face was presented to Lucy. "Did he say so?"

"Brothers never tell their sisters anything," replied her friend lightly, regretting her intervention as she watched the light die out of Gemma's eyes. "Let's trot," she suggested, giving Smoky a nudge with her heel.

Two things happened nearly simultaneously at that instant. A loud hail came from the field on the right, and a hare ran across the path within five feet of the gray.

Lady Gemma turned Fleurette easily and put up a hand to shield her eyes from the sun. "Here's your brother, and I believe that is Lord Oliver with him. Did you know he planned to return to Wiltshire, Lucy?"

Miss Delevan, however, was in no position to answer, if indeed she even heard her friend's question. She had jerked the reins at the shout and the gray had started to respond when the hare spooked him. The pair had veered into a field and were many yards away when Gemma looked over her shoulder.

Turning Fleurette around, she gave her her head and set off at a gallop in pursuit. "Pull him up, Lucy," she called imperatively, but it became apparent from Lucy's position that she had lost the reins and was clinging to the horse's mane to keep her seat. Out of the corner of her eye Gemma saw two riders heading across the field at an angle, and her ears were filled with the steady drumming of hoofbeats, her own horse's included, as she bent lower over the chestnut's neck.

The men were going to overtakc the runaway before she could, but she could only pray it would be before the gray reached the hedge dividing two fields that was looming dangerously close. Lucy was no jumper under the most favorable conditions—there wasn't a chance

that she'd negotiate the leap safely. Gemma didn't
realize she was holding her breath until Lord Oliver on
the powerful bay rode up on one side of Lucy a second
before John could reach her from the other. The former
seized the bridle and wrenched Smoky to a walk
gradually enough that Lucy managed to maintain her
position and eventually sit upright again.

Lady Gemma, coming up a bare instant later, pulled
the mare up and gazed in openmouthed astonishment at
the sight of her friend tumbling off her horse and
casting herself half-sobbing into the arms of her rescuer.

"Oliver, Oliver, do you realize what you have done?
That was your *left* arm!"

"Are you all right, sweetheart? You are not hurt?"

"Never mind me, I'm fine. Don't you understand?"
shrilled Lucy, shaking as much of him as she could
encompass. "You stopped that horse with your *left*
hand. How does it feel now?"

An ashen-faced Lord Oliver clenched and unclenched
his left fist. "Like someone is jabbing a thousand
needles into me," he admitted wryly. Then, disregarding said needles, he pulled his fiancée to him,
wrapping both arms tightly around her willing body.

John edged his mount closer to Fleurette, whose
dazed-looking rider was absentmindedly patting her
neck.

"Shall we leave them alone for a bit?"

He headed back toward the glen at a slow trot.
Gemma followed mechanically until they were out of
hearing range of the others. At the edge of the trees he
waited for her to join him and they proceeded at a walk.
Neither spoke for another minute or two. John's head
was angled so he could watch the changing expressions
on Gemma's face as she tried to assimilate the recent
happenings. The initial shock had given way to
frowning puzzlement, which was succeeded in turn by
sudden suspicion. Her mouth was open as she swung
toward him, but John nipped in first.

"I do approve of happy endings, do not you?"

Gemma was not disarmed by his best smile and nonchalant tones. "You knew about this, didn't you?" she challenged.

"I was as surprised and delighted as you must be to learn that Lord Oliver has recovered the use of his arm."

"You know that is not what I meant! Not that I am not excessively happy for him—of course I am, poor man!" she amended quickly. "You knew about Lucy and Lord Oliver before today, didn't you?"

Her voice had lost its aggressive tone, and a trace of hurt feelings came through.

"Yes," he admitted. "Lord Oliver proposed to Lucy the day he left to visit his parents."

"She never mentioned a word to me, never let fall a hint that she was in love with him."

John heard the quiver in her voice and wished that Lucy had taken her friend into her confidence, though he thought he knew why she had remained silent this last week. He could feel Gemma's pain and realized that this was part of loving her; he would always feel her pain. He took a deep breath and addressed her averted head in gentle tones.

"I am persuaded, my love, that, knowing you have not been very happy just lately, Lucy shrank from making a parade of her own happiness. At another time she would have shared her news with you gladly."

Hot color flared over Gemma's cheekbones, and her head went up proudly. "I don't know what you mean. I am perfectly happy!"

The horses had come to a dead stop, though their riders scarcely noticed.

"Perfectly happy?" queried John, looking straight at his flushed companion.

"Yes, of course. Why should I not be?" There was more than a hint of bravado in her manner, and her eyes were wary.

"Because I have been perfectly miserable, and a . . . friend could not be happy when someone is miserable."

Gemma barely moved her lips as she whispered, "Why should you be miserable?"

His eyes compelled hers, would not release them. "Because the girl I love has turned against me."

"Oh, no! You don't love me, you know you don't!" She put out a hand in a gesture of repudiation and had it captured in his. She tugged unavailingly to free it, then accused unsteadily, "You only came here because your father wished you to marry me."

"And I stayed because *I* wished to marry you."

He had her full attention now. Brown velvet eyes stared into his, begging to be convinced but unaware of their self-revelation.

"I planned to stay for a few days for my father's sake and then take my leave. You may conceive of my surprise when I found you not only informed of the marriage scheme but turning me down at the outset. I should have felt vastly relieved, but instead I was devastated."

"Fustian! After one day?" demanded his love disbelievingly.

"After one look from the most beautiful, mischievous eyes in the world. Use your wits, my darling girl. Why would I stay around with George Godwin in the vicinity unless I had fallen desperately in love with a girl who thought herself in love with another man?"

"I wasn't—I mean, I'm not in love with George."

"I know that. What I don't know is whether you could ever be in love with me."

If Gemma heard the questioning intonation, she did not reply. In fact, she had evidently been struck immobile. Thick black lashes descended onto her cheeks and she stared down at her hand on the reins of the quiet mare. The hand in John's trembled slightly but she made no effort to withdraw it. The glen was suddenly filled with sounds that hadn't impinged on their consciousness before: rustlings of branches, scampering of unseen little animals, the creak of leather as John shifted in his saddle. The pressure on her hand was increased, but she refused to look up until he said coaxingly, his voice infinitely tender, "Come, little one, you have never been wanting in courage before. There is only one way that I can marry you. Much as I adore you, I won't take your hand without your heart. Where you are concerned, my greed knows no bounds. Are you going to give me your heart or must I give back this hand?"

Gemma did not reply in words, but when he sighed and would have released her hand, he found his fingers clutched convulsively. His swift understanding needed no more positive sanction to lean forward and press an urgent kiss on her lips.

"Yes?" he asked, lifting his mouth an inch to smile into soft eyes.

"Yes," she breathed, her dimples released from captivity and her face suffused with wonder. Being a more proficient horsewoman than Lucy, she was able to keep her seat while flinging an arm around his neck to return his kiss.

With the cooperation of the patient horses, the newly betrothed pair managed to exchange an uncomfortable but promising embrace and might have done even better with practice had they not been interrupted by the arrival on the scene of Lucy and Oliver.

"This love business is like the influenza, very infectious," observed Lord Oliver with a teasing smile that threw Lady Gemma into blushing confusion for a moment or two. Eventually she recovered enough to add her felicitations to John's on the miraculous recovery of his paralyzed arm and to wish him and Lucy happy. This new, smiling Oliver was a stranger to her and she was shy of him at first, but the lovely glow of happiness radiating from Lucy was guaranteed to predispose her in his favor.

"Dearest Gemma, I can't tell you how thrilled I am that we are going to be sisters," Lucy declared. "I have been casting spells in my head for weeks and praying for just this conclusion to John's visit."

"Amen to that," said her brother, looking at his beloved in a proprietary fashion that had the strangest effect on her, reducing her bones almost to pulp and interfering with her breathing mechanism.

Altogether it was a mad party that meandered into the stable yard a half-hour later and then strolled two by two toward the ornamental lake as if determined to defer as long as possible the moment when they must return to a world inhabited by others.

At an upstairs window, Her Grace of Carlyle was pulling up the blinds in her boudoir when she noticed the two couples making their separate ways through the gardens. Her first reaction was one of regret that they would no doubt be losing Lucy soon now that Lord Oliver had returned. She would miss her delightful company almost as much as Gemma would, she thought a trifle sadly.

Her attention shifted to the second couple, only a few paces behind but seemingly isolated. Her gaze sharpened. Surely this was the first occasion in a very long time that Gemma and John had been alone together. Could it mean . . . ? Her grace bent nearer the window, unaccountably excited by some intangible impression conveyed by their bearing. At that moment John threw back his head and laughed at something Gemma said. Before the duchess's suddenly misty vision, he reached out and caught Gemma's chin in one hand and kissed her swiftly before they resumed walking, hand in hand now, toward the lake.

With a prayer of thankfulness on her lips and tears of relief and joy in her eyes, Her Grace of Carlyle lowered the blinds and left the window.